NEVER KISS A SCOT

The League of Rogues - Book 10

LAUREN SMITH

Copyright © 2019 by Lauren Smith

Font and Print Layout design by Cover by Combs

ISBN: 978-1-947206-60-1 (ebook)

ISBN: 978-1-947206-61-8 (mass market print)

E

xcerpt from the *Quizzing Glass Gazette*, June 30, 1821, the Lady Society column:

LADY SOCIETY HAS BEEN HEARING THE MOST DELICIOUS tales. Dare I say rumor has it that Lord Kincade—a Scottish earl—and his two brothers have recently come to Bath and are setting the fans aflutter and the matrons atwitter? I'm tempted to suggest matches for these Scottish rogues, but then again, if I know anything about Scots, they will take what they want, when they want it. Ladies of Bath, if you desire one of them for a husband, I wish you the best of luck!

HAMPSHIRE, JUNE, 1821

. . .

THE WILD HIGHLAND LORD GRASPED THE WOMAN IN HIS arms, pressing his lips to hers. Wind tore at her skirts as they stood upon the highest point of the heather-covered hill, embracing each other. There was nothing so wondrous as this, nothing so fulfilling as a perfect kiss...

"A perfect kiss?" Joanna Lennox glared at the last page of her Gothic novel, *Lady Jade's Wild Lord.* "There is no such thing as a perfect kiss." A perfect kiss was a myth. She was sure there wasn't, because if there were, she would have been kissed by now and known that, wouldn't she? Yet here she was at twenty years old, unkissed, uncourted, and utterly *alone.*

She stared into the depths of the fireplace in her library, her heart empty. After three arduous seasons in London, she was a failure as far as the standards of the marriage mart were concerned. The rumor mill had begun to spin tales of why she was still single. London society loved to mock a woman who could not catch a man, especially a woman with a large dowry. Desperate men would overlook any number of problems with a woman so long as her dowry was bountiful.

So what is it that I lack that sends even fortune hunters running to the hills?

It wasn't that she hoped to be married for the sake of marriage itself, or to stop those silly peahens from gossiping. She was an independent, intelligent, opinionated woman. Yet something was missing within her, some grand secret that only someone in love was privy to. At least, if the books she had read were any indication. She wanted to love and be loved by a man, but she knew just how rare love matches were.

She tried to focus on the book in her lap as she pulled her tartan shawl tight around her shoulders. The library in her old country home was a little chilly, even with the fire lit. She usually could lose herself in a book, but not tonight. Her older brother, Ashton, had fallen ill with the grippe, and his fiancée, Rosalind, was tending to him. But the house was quiet, an awful quiet that lent itself to restless nights and melancholy thoughts.

Joanna had witnessed Ashton banish the depths of his coldness and shed the burdens of the past so that he might embrace a warm future with his bride-to-be. It was clear that her brother loved Rosalind dearly, even if he was too damn stubborn to admit it.

Will someone ever love me like that? She blew out a frustrated breath. It wasn't as though she hadn't *tried* to find the perfect gentleman. She'd been charming, polite, and endearing. Men loved to engage her in conversation, yet no man came to call on her, and none sent flowers. There was not one flicker of hope that she was to be courted.

The worries plagued her more and more, leaving her sleepless at night and irritable during the day. But she wasn't the sort of woman to sit and mope, which was why she found her current mood most irritating. Joanna knew she ought to be doing more to distract herself from these doldrums.

Perhaps the Society of Rebellious Ladies would appreciate another member.

Joanna giggled at the thought and turned to the last page in her book. That would at least keep her distracted from her unsuccessful husband hunt. The society was a secretive and increasingly sought-after group for young ladies of the *ton*, and yet joining it was also considered scandalous—which was part of its appeal to those who were members. Rumors suggested that the Society was always in the midst of schemes, some of which even graced the pages of the *Quizzing Glass Gazette*, and they seemed quite happy to be off on adventures of their own without men shadowing them. Their husbands hadn't the faintest idea that the balls, teas, and dinners were often a ruse for the Society's activities.

Since Joanna had no man who was eager to shadow her, she would be a perfect candidate to join the Society. They had been known to accept single ladies, married women, and even declared spinsters among their ranks. Each member of the Society had to possess the characteristics of strength of will and purpose, and they understood that loyalty to the other members was paramount.

A sudden creak of the wood floor startled her. No one should be about at this hour, yet there were any number of reasonable situations in which someone might be. She was still up, after all. Slowly, she peered around the edge of her chair.

A tall, broad-shouldered man in black trousers and a long black shirt stood in the doorway, staring at her. His eyes were a mercurial grayish-blue, and intensely focused on her. For a moment, Joanna was arrested by the sight of his chiseled jaw and aquiline nose, his dark hair a tad too long to be considered respectable.

A splash of clarity hit her. A strange man had just walked into the library close to midnight—and she was there alone. She kept calm. If she needed help, she could cry out. A servant would hear her, surely.

"Who are you?" she asked. He wasn't one of her brother's friends. Ashton belonged to an infamous band of English peers known in some circles as the League of Rogues. She knew nearly all of his friends, as well as the members of the League, and this man was neither. So who was he?

"It doesn't matter who I am. Who are *you*?" His voice was low, silky, yet the brogue was thick enough that she knew he had to be Scottish. Was he perhaps tied to Ashton's fiancée? She was Scottish.

"I'm Joanna Lennox." She closed her book and set it aside with her blue tartan shawl on the chair as she stood.

"I know that clan," the man said, noticing the tartan. "MacLeod. Are you Scottish?"

"What? Oh no, my family has relatives who are, but

not me." She thought of how very *not* Scottish she was, and the idea amused her. She had to admit she'd often dreamt of living in the Highlands, not caring a whit what London society or its damned rules thought about her. She put those thoughts aside to focus on the stranger in black. She came closer, wanting to see him better. Logically, she knew she ought to be shouting for help, but she didn't feel as though she was in any danger. "You didn't answer me. Who are you?"

The man glanced about, clearly struggling to think of an answer.

"I..." He hesitated, and then his eyes narrowed. "Is Lady Melbourne here?"

"Why yes, she's—wait a moment." Joanna knew then why she was so fascinated by him. There was something acutely familiar about his eyes, that same serious shade of grayishblue. And the way he frowned was so like Rosalind, who was quite a serious woman.

"Are you one of her brothers? Did you come down for the wedding?" That had to be it. In all the excitement of her brother's unexpected engagement and then his sudden illness, they must have forgotten to tell her that Rosalind's three brothers had been invited from Scotland for the wedding.

"Aye. I received a letter from my sister and came down to attend the wedding. I only just arrived and didn't wish to disturb the household." He widened his stance, the move strangely aggressive. Joanna had the sudden concern that he might try to grab her, but that was silly. He was Rosalind's brother, not some villain, even if he was dressed like a highwayman. Perhaps he'd only just arrived and wasn't prepared to meet her, which would explain his interesting choice of clothing. He would be exhausted from travel and need time to rest, and here she was judging him as though he was a man sent to cause trouble.

"Oh dear, you must be tired after such a long ride. Have the servants taken your things to your chambers?"

"Thank you, my lady, I've already been seen to. I was just looking for a room to warm up in a bit before going to bed." His gaze searched hers, and she had a suspicion he was expecting her to challenge him, but she had no reason to. He was Rosalind's brother and quite welcome here.

"Well then, come sit by this fire. I just finished my novel and was planning to retire soon. I'd be happy to lend it to you—if you enjoy novels, that is." She returned to her chair and picked up her book, then came back and placed it in his hands. "It's one of my favorites."

He stared at the title. "*Lady Jade's Wild Lord?* Thank you."

It was an L. R. Gloucester novel, a torrid Gothic novel, and he was staring at it with a reverent expression that tugged at her heart. Like a man who hadn't held a book in his hands in years.

"I'm afraid I'm still at a loss as to your name. Which one of Rosalind's brothers are you?"

His storm cloud colored eyes darted around the room before they came back to her. "How do you know about us?"

"Oh, she told me all about the three of you. Let me guess..." She tapped her chin, grinning. "Are you Aiden, Brodie, or Brock? I shall guess...Aiden."

He snorted. "Like hell. Do I look like some young pup?"

He certainly didn't. He looked more like a Scottish Highlander out of her girlish fantasies.

"Brock then," she said. "You look like a Brock. It's a very old name, Brock. I like learning about names and their meanings. Did you know Brock means badger?" She stared at his lips, surprised at how full they looked. Then she wanted to kick herself. She should not be dreaming about this man's lips. He was a guest, and she needed to act like a proper lady, not some wanton creature obsessed with someone's mouth.

"Badger?" He tilted his head. "I didn't know that." Those full lips curved into a smile, and she couldn't help but grin back. Her heart raced wildly as she met his eyes. His devil-may-care grin hit her so hard that she had trouble standing. Brock set the book down and suddenly caught her by the waist, pulling her flush against his body.

"It's a custom from my village to offer a kiss to those whose families are about to be joined."

A kiss? Excitement shot through her like quicksilver. Perhaps she would finally get to know whether her Gothic novels were telling the truth about kisses.

"Really? I've read about parts of Scotland, but I've never—"

His arm around her waist tightened, and she pressed against his body, feeling the hard muscles of his tall frame against her soft curves.

"Shush, lass, and let me keep with tradition," he whispered, then bent his head and slanted his mouth over hers.

His taste exploded upon her tongue, seducing her with dark excitement. A hint of brandy was still on his lips, and she relished it. One of his hands dropped from her waist to cup her bottom. She squeaked in surprise against him and then moaned as he fisted his other hand in her hair, pulling her head back so he could deepen the kiss. Her knees buckled treacherously, and she tried to think, but it was hard to be rational when her stomach was filled with such a wonderful swooping feeling. She was kissing Rosalind's brother...

Joanna pulled herself away enough to separate their lips. She was amazed at the riotous sensations she was experiencing from just a single kiss. Maybe kisses really could be perfect. How could she feel something invisible yet so tangible when she didn't even know this man? It didn't make sense, and she liked things to make sense. *Get control, Joanna—you don't swoon at kisses. Kisses can't be nearly as good as they are described on paper.* Yet Brock's kiss had been exactly that—devastatingly perfect. Of course, she had no way of knowing if all kisses were like that or just his, given that this was her first.

"This is traditional where you come from?" If all the ladies in Scotland were kissed like this upon meeting a man...*Lord*...

His lips twitched. "Old as the bones in the hills."

She kept her palms pressed on his chest, knowing she ought to push away, to behave like the English lady she had been raised to be. But part of her, a much stronger part, wanted to toss the rules of good behavior aside and do anything for just one more kiss. She looked up, gazing into his grayish-blue eyes.

"And I suppose it would be rude of me to break with tradition."

His now arrogant smile would've made her slap him if she wasn't so desperate to lose herself in his kiss again.

"Incredibly rude. You'd be insulting my entire clan."

Her pulse fluttered, and she sucked in her lower lip briefly as she anticipated another kiss. "Well, Mother did raise me to respect other cultures." She slid her palms up his chest and curled her fingers into his black shirt as their mouths met and that addictive fire burned through her all over again. She clung to Brock, exploring his mouth with hers, their tongues touching gently before the kiss became more insistent.

His hands moved back to her waist, tugging at the blue sash above her hips as his other hand pulled pins loose from her hair until he was able to slide her hair ribbon free. Then he was pulling her wrists together, winding the sash around them. Her body melted at the sudden domination and the thrill of him binding her, but she tried to react rationally.

"What are you doing?" she asked in a breathless mixture of anger, fear, and arousal. "This can't be traditional." She tugged on her now bound wrists, staring at him, hoping he would explain himself.

"I'm sorry about this, lass, but I can't have you calling for Lennox."

Lennox? He had to mean her brother, but why was he restraining her?

"Call for—" She was silenced as he slid her hair ribbon between her parted lips and tied it around her head, gagging her. With gentle hands, he guided her to the chair by the fire and pushed her into it. She fell back with a muffled cry, not one of pain but indignation. How *dare* he truss her up and—

"Move from here in the next few minutes and I fear you will regret it," Brock warned.

She tried to curse him, but the gag muffled the noise. He gazed down at her a moment longer, a sharp flash of regret in those gray eyes that made her still. He didn't want to leave her tied up. This wasn't part of some game of seduction, so why had he? More importantly, what was the thing he was about to do that he clearly did not want her to see? A cold wave of dread swept through her, but she dared not move, not until she saw him vanish through the library door and into the corridor outside.

Joanna waited only a moment before she leapt up from the chair and rushed to the door. She pulled at the handle and stumbled into the hallway, tripping over a wrinkle in the carpet and twisting her ankle. She yelped as she took a step on the injured ankle.

At the sound of footsteps, she glanced up, expecting to see Brock, but instead it was Charles Humphrey, or as London knew him, the Earl of Lonsdale. Charles was a member of the League of Rogues and one of her brother's closest friends.

He jerked to a halt when he saw her hands were bound and her mouth gagged. "Joanna? What the devil?" He tugged the ribbon free from her lips and unbound her wrists. "What happened?"

"There's a man here...one of Rosalind's brothers..." She tried to explain, but she honestly had no idea what was really going on.

"You mean a Scotsman is in this house?" Charles snapped.

"Yes, he said he was invited to the wedding, but then he tied me up and—"

"He's not invited. The bloody bastard shouldn't even be here. We must tell Ashton at once."

"What? Why?"

"Because Rosalind's brothers are damned dangerous. They've come to take Rosalind back to her father in Scotland. He's a rotten excuse for a human being." Charles looked her over. "The man didn't touch you, did he? I mean, aside from binding you?"

Joanna swallowed hard and shook her head. She wasn't about to admit that she'd been passionately kissing a dangerous Scotsman.

"Thank God. Your brother would never let one of those brutes hurt you," Charles muttered as he helped her down the hallway. She clutched the silk sash that had been around her wrists as they strode down the hall, calling for her brother.

"What sort of a man is her father?"

"The sort who beats his own defenseless daughter."

"Did her brothers hurt Rosalind? Or was it just her father?"

"Just her father, as far as I understand. But I've tussled with them once before. One of the bastards broke a chair over my back."

"My God! What was that all about?"

Charles hesitated in answering, but not for long. "As you might expect with me. A woman. Take my word on this—you don't ever want to be alone with any of them. They'd seduce you before you had a chance to think."

Joanna swallowed the sudden lump in her throat. Brock was dangerous? She shouldn't have been surprised. Any man who could kiss like that had to be. It was just her luck that she found a man who made her feel alive, and he was someone she should never marry.

Bath, *one month later*

"She'll never marry, not that one, unless she sets her sights low, and maybe not even then." A society mama *tsked* a little too loudly as Joanna passed by her in the assembly room.

"Quite right," another woman whispered back. "No one ever asks her to dance. Must be something wrong with her." The words cut deep because Joanna knew the woman was talking about her, and she knew the woman was right.

There was only one man in England who seemed to be interested in her at all—a rather boring but decently attractive man named Edmund Lindsey. He was only a gentleman, no title but plenty of fortune. Still, Joanna was hesitant to consider him. She felt no passion for him, no great fire in her belly or flutter in her chest. She didn't want to marry Edmund simply because he was her *only* choice, but what else could she do?

The one man she had wanted to marry had given her a wonderful, perfect kiss and then vanished into the night like the rogue he was. It was the sort of thing that ruined a woman for all other men because no man would ever compare to Brock Kincade. And she'd been a fool to think he might come back for her after the disagreement between Brock and her brother had been settled but he hadn't.

Because there's something wrong with you... The thought slithered from her brain deep into her heart.

She tried to move through the crush of people near the dance floor, not that it mattered. Her card had the next three dances empty, and what few dances she did have on her card were with married men who were older and business acquaintances of her brother's. She shouldn't have come tonight, but Ashton and his fiancée, Rosalind, had wanted to spend some time enjoying Bath before the wedding.

Joanna's mother had all but given up on her finding a man to seriously court her, and she'd essentially left her alone. That meant Joanna had avoided most social engagements and instead chose to tuck herself away in the circulation room of Meyler's library—mostly to avoid Edmund. He'd learned she'd come back and was doing his best to run into her in every tea shop, every assembly room, and even on the street while she tried to ride. It was frustrating. All she wanted was to be left alone to consider her options.

It hadn't escaped her notice that she was not the only young woman using the hidden magic of books to escape the social scenes of the city. Only yesterday, she'd run into a friend from London, Lydia Hunt, at Meyler's. They had commiserated over their shared matchmaking woes. Lydia's younger sister, Portia, was a true beauty and quite full of trouble, which meant Lydia spent much of her time declining invitations from young men who were interested in her because her little sister would try to steal them away. Given that Lydia's father openly supported Portia's desire to marry before Lydia, Lydia had given up hope of a match because any man she desired would be turned toward Portia instead.

Joanna didn't have the excuse of a scheming younger sister, however. She simply wasn't *wanted* by any man except Edmund.

A crowd of young men stood around the refreshment table drinking ratafia and laughing raucously, in spite of the group of disapproving mamas who watched from a distance. One of the men glanced her way and offered a smile, but he did nothing more to encourage her. She'd never felt more invisible in her life.

All she wanted was to be loved, to share the passions of life with a man, yet none would consider her. She'd wondered from the moment her first season had passed whether the debts and scandals her father had created before his death had left her name blackened somehow. Was it possible that the past was ruining her future? What other reason could there be for men to avoid her like this?

Ashton had restored their family fortune, it was true, but as the daughter of a baron and now sister to one, she was, to be frank, at the bottom of the ladder when it came to the peerage. Most men wished to marry up, not simply acquire fortunes. And Ashton wouldn't allow the more attractive fortune hunters anywhere near her—not that many had tried. Most men seemed content enough to smile and talk with her, dance once or twice, but never anything more. Even those who showed initial interest one evening would ignore her the next as if they'd never met her.

All that remained was Edmund Lindsey, and her brother had laughed in his face when he'd expressed his interest in Joanna. Her brother's open dislike of Edmund hadn't made sense, but when she'd questioned him about it, Ashton had simply told her not to bother with Lindsey, that there would be a good man out there for her to marry someday. Yet despite her brother's callous and dismissive treatment, Edmund remained persistent.

Joanna hastily made her way to the corridor outside the assembly hall, resting a gloved hand against the wall to catch her breath. So far, she'd successfully avoided Edmund. He was here somewhere, but Bath was flooded with people this time of year, and there were hundreds in attendance tonight. It was easy to get lost in the crowd when one wanted to. When she heard voices, she ducked around the corner into a small corridor off the main rooms, afraid Edmund had found her. But it was only a pair of ladies, and their voices echoed down the hall, clearly audible to her.

"Have you seen *them?*" one of them whispered.

"Them?"

"The Kincades—those Scotsmen. The brothers of Lady Melbourne. She's marrying Lord Lennox in two days, you know. It's all very scandalous..."

Joanna sucked in a breath and waited, listening hard. Could it be...?

"Why is that so scandalous?" the other woman asked.

"Lord Lennox is one of those *rogues*, my dear, you know the *League*. But if you ask me, it's the Kincade men who are far more wicked."

"Yes...wicked *how?*" The second woman was clearly frustrated by her friend's failure to provide details.

Joanna could tell them just how wicked one of the Kincade brothers was.

He had kissed her and then ridden off into the night with his brothers and sister. Ashton had traveled all the way to Scotland to convince Rosalind he loved her. When that was resolved, Brock and his brothers had stayed in Scotland while Rosalind returned to England. They had been invited to the wedding, which was only a few days away. Had they accepted the invitation? No one had mentioned it to her if they had, of course. No one seemed to notice her at all these days. Her mother was busy fussing over Ashton and his future bride, and her other brother, Rafe, had left for London without so much as a word except a single promise that he would return for Ashton's wedding.

The ache only grew deeper in her heart. *I am alone.*

"Well, if you *must* know..." The first woman's voice then lowered to the point where Joanna could no longer hear. Cursing silently, she peered around the edge of the hall to get a better look at them. The two ladies wore turbans festooned with ostrich feathers, and as their heads bent to gossip, the feathers wavered and danced in the air. It would have been comical enough to make Joanna laugh, but she truly desired to hear what they were saying.

"No. You believe it's true? That he really...?" Again, the conversation dissolved into whispers. "And they are here tonight?" the second woman suddenly blurted out.

"Yes! In the assembly rooms. Not dancing, of course, but prowling about. All three of them are like wolves. I won't let my daughter near them."

"I should think not," her friend agreed. "Are they wife hunting?"

"Wife hunting? Those scoundrels? I doubt it. They're more likely skirt chasing. They are trouble, mark my words."

"Trouble indeed," Joanna agreed in a mutter. After

Brock Kincade had stolen a kiss, she had been unable to think of any other man, let alone someone as dull as Edmund Lindsey.

Damned Scot! The despair within her was transformed into anger—anger at Brock. They hadn't seen each other since that night, and it was about time she changed that. She had quite a lot she wished to say to that wretched man. One could not go around kissing ladies in libraries at midnight and not expect them to be affected. Not a word or an apology given after—it was unconscionable.

Joanna squared her shoulders and headed back to the assembly room, determined to find Brock and give him a good telling off. That at least would unburden herself of these feelings building up inside her. Then she would only have to put up with him for a few days during the wedding festivities, and she would be free of him. She would likely never see him again, which was just fine by her.

The assembly hall was still crowded; the couples in the center were just finishing a dance. She searched the faces around her, but there were at least a hundred guests in the dance hall. She spotted her mother and Rosalind talking with friends. Ashton and Charles stood in conversation near the refreshment table. Joanna bit her lip. She felt like she belonged with neither group, and the thought only made her mood bleaker.

And then she spotted them. A trio of tall dark-haired men wearing simple buckskin breeches and waistcoats lounged against a pillar by the orchestra. Brock, Brodie, and Aiden Kincade. Infamous devils the lot of them, if the gossip she'd heard about them was correct.

She had not yet had the pleasure of meeting Brodie and Aiden, but there was no mistaking the three as brothers. All had dark hair and stormy eyes, with strong jaws seemingly carved of marble. They were handsome men who would tempt any woman to be reckless with her virtue.

I was certainly tempted. She thought this with a scowl as she stared at the trio.

Several couples moved out of Joanna's way as she strode toward the Scotsmen. But before she was halfway, she was waylaid by a short masculine form who stepped directly into her path.

"My dear Miss Lennox! What a pleasure it is to see you here tonight!" Edmund Lindsey exclaimed.

God's teeth! Joanna forced a smile on her face as she turned her attention to Edmund. He bowed his head to her, and she couldn't help but note his unfashionable hairstyle, a decade out of date, and the rather foppish style to his clothes. While his face and features were genuinely considered fine and attractive, it did nothing for his personality. His cravat was far too elaborately folded and was wilting in the heat of the room like a hothouse flower losing its bloom. He struck her as a rather pathetic creature, and Joanna suffered a twinge of guilt that she could not find it in her heart to like him.

"Mr. Lindsey," she said on a sigh. "How are you?"

"I am well, now that I've had the good fortune to run into you." He preened beneath her gaze, and she resisted the urge to roll her eyes. His open flattery, once tolerable, had become quite irritating. "I don't suppose you have any dances open?"

"Why...no. I'm so sorry." It was a lie, but she was not about to dance with him, even though he seemed to be the only man in England who wanted her. Yes, it was completely rude to lie about one's dances like that. Everyone knew a young lady ought to accept any dance offered, no matter who the man was and whether or not she liked him, but she couldn't bring herself to accept.

"Then perhaps I could fetch you a glass of ratafia?"

"Er, yes, I suppose that would be all right." It would at least give her a few minutes alone, and she could plan her escape from the hall. It would be easy enough to flag down a hackney if she could make it outside without Edmund following.

"Be right back, my dear!" Edmund bustled off, nudging his way through the crowds. Joanna sighed in relief before she located Brock once again and headed toward him and his brothers.

Brock seemed to notice her when she was within a few feet of him because he pushed off the pillar and stood straight as she came up to him. He did not bow, nor did he incline his head or provide anything other than a civil greeting. Her heart pounded against her ribs as she glared at him. By God, she was going to get an answer from him, scandal be damned.

What was the worst that could happen? Yet another empty dance card? No bouquets of flowers? No eager gentlemen upon her doorstep? She was used to such disappointments already, except for that damned Edmund. But that was a whole different problem to deal with.

He was wealthy and quite connected in society, but those qualities held little interest for her. Plenty of other women had made it quite clear they would marry him, so why couldn't he turn his affections toward one of them? There was just something about Edmund—the way he looked at her when he thought she wasn't watching—that unsettled her.

An idea occurred to her. Perhaps she could create a scandal to scare him off? By this point, it seemed to be her only option.

Better to be alone than Edmund's bride. The thought threatened to drown her with its bleak outlook. She understood that many women married for security, but she could not. The idea of marrying a man, sharing his bed, sharing in his life when she did not feel a passion for him... Her stomach rolled again, but she kept her composure.

"So you've returned?" she asked, not caring that people were already starting to turn and look her way.

"Aye, I have," Brock answered in that soft, dark voice

that made her insides melt. It was a lover's voice—not that she was supposed to know such things.

"And you did not think that perhaps you ought to pay a call to my brother...or *me?*" she added, trying to hint at what he had done to her without letting her hurt and anger flare too openly. He had *kissed* her, for heaven's sake. The least he could have done was to come back to make things right between him and Ashton and...*kiss me again.*

"We came down for the wedding. And I did pay a call to your brother when we first arrived two days ago."

"You've been here *two days?*" She hated how shrill her voice sounded.

"I would have come sooner, but I canna leave my lands alone for long. There's much that needs looking after."

He didn't want her, then. Nothing about their encounter seemed to have remained in his memory. The kiss had been nothing more to him than a means to silence her so he could rescue his sister. She staggered back a step, the fresh pain from this blow being all too unexpected. Brock stepped close, catching her hand and lifting her dance card out where he could see it and the bare spaces where men's names ought to have been.

"Empty? Did you arrive late?" His eyes searched hers for answers.

She swallowed a harsh laugh. "It's *always* empty. I'm not worth a dance."

A spark of fire lit his eyes. "Not worth a dance?" The edge in his tone was unnerving, as if the words she had spoken offended him. Then he gripped her hand and dragged her out into the middle of the couples lining up for a dance. Too stunned to refuse, she got in line with the other ladies, still staring at him as he shoved his way between two gentlemen to pair with her. The music began, and they started to follow the steps, twirling, clapping, marching, but all of her focus had fallen on him and the way he never took his eyes off her. He was a wonderful dancer, which surprised her.

In the last month, she'd conjured up all sorts of silly dreams about him and what he was like. A dashing Scottish warrior, a brute, even a highwayman, but never a fine dancer. Rosalind had spoken a little to Joanna about her past and the cruel world her father had created for her and her brothers. Joanna knew that Brock had often taken beatings meant for his younger sister to protect her. In a grim world like that, how could he have learned to dance like such a gentleman? It was one mystery that she would likely never have answers to.

The dance ended, and the couples around them began to pair with new partners, but Brock stayed close to her.

"Another?" he asked.

"But... We shouldn't. People will talk..."

"Talk doesn't bother me." And it apparently didn't. His eyes never left her face, even though quite a few people now stared at them in wide-eyed shock. It was completely forbidden to dance with any man more than once. Yet she didn't find it in herself to care in that moment what rules she was ready to break for this man. His intensity and the way he didn't seem to care about anything but her made her feel wild and reckless, like when she'd been a child and had toured part of the countryside near Cornwall. She'd stood on the edge of the cliffs, feeling the wind buffet her body hard enough that she'd almost fallen to her death. The spark of fear and excitement of that moment and this were almost the same. She didn't want to stop feeling so...*alive.*

"Very well." She let him dance with her again and again, and then, when that dance was done, *again.*

By the fifth dance her feet were aching, but Joanna couldn't have cared less. Dancing with Brock had erased her black mood. She'd been smiling, laughing, not caring in the least about the attention focused upon her as each dance progressed. Only when the music stopped did she finally feel the hundreds of eyes upon her and the whispers spreading like wildfire in the crowd.

"No wonder she hasn't found a match. *Five* dances..."

"Must be his mistress..."

"Too improper, dancing with that Scotsman..."

"Her mother will be ashamed..."

Everywhere Joanna looked there was judgment and callous disregard for her feelings. What had she been thinking? Courting scandal by dancing with him? Even if this scared off Edmund Lindsey, was it truly worth it? What of the gossip that would hound her in hushed whispers wherever she went? A man like Brock wouldn't marry her. She was simply a toy for a reckless Highland lord to play with when it suited him. Just kisses in libraries at midnight and dances to stir the scandal sheets.

"Lass..." Brock whispered, holding out his hand.

She stared at him, and before she could think twice, she'd wound back one hand and slapped him hard across the face. The assembly hall fell into a silence punctuated by the violins coming to a halt when the players dragged their bows discordantly over the strings. Everyone, it seemed, was gaping at her. Brock didn't move, didn't so much as flinch, even though a soft red shade was forming on his cheek.

Oh Lord, why in heavens did I do that?

The thought made her hysterical enough that she was torn between laughing and crying. She'd just slapped Brock in front of half the *ton*. If she wasn't going to be at the top of the scandal sheets for dancing too long with him, she'd surely end up there now for striking him in public.

Joanna turned and fled. She was going to be the laughingstock of all England.

She flew down the steps to the front of the assembly hall and onto the street, clutching her reticule as she prayed her family wouldn't notice her absence. But how could they not? Everyone had been staring at her by the end of the fifth dance, and then she'd gone and slapped Brock in front of them all.

She waved at a hackney driver a dozen feet away. He picked up his whip and gave a gentle flick to his horses and headed toward her. A breath of relief escaped her.

I can go home and forget about tonight...I hope...

Just then, someone grabbed her from behind, a hand covering her mouth. She yelped as she was raised up and shoved into the coach she had summoned.

"Oi! What are you doin'?" the driver shouted.

"Just take us to Finchley Street! I'll pay double the regular fare," the man who held her said. Joanna stilled for a brief instant as she realized that the man who'd grabbed her was Brock.

"How *dare* you?" She tried to escape, but Brock blocked her path as he climbed inside with her.

"Hold that temper, lass. I'm not going to harm you, which is more than you did for me back there," Brock snapped. His hands captured hers, pinning them to either side of her head against the cushions behind her on the seat.

"Let me go, Lord Kincade," she demanded. His handsome face was a mask of moonlight and shadows in the dim coach interior as his lips curved into a grin.

"Not just yet. You and I need to talk." The smile faded, and he looked deadly serious now. If he hadn't been holding her wrists, she would have slapped him again.

"*Talk?* You should have talked to me a month ago. But no, you left me tied up in a library and kidnapped my brother's fiancée!"

"I didna kidnap her. I was *rescuing* her," he corrected.

"Well, you might have been rescuing her, but you *left* me," she said with a growl. "You cannot go around kissing ladies like that with no consideration for their feelings. And then you convinced me to dance and you danced so wonderfully that I forgot to stop and now *everyone* is talking because you're a known skirt chaser and a rogue, and then I slapped you and it will be all over the papers tomorrow. I'm ruined, and it is entirely your fault..." She struggled to get free, fury raging through her, but she couldn't get him to let go.

"Lassie, you talk too much." That was the only warning she had before his mouth slanted over hers and the world exploded around her in delicious sinful fire for the second time in her life.

3

Brock smiled against Joanna's lips as she melted against him. She was just as wonderful as he remembered. He kept her wrists pinned against the back of the coach for a moment longer until he felt her surrender to his kiss. When he released her, she curled her arms around his neck. Every time his mouth covered hers, he felt unable to get enough of her natural sweetness or the dreamy intimacy that settled around them as they embraced. His stomach flipped with boyish excitement as he pressed against her. He had his lovely English lass back in his arms where she belonged.

In the month since he'd first met her and had to abandon her to rescue his sister, he had been reliving that heated encounter in the library of Joanna's country home. He had vowed to come back for her to make her his.

The time had come at last.

He longed for a bride, one who could share his bed, make him laugh and smile with her lively talk and brilliant mind, and whose dowry would help repair his crumbling castle. Joanna was that woman. But there was a problem—her brother would kill him if he asked for her hand in marriage. They were on civil terms after the matter with Rosalind, but they could not be considered friends.

So how then to get his beautiful blonde siren away from her protective guard dog of a brother and his damned band of rogues?

An elopement, perhaps? Yes, that would do nicely. A race to Scotland. He knew the roads better than any Englishman and could travel faster, even with Joanna in tow, assuming he could convince her to marry him.

"Brock," Joanna whispered against his mouth between kisses. "You are...the most wicked man I've ever met." Her breathless accusation held no real venom, only sensual delight and surprise.

"I've not even started to kiss you properly," he said with a chuckle, brushing the backs of his fingers over her cheek.

She gazed up at him. "You haven't?" Those blue eyes, deep and mysterious as the loch by his castle back home, were so damned lovely and wide-eyed with innocence.

A bone-deep ache grew inside him whenever he looked at her. This wasn't simple lust; she filled him with a longing for things he'd dared not to dream of since he was a lad. She was a ray of sunlight, a hearty laugh, a wink and a smile all rolled together. She was everything good and pure in life, and he *wanted* her—wanted her more than he'd ever wanted anything before.

She must be mine, at any cost. It was a greedy thought, he knew, to think he could possess her when he didn't deserve such a beacon of light in his life, and once she realized she was kissing a damned devil she would hate him. Yet he couldn't bear to face that truth just yet.

His father's cruelty had destroyed so much of him that even his heart was made of stone.

"When I kiss you properly, lass, you will know." He nuzzled her throat before he pressed a slow, languid kiss above her collarbone. She sucked in a breath, struggling against his hold, but it wasn't an attempt to get free—it was an attempt to get closer.

"Where are we going?" she asked between gasps as he moved his lips back up to her throat.

"To my home, at least for now. My brothers and I are sharing a residence on Finchley Street for the duration of the festivities."

"Your...home?" Some of the drowsy lust in her voice faded. "No, we mustn't..."

This time when she fought his hold, he allowed her to pull herself free. She shrank away from him on their shared seat. "You must take me home at once."

"Joanna," he whispered. "Surely you know why I have come."

"For Rosalind's wedding," she said coldly.

"That is only one reason. The other is *you*." He reached for her, but she slapped his hand away.

"You left me alone for a month! You kissed me and left me without a word! And now you want me to believe that you're here for me? I doubt you thought of me at all before you saw me at the assembly."

The hurt in her eyes wounded him, but there was no way to make her understand. The night they had met had been dangerous, and he couldn't have done anything more than kiss her. He could not have made it back to Scotland with both Joanna and his sister. And he could not have written to her or sent word, because her brother no doubt had been watching her ever since that night.

Brock had convinced himself—or tried to—that leaving her alone was better, that she belonged with a man who could love her. But he had been a damned fool to think that he could stay away from her, though, not once he saw her again.

"Marry me," he blurted out.

Her eyes widened. "What?"

"Let me take you to Scotland, make you a proper bride."

She gazed at him, mute, trying to process his words. "But..." He could see the indecision in her eyes.

"We still have two days before the wedding. You dinna have to decide now." He opened the coach window and gave the driver her brother's address. Once the coach turned around, he sat back on the seat across from her and tried to remind himself that she needed time. Taking her into his arms for another kiss wouldn't necessarily change her mind. Women needed more than passion in their lives; they needed stability, a common ground. He could offer none of that. His past had been vastly different and far harsher than hers. But it didn't stop him from wanting her enough that it made him ache inside to think of letting her go.

When he and his brothers had arrived for the wedding, he'd hoped to see her sooner, but her damned brother had kept her safely away each time he'd tried to visit, though always making it seem coincidental. Even with their differences settled there was a cat-and-mouse game of civility between them. It had only been luck that he'd seen Ashton disappearing out of the assembly hall when Joanna had approached him to dance; otherwise, he never would have had the chance to talk to her, let alone share five dances with her. He'd expected her brother to storm in at any moment and drag her away, but he hadn't. The overprotective fool had slipped up in Brock's favor, but Brock wasn't stupid enough to believe that Ashton wouldn't figure out where his sister had gone and who had chased after her.

He knows I want her, and he's protecting her, just as I tried to protect my sister from him. Brock was never one to enjoy situations of irony, and this one made him want to punch a stone wall.

"Why do you want to marry me?" she asked after a long silence.

"Why?" he echoed, confused.

"Yes. Why? Do you love me?"

He stumbled in his response. "Well... I mean..."

"Right, you don't, because we don't even *know* each other. Marriage should be based on love, not lust."

He laughed. "Love? Lass, you are far too innocent. I've met only a few people who ever married for love, and those marriages didn't end well." His parents had married for love, but his father's greed for power had been stronger than his love, and it had broken his mother's heart. He would never forget what she'd told him only a few days before she died.

"Love, true love, fills the heart so completely that there is no room left for hate or greed. I thought I was enough for your father, but I wasn't..."

Brock didn't believe he could ever love someone that much—not because he didn't want to but because his heart had been hardened by hate and anger. It was weighed down with stones of the past. There was a darkness inside him, one that he could not banish. A man like him could never be filled with love and nothing else. Because if he did love fully and all-consuming, whoever held his heart would make him pay dearly for it. She would crush him the way his mother had been crushed. His spirit would be broken and his will to live destroyed when he would not be loved back. Joanna was a danger to him, and she didn't even know it. She could leave Scotland, return to her family and friends in London, and leave his castle empty and his heart in pieces on the floor. No...if they married, he would have her heart and body, and she would have his body and affection, but no love. It was too dangerous.

"I won't marry you." Her soft reply stung worse than any blade sinking into his chest. He hadn't expected her to reject him.

He had been listening tonight at the assembly hall, had heard the mocking whispers that she would never find a husband, that something was wrong with her.

There was *nothing* wrong with Joanna. What was wrong was that the damned *Sassenachs* thought their women should be meek as lambs and silly as geese. Sweet Joanna was fierce, intelligent, and had her own mind, and those bloody English fools knew it.

"I'll ask you again after the wedding," he said as the coach stopped at Lord Lennox's residence.

She frowned, and the furrow between her brows made her look adorable. "I won't change my answer."

He smiled. "You might. A man can hope." He opened the coach door and assisted her down, holding her close as he set her on her feet. She stared up at him, her blue eyes like dark pools beneath the muted light of the streetlamps. A loose curl of pale-blonde hair brushed the tops of her breasts, and he slowly stroked her silken strands back with his fingers. Her breasts rose in response as she took in a sharp breath.

"Sleep well, fair Joanna, and dream of me tonight."

She scowled. "I most certainly will not."

He cupped her chin, tilted her head back, and feathered a lingering kiss on her lips before he stepped back and climbed into the coach. "Aye, you will."

She would change her mind. Brock had two days to convince her that marrying him was something she wanted. He would be a good and loyal husband, and he would see her well cared for and well satisfied, in bed and out.

So long as I can keep her safe from my family's past.

He hadn't forgotten what Rosalind had shared with him. Their father, Montgomery Kincade, had betrayed his fellow Scotsmen by helping an English spy assassinate the leaders of a rebellion more than twenty years before. That spy was still alive, and Brock's father had threatened him with proof of their dealings being made public before he died. Rosalind had found that proof and had given it to Ashton to use against their sworn enemy. Instead, Ashton had chosen to burn it to protect her.

Brock didn't believe that was enough. He didn't trust the English, and he fully believed that the Kincade family and anyone they cared about would be in grave danger if the truth about their father ever came to light. He had to find a way to protect his family and his future bride from the bloody hands reaching through the mists of time, hoping to drag him down into darkness. But how could he stop a powerful English spy or his own countrymen if they cried out for vengeance?

I am not my father. I will not hurt Joanna. I will protect her with everything that I have.

EDMUND LINDSEY HELD THE GLASS OF RATAFIA, frowning as he searched for any sign of Joanna Lennox in the ballroom. He'd gotten used to finding her quickly in a crowd over the last few months. She was taller than most ladies, and her pale-blonde hair was like a shining beacon beneath the chandeliers.

"Lindsey, you continue to disappoint me," a cold voice said from behind him. Edmund spun to face a handsome aristocrat with dark hair and even darker eyes. The man had appeared from a shadowed corner of the ballroom, unseen by the nearby guests. Edmund glanced about, expecting to spot a door or some pathway to explain the man's sudden appearance, but there was no such place from which he could have emerged. It reminded him of just how skilled the man was and that he was not to be trifled with.

"Sir Hugo." He bowed his head at the man who had

been sending him his orders for the last three months. Those orders had been clear—that he must seduce and marry Joanna Lennox. How he had found himself in that position was a matter he preferred not to dwell upon.

"I did not spend my time and resources trying to convince the eligible bachelors in the country to avoid Miss Lennox just so you could somehow drive her off."

Edmund tried to puff up his chest, taking some professional pride in his abilities. "I am on the verge of winning her over. In fact, I was about to ask her for a moment alone so I might confess to some of our shared interests—the ones you so kindly provided."

"That will be difficult, seeing as she is no longer here. She fled with that Scottish brute, Kincade. It's been three months. I was informed you had ways of winning women over, but it appears those rumors are simply that —rumors."

The verbal slight didn't go unmissed. Edmund would have thrown the ratafia in any other man's face, but not Hugo Waverly. Waverly held power far beyond what his title would suggest. If it hadn't been for the excellent funding he had received from the man, Edmund would never have taken this task on.

"Perhaps I should have picked a more aggressive man to woo her," Hugo said, then looked Edmund up and down. "Taller as well. But I thought by now she would be more desperate. I had dearly hoped to see her shadowed with self-pity as she accepted your proposal. It seems I miscalculated either her desperation or your effectiveness."

Edmund knew better than to react to such an insult. He knew he was attractive, and while not particularly bulky in muscle, he offered pleasure to any woman in his bed. Plenty of women had learned quickly enough that what he lacked in height he made up for in other ways. Yet Joanna had not even given him the chance to show her his charms. The little chit could barely contain her open dislike of him, and it filled him with a frustration that he barely concealed in his polite manners. Such constant rejection was no good for one's self-esteem.

"It's clear she will not choose me," Edmund confessed. Oddly enough, saying the words out loud came with a strange sort of relief. "Perhaps you ought to bribe the Scot?"

Waverly's cruel mouth twisted with a venomous smile.

"I'm afraid the Scot is not for sale. But you have given me an excellent idea. I had intended for you to make her miserable as a husband, but perhaps my plans were not ambitious enough. But that man's father and I have a history. It opens certain...possibilities."

Edmund repressed another shudder. Now he was grateful for Miss Lennox's rejections. Hugo's plan no doubt would have made them both miserable, and money could compensate for only so much in life.

Whatever Waverly was planning, Edmund wanted

nothing more to do with it. He preferred staying alive. Waverly had protection from the Crown, it was true, but Edmund had no such luxury. And if someone died from Waverly's games, well, Edmund might be the one to hang for it.

"Should I assume our business is concluded then?" Edmund asked quietly.

Waverly stroked his chin, his black eyes looking at something in the distance that Edmund could not see, and for a moment he feared he might have to repeat his question.

"Yes, I am done with you. My office will tender a final payment in the morning, and I will see no more of you."

Edmund couldn't agree more on the last point. He hastily retreated into the crowds, smiling at his good fortune. Another thousand pounds would be lining his pocket, and all he had done was chase Joanna Lennox into the arms of someone else. Lady Fortune was smiling upon him, at least.

He tried not to think whether or not Fortune would soon frown upon Miss Lennox.

⚘

HUGO STOOD AT THE EDGE OF THE BALLROOM, lurking in the shadows kindly afforded by an unlit lamp in his corner of the room. He watched the oblivious couples dance. His wife was out there tonight, no doubt dancing with some fool. He didn't care if married ladies weren't supposed to dance except with their husbands. His wife enjoyed dancing, and since he could not give her the time for a dance, not while seeing to his plans, he was content to let her have her amusement wherever she could find it.

A flash of pale-blond hair caught his attention, and he had to keep his heart from racing as he saw Ashton Lennox on the dance floor, his Scottish bride in his arms.

My prey...so close. He had to keep himself from reaching for the small blade he kept on him at all times. The dagger that he dreamed nearly every night of plunging into the hearts of every last member of the League of Rogues.

Only a few days ago they had held the key to destroying him in their hands, and yet they had chosen to burn it. He still could not reason out why. Not that it mattered. He would not stop; he would not show mercy.

I will bring you down, one by one, with a death of a thousand cuts. And one of those cuts will be Joanna Lennox.

All he had to do was let it slip to the right Highland clans that Lord Kincade's father had betrayed his countrymen, and that the Englishman who had helped him was Ashton Lennox. And he knew which clans held their grudges for generations.

They would kill Joanna, Lord Kincade, and likely

Ashton as well. Even if Ashton somehow survived Highland justice, losing his sister would destroy him. The sweet irony would be that Ashton himself had just destroyed the very evidence that might have saved her.

And no one will be the wiser that I played a part in any of it.

It was so easy to be the devil at times—so very easy.

4

Joanna slipped into the silent, still house. Everyone was likely still at the ball. Her shoulders dropped in relief. She would have some time alone to collect herself after the disaster she'd created after that last dance with Brock. She thanked the footman who met her at the door and snuck down to the kitchens where their cook, Mrs. Copeland, was kneading some bread for the next day. The cook's dark-brown hair, streaked with gray, was tucked beneath a white cap, and her cheeks were red with her exertions as she kneaded dough on a counter.

"Miss Joanna!" The cook grinned and retrieved a small wet cloth to wipe the flour off her hands before she hugged Joanna. Mrs. Copeland was like a favorite aunt to her. She'd always taken good care of the Lennox children and had been their cook for more than fifteen years.

"Mrs. Copeland, do you have any peach tarts?" Joanna glanced about the tidy kitchen, hoping to find at least a little something to eat before bed. She, like some ladies, was often too embarrassed to eat at a ball. She wasn't plump by any means, but she was very conscious of her figure, and it seemed a bad thing to appear to hover about the refreshments when men were watching.

Mrs. Copeland chuckled. "Do I have peach tarts?" She walked over to the cooling rack and lifted up a blue-and-white plaid cloth off the plate, revealing several glistening, sugary peach tarts.

"Take as many as you like." Mrs. Copeland winked at her. "And there's a bottle of sherry in the cupboards if you'd like a wee nip before bed."

Joanna grinned and fetched the bottle. "Only if you have a glass with me." She retrieved a couple of small sherry glasses and filled them. Mrs. Copeland put up only a small protest before taking her glass, her hazel eyes twinkling. It was a post-ball ritual to have a tart and a glass of sherry with the cook.

"Now then, how was the dancing?" Mrs. Copeland asked after Joanna daintily cut into her tart with a fork.

"It was..."

Divine.

Wretched.

Dancing with Brock had been simply wonderful, but

what had happened afterward... Shame burned the back of her throat, and she blinked away tears.

"What's the matter, dearie?" Mrs. Copeland patted one of her hands. "You look ready to cry. I thought balls were supposed to be wonderful."

Joanna banished the tears. The last thing she wanted was to appear foolish. Even though she'd been friends with Mrs. Copeland most of her life, she had never dared to tell anyone in the house her troubles with suitors—or the lack thereof.

"Do you believe in perfect kisses, Mrs. Copeland?" she asked.

It was something she dared not ask her mother. Regina Lennox was a lovely woman, Joanna admitted that readily, but the idea of asking her mother about such things seemed terrifying. Her mother would likely question her fiercely as to what she meant by asking and whether there was a gentleman out there whom Ashton should be bring to heel as a husband.

"Perfect kisses?" Mrs. Copeland's eyes narrowed slightly. "Have you been kissing some young buck, Miss Joanna?"

"I...no," she lied. "I was just thinking about them, you know. It's not as though I have a beau with whom to practice."

"Practice?" The cook snorted. "'Tis only the men who need *practice*. If the kiss isn't perfect, blame the man, I say."

There was no blame she could give at all to Brock.
His kisses *were* perfect. And that was exactly the
problem.

"Mrs. Copeland, did you marry Mr. Copeland for
love?" The cook's late husband had been the head groom
for their horses in the country. After his passing, Ashton
had insisted on the cook traveling with them. Joanna
had suspected it was because Mrs. Copeland missed her
husband and the country house reminded her of him
almost everywhere.

"Love? My Albert? Lord no, not at first. He was
simply a handsome lad with straight legs, dark hair, and
all his teeth. And when he smiled," the cook said with a
sigh, "I fairly turned to a pot of butter melting in the
sun." Mrs. Copeland added, her tone softer, "Love,
though, that came after." Her eyes crinkled at the
corners as she smiled.

Joanna clung to the words. "Love came after?" Could
it be possible to marry someone and let love follow? She
believed it might be possible for her, but she wasn't sure
if Brock could fall in love with her in return.

"When I was young, I married 'cause I had to in
order to support my younger siblings since my parents
were dead. Albert was strong, had a good position with
your family, and your mother and father had no issue
with their cook being married to their groom. It was a
match that suited everyone. Albert was handsome, as I
said, and it made bedding pleasurable. But it was the

small things that came later, the things you may not notice at first, mind you, where he began to show his love for me, and I for him."

Joanna took another bite of her tart, fixated on Mrs. Copeland. "What kind of small things?"

The cook sipped her sherry. "He would sneak into our room before I was done in the kitchens and have a footwarmer under the sheets, and he'd have a fine fire lit to keep our room warm in the winter. I used to make sure his boots were polished each night after he came to bed. They would get so dusty in the stables. Just before bed, he would cuddle me close and whisper, 'Have sweet dreams, my Nellie.' Then he kissed my temple." Mrs. Copeland sighed, her eyes overbright with tears and her voice a little rough.

This time Joanna was the one who patted Mrs. Copeland's hand.

The cook wiped her eyes and cleared her throat. "Now, you tell Nelly, what's all this talk of kisses and love? Have those silly gentlemen finally gotten wise to how pretty and intelligent you are?"

"No," Joanna said. That was the truth, as far she knew. Brock had offhandedly proposed to her, but that didn't mean he thought she was pretty or intelligent. He wanted her, yes, but he was so impulsive about it all that she wasn't certain why.

"What the devil is wrong with those men?" the cook said with a huff. "You're pretty, you're intelligent, and you're far too sweet." Mrs. Copeland waved the glass of sherry to accentuate her point.

Joanna finished her tart, feeling no more decided on Brock and his proposal than before. She had hoped that when a man she cared about finally got around to asking her, there would've been...trumpets blowing, she supposed, vows of undying love, something worthy of the quest to win her heart. A marriage proposal should not have been thrown out in the middle of an argument in a dark carriage with a man she had just slapped in front of all of Bath.

Weariness filled her with a heavy fog as she tried to think of what she should do, not just about Brock but about her future.

"Why don't you go to bed? You look dead on your feet, dearie." Mrs. Copeland took her plate and gave her a gentle shove toward the door leading out of the kitchens. Joanna paused only long enough to look back as Mrs. Copeland put away the sherry, the cook was still wiping her eyes.

How lucky Mrs. Copeland had been to have a love like that. Joanna turned away, and with dragging, defeated steps she sought refuge in the library. Sometimes she was too exhausted to sleep, and a good book would help relax her mind. The library of their townhouse in Bath was smaller than the one at their manor house in the country but still large enough that she could wander between the tall shelves and lose herself within the land of books. As a child, she'd often imagined that a doorway between the shelves would open up and she could step inside the pages of a story itself. Now she wished more than ever that she could do just that. Step into a world apart from this one and forget her troubles.

Joanna took a candle from the table by the door and lit it with a taper from the fireplace. Then she perused the shelves, studying the various titles. Nothing immediately drew her attention, but she continued to look as she moved deeper into the shelves toward the back of the room. If she was being honest with herself, all she could think about was being kissed deliriously by the man who haunted her thoughts now. She touched the spine of a nearby book as if it held the answers she longed for, such as why Brock was back in England now and callously proposing marriage at the worst, least romantic time. Furthermore he didn't love her, didn't believe in love matches. What the devil was she to say to that? She believed in love matches and every wonderful thing that came with them.

None of these books would do to distract her. Damned Scot! How dare he wreck a perfectly good night! She might as well just head up to bed. She started back to the edge of the nearest bookcase but froze when she heard voices close by.

When the door to the library opened, the voices

echoed along the spines of the books. Her breath stirred the flame of the candle she held close to her face.

"Ashton, we must speak," Regina, their mother, said. "Please stop walking away from me. It's important."

"Mother." Ashton's aggrieved sigh would have made Joanna smile, but her mother's next words forced her to remain silent and out of sight behind the shelf.

"I'm worried about Joanna. You saw her tonight, how irresponsible. So many dances with Lord Kincade..."

"I heard," Ashton said bitterly.

"And then to strike him? If she had any chance of a match before tonight, she has none now."

Ashton's booted steps sounded as though he was pacing before the fire.

"I am worried as well, but not because of tonight. Joanna was pushed to her limits—her frustration at her situation is quite clear. I do not fault her in the least for hitting Kincade. He had no intention of letting her go to another man for the rest of those dances. My concern lies in that no man will take her now, as she is. I put out discreet offers to the best gentlemen, but the moment I utter her name, the men flee. I've emptied entire card rooms at my club. I do not understand it."

Joanna bit her tongue painfully and closed her eyes, feeling very small and useless. Her own brother was trying to sell her off, and not even then would any gentleman take her. Shame closed her throat, and tears burned her eyes.

"If she wants to remain unmarried, that is quite fine. I'm all for women leading an independent existence if they so desire, but Joanna has always wanted to be in love. It's so clear that she's unhappy." Her mother's voice was closer to the shelf that Joanna hid behind now, and Joanna held her breath, afraid of revealing her position. The shame would only double if they discovered her eavesdropping.

"What if..." her mother began. "What if she were to marry Lord Kincade? He looked most bewitched by her. I daresay five dances is quite an indication of a gentleman's interest."

Joanna's heart leapt with forbidden hopes. Had her mother seen something in Brock's actions tonight that suggested he might actually care for her? Or was it simply in his nature to cause scandals and break hearts? She desperately wished it was the former, but how was she to know for sure?

"Gentleman? Have you not forgotten that he kidnapped my fiancée? In the middle of the night, no less, while I lay at death's door?" Ashton's tone was hard.

"Ashton, dear, you exaggerate. Death's door indeed. And need I remind you that you kidnapped Lady Essex, before she became Lady Essex?"

Ashton snorted. "*Godric* kidnapped her."

"With *your* help." Their mother's tone was full of amusement and a little judgment. Joanna wrinkled her nose, frowning. Ashton had indeed helped the Duke of

Essex kidnap his future wife, and he certainly shouldn't be casting stones when his own house was made of spun glass.

"Perhaps I'm mad, Mother," Ashton replied. "But I don't want to entrust my youngest sister into the hands of an irresponsible brute. I wasn't old enough to protect Thomasina when she married Lord Reddington, and he had quite the reputation as a scoundrel back then. Thankfully, he turned out all right. But Lord Kincade? He's irresponsible and reckless. What if Rosalind had fallen ill from tending to me after he and her other brothers had taken her? They were sleeping on the ground in bloody bedrolls. If she'd taken ill, without proper care, she might have died. I dread to imagine how Kincade would treat a wife."

"Ashton"

"And don't forget the state of the castle. It's crumbling to bits. If Joanna were to live there, she would catch her death in winter from those drafts."

Joanna took a chance to peer around the edge of the bookcase. Ashton was pacing back and forth by the fireplace, his coat discarded and his sleeves rolled up as he moved. Their mother stood close by, playing idly with the fan that hung from her wrist. Both looked upset.

Joanna scowled. She was the one who should be upset, not them. They weren't the ones with no certain future ahead of them and no chance at love.

"Why do you think he's a brute?" Regina asked, her

tone quiet, more colored with worry now. "You think he's like Rosalind's father?"

There was a hesitation, thick and heavy, before Ashton responded. "I don't believe so, no. But he and the others, they don't seem *civilized*. Aside from Edinburgh, Scotland is a land of deep forests, wooded hills, and rivers, populated by fierce people. Joanna is refined and cultured. What sort of life would she have there? She'd be lonely in that dank castle. No more balls, no more parties, no more society." Ashton had stopped pacing now.

All of that sounded perfectly lovely to Joanna, but if Brock didn't love her, then she couldn't agree to marry him.

"I hadn't thought of that," their mother said, her tone soft with regret. "But if not Kincade, then who? I don't want my child to be lonely. You have Rosalind, Rafe is..." Regina sighed and chuckled. "Rafe is likely to be a bachelor forever and quite content with that. But Joanna is like me, a woman who craves love. I simply want to see her happy."

"As do I," Ashton agreed. He scrubbed a hand over his jaw, and his shoulders slumped with the weight of his responsibilities as head of the Lennox family. "Come, it's late, and we should both get some rest."

"Yes. So much to do," Regina agreed. "The wedding is the day after tomorrow, after all. Everyone is coming. And I do mean *everyone*."

Ashton laughed, and Joanna heard the warmth of it, and despite her own sorrow, she was glad. Ashton and her mother had finally repaired a broken bridge between them. Brock's sister, Rosalind, had so much to do with that.

"Let's hope not *everyone*," Ashton replied, still chuckling. "Mrs. Copeland doesn't have the capacity of feeding the entire city."

"Oh, hush, don't let her hear you say that. She'll take it as a challenge."

Joanna heard the creak of the library door as her brother and mother exited. She stayed hidden awhile longer, her heart beating hard but slow, each sound echoing in her head. She gazed at the small yellow-and-orange flame wavering on the candle she held.

Was she lonely? She hadn't wanted to admit it to herself, but she was. All of her friends were married now, some even with babes on the way, but not Joanna. She felt frozen, yet she could feel herself aging every day with no husband, no children, nothing to show for it. Her friend Lysandra Russell was seemingly content to be alone. She was obsessed with astronomy and never wanted to attend any balls or dinner parties. Joanna's passion was reading. Perhaps she could become a novelist, like Jane Austen and spend the remainder of her days writing books. That wouldn't be so terrible, would it?

The memory of Brock's mouth on hers, the mingling of their breath in the quiet darkness of the coach and feel of his large, strong hands touching her hips sent a swift, powerful flood of heat through her from head to toe. She wanted that, the wild fluttering excitement and the following heady, dizzying feeling of being in a man's arms, but not just any man. She wanted Brock. She had to admit that to herself, even if nothing came of it. But could it? Had he truly been serious about proposing to her? Could she trust him, or had it been a ploy to woo her so he might bed her and look for another lady on the morrow to sate his lusts?

No...she didn't think so. There had been a note of honesty in his gaze that seemed to tell her the proposal had indeed been real, if perhaps unplanned.

Two days. She had two days to decide what she wished to do.

Joanna abandoned her quest for a book, knowing that she would never have a chance to read now. She would spend all night running through every possible decision she could make about her life and her future. She blew out her candle, watching the smoke curl up from the blackened wick in ghostly tendrils. Then she headed up to her bedchamber with thoughts of Brock in her mind and the touch of his lips over hers.

She knew it was going to be a very long night.

5

B rock woke late, the sun pouring through the sash windows of his bedchamber. He rather liked the multipaned glass of the windows. They were commonplace in England, but not back home. He blinked, bleary-eyed, as he remembered he was not in Scotland. He was in England for Rosalind's wedding. He winced as he remembered last night at the ball. Joanna. She'd slapped him, and then he'd tossed her into a coach and almost brought her here to this residence.

If Rosalind ever found out what he had tried to do, she would toss him and his brothers out on their ears. She had helped him and their two younger brothers, Brodie and Aiden, secure this townhouse. She called it *decent*. He called it extravagant. It would indeed have been a fine place to bring Joanna last night, but alas, he'd decided against compromising her to get what he wanted—her as his wife.

Brock lay still, staring up at the dark green brocade canopy of the expensive bed he'd slept in. The furnishings were new and fashionable, the house was well staffed, and the rooms were large and warm. It wasn't what he was used to at all. Although Castle Kincade was vast, he only lived in a small portion of it, and what furniture they had left wasn't in decent condition. The thought made him wince.

Brock sat up, noticing he had foolishly dragged a handful of blankets to bed, expecting drafts, only to have kicked the blankets to the floor in the middle of the night when he'd gotten too hot. Last night had been positively stifling. *Bloody English weather.*

This house on Finchley Street wasn't home. It was more comfortable, cleaner, less crumbly, but it wasn't *home*. Brock slipped out of bed and walked over to the washbasin on his dresser. He splashed cold water over his face and brushed his knuckles along his jaw, feeling how rough his beard was, or at least the scruff that had grown overnight. There was enough to scrape his skin. That wouldn't do.

He had every intention of trapping and kissing Joanna Lennox in some corner today, and he wanted his skin as smooth as a bairn's bottom in case he had a chance to steal another kiss. If he didn't shave, she'd have a redness about her cheeks that would give away the fact that he'd been kissing her. The last thing he needed was to get in another fight with Lennox before Rosalind's wedding. His sister would never forgive him. He unfolded the leather wrap on the dresser, revealing his pot of shaving cream, brush, and razor. Then he set about the task of shaving. He was only two strokes in when his bedchamber door burst open and Brodie rushed inside, grinning.

"Ach, good, you're up, man. I feared you'd sleep the day away."

Brock, razor still frozen against his skin, was never more glad that being the eldest had trained him not to startle easily. He hadn't cut himself.

"Brodie, you know they make doors for a reason— so younger brothers knock. What if I hadna been alone?"

His brother chuckled, his grayish-blue eyes glinting. "But you *are* alone. No doubt you were mooning over that wee Joanna all night."

"I dinna moon," Brock growled, narrowing his eyes as his brother walked over to the bed and sat on the edge, looking far too smug for his own good.

"Aye, you do." Brodie crossed his arms over his chest. "Oooh, Joanna, sweet pretty Joanna," he mocked in a silly, high-pitched voice.

Brock met his brother's gaze in the reflection in the mirror behind him as he continued to shave.

"It is not wise to mock a man armed with a blade, brother."

Brodie chuckled, ignoring the threat. "Well? Did you catch up with her?"

"Who?" Brock moved his razor to the other side of his face, the side that Joanna had slapped—quite hard, in fact. He rather liked that she was a strong lass, but he wanted to give her no cause to strike him a second time. Although he admitted he deserved it the first time.

"Joanna!" Brodie exclaimed in exasperation. "Lord, are you even listening to me? I saw you run after her when she fled the ball. Everyone was talking about it. You danced with her too much, it seems. Apparently, the English think that's scandalous." Brodie smirked, and Brock knew that smile all too well. Whatever Brodie thought was scandalous would be disastrous for a normal man or woman.

He hadn't danced with her enough, but once they were married he would remedy that. He would dance with her every night if he had the chance.

"So...did you catch her?" Brodie persisted.

Brock finished shaving his throat and nodded. "Aye, we had a wee talk, but she is still upset about our first meeting."

His brother grinned again. "When you kissed her and left her trussed up? I can't imagine *any* reason why a gentle lady would still be upset." Brodie's amused sarcasm made Brock's temper flare.

"What do you want, Brodie? If it's to needle me all day, you must have better things to do."

"We have tea at Lennox's house. You'd better dress and be ready in an hour." Brodie got off the bed and left Brock alone to scowl as he wiped his face clean.

Tea at Lennox's house. T'would be heaven and hell as he tried to mend the tenuous trust he and Lennox had been building, and most importantly, it was an opportunity to see Joanna again. This brought a smile to his lips, then a frown. Lennox would be there, no doubt keeping an eye on him and making plans to keep Joanna far away. Brock had every intention of doing something about that.

Brock finished dressing alone, much to the dismay of the valet his sister had provided for him. He'd grown used to existing with a small staff at Castle Kincade. They had only a cook, a steward, two footmen, one maid, a groom, and a coach driver. It was enough for a townhouse, but not an ancient castle. But once he married Joanna, if she was agreeable to it, he would like to hire more staff.

He fetched his hat and coat and left his bedchamber. Brodie had gone ahead it seemed, but Aiden was waiting for him in the hall by the front door. Aiden was the youngest, and he was both quieter and less boisterous than Brodie. He had suffered most at the hands of their abusive father, and with the man only recently in his grave, Aiden was still quiet—not quite sullen, but more melancholic.

Brock did his best to cheer his brother up when he could, but Aiden preferred to be left alone. Only the company of the wild animals he rescued drew his focus these days. Brock often wondered if Aiden's obsession with the beasties was out of some belief that he could save creatures as no one had been able to save him. The thought left Brock with a dull ache in his chest. Once he had Joanna as his wife, he'd turn his attention to Aiden, and see if he couldn't lift his brother's spirits.

"Ready for tea?" Brock asked.

Aiden shrugged. "Tea is tea, isn't it? But I will be happy to see our sister."

They climbed into the coach after giving the driver instructions to Lennox's townhouse. When they arrived, Brock was surprised to see dozens of other coaches lined up along the street and at least a dozen people walking toward Lennox's front door.

"Is the man having tea or holding court?" Brodie joked as he met them at the door, but no one laughed.

Aiden shrank back, and Brock gently nudged him in the back.

"It will be fine. You can go inside, greet Rosalind, and then go into the gardens. Fewer people are likely to be there."

Aiden squared his shoulders and nodded. They followed the crowd to the door and filed in behind several ladies in fine colorful tea gowns. Aiden blushed as one of the young ladies glanced back at him and smiled, then whispered something to her friends, and they broke out in barely hushed giggles.

"Come on." Brock ushered Aiden past the ladies who lingered in the entryway, still smiling at his little brother.

"There are so many," Aiden muttered. "Just like last night. They make me nervous."

"Women have a way of doing that, no matter where you are," Brock said with a chuckle. He and Brodie were more used to women's ways as they both spent much time in Edinburgh, but Aiden avoided society, preferring the rocks, hills, trees, and animals as his way to commune with nature.

"Brock!" Rosalind came sweeping down the stairs, looking radiant in a bright-orange gown with a teal-blue sash that made her appear like a colorful songbird. He caught her up, swinging her around in his arms before he set her down so she could embrace Aiden. Her wide smile was full of joy, and Brock's own heart was bursting at the sight of his little sister's happiness. If Lennox made her feel this way, he couldn't be that bad of a fellow. But that didn't mean he completely trusted the man.

"Aiden, the Duchess of Essex is in the garden with her foxhound, Penelope. Would you mind offering her some advice on training her dog?"

"I'd be happy to." Aiden's open relief was obvious as

he rushed off toward the back gardens. Rosalind watched him go and then turned back to Brock.

"How is he?" she asked, her tone softening so as not to be overheard by any of the guests nearby.

"No worse. No better," Brock admitted. "Father left wounds on all of us—his are deeper than ours."

Rosalind bit her lip. The joy he had seen moments earlier began to wane.

Brock scanned the crowd. "So, where's Lennox?"

"The dining room. We had so many guests we had to have the tea service set up there. His friends are already here."

Lennox's friends? Brock wanted to groan. The papers called them the League of Rogues, and that they were. Bloody meddling *Sassenachs*. He'd met a few of them a few years back in a pub outside of Edinburgh. That encounter had cost both sides some coin to repair the broken furniture from the brawl. The memory brought a sudden, unexpected smile to his face. It had been a good fight.

"If you break even *one* chair..." his sister warned.

Brock raised his hands in mock surrender. "I swear to be on my best behavior."

"Speaking of behavior." Rosalind's gray-blue eyes sparked a fire. "What were you thinking last night? Joanna has been desperately trying to find a husband. After what you did, I worry that she has no hope."

"Good," Brock said, and almost laughed at the look of incredulity on Rosalind's face.

"Good? Why pray tell is that *good?*" she hissed. "Joanna is a sweet woman and one of my dear friends. I don't want you hurting her."

"'Tis good because I intend to marry the lass." He grinned when his sister's mouth opened but no words came out. She blinked several times, and then without warning, she punched him hard in the shoulder.

"Ow!" he snapped, surprised that the blow actually stung.

"Brock Angus Kincade, you had best be teasing me."

"I am not." He sobered. "She's everything I want in a wife, and 'tis time I married. What's wrong with that?"

"But..." Rosalind continued to stare at him. "Do you even know her? I mean, truly? Her favorite color, her favorite flower, what she likes to do for enjoyment?"

He didn't, and as he realized this, he frowned. He *wanted* to know all of those things.

"I will find out," he promised Rosalind.

"You cannot go up to her and simply *ask*. You must let it flow naturally."

Brock scowled at his sister. "How about that woman you mentioned, the duchess? I heard her courtship was far from natural."

"Yes, well, that's different."

"And I seem to recall that your courtship with Lennox did not flow *naturally*."

Rosalind's cheeks turned a fiery red. "Yes, well, things were different with Ashton and me. We always had..." She struggled for a word. "A spark, a fire that burned hot between us. Learning about each other came after."

"'Tis the same for Joanna and me," Brock said, thinking of how when he held the woman in his arms there was so much more than a simple spark between them. It was an uncontrollable blaze.

"Brock." Rosalind caught his arm, her face earnest, her brows drawn together. "You must take care, especially with Joanna. She is Ash's youngest sister and my friend. I don't want to see her hurt."

"You are *my* sister, and Lennox took you."

"Is that what this is? Revenge for marrying Ashton?"

"Of course not." He bristled like an irate badger. "I'm merely pointing out that Lennox has made you happy, and I'm willing to let him marry you. Why canna you do the same for me?"

Rosalind's eyes brightened. "Do you love her? She *needs* love, Brock. She's like me—she wants to be loved, madly, wildly. I remembered that you always said you would never love, because love would make you vulnerable. But Father is dead. He cannot reach us from the grave. You must be able to love her."

Brock's throat tightened. He didn't want to lie to Rosalind, didn't want to say he would love Joanna. He would care for her—he already did, in his own way—but love? He could not promise that because he did not know if he was capable of it anymore. Certainly not the kind of love Joanna no doubt read of in her Gothic novels. Love was not something that made you swoon and sigh. Love destroyed a person. It burned away at them inside until disappointments robbed them of their last gasping breath. Just as it had killed his mother.

I won't let that happen to me. I will never allow myself to love anyone like that.

"I will care for her, Rosalind." It was all he could say. His sister frowned in a way that reminded him with a stab of pain of their beloved mother. She'd always been able to sense when he wasn't being truthful, and she would make exactly that same expression Rosalind was making now.

"Brock..." she said again, worry in her tone. Before she could speak further, Regina Lennox called Rosalind's name, waving her over to a twittering crowd of ladies who were gathered around Brodie.

He was grinning devilishly, no doubt regaling the ladies with some scandalous tale or another. Brodie had never met a woman he didn't like. While Aiden preferred animals to people, and Brock had a stone wall around his heart, Brodie's way of dealing with their abusive father had left him hungry to be loved by all without truly loving anyone in return. If Brodie wasn't careful, he'd find himself at the end of a dueling pistol before long.

The moment Rosalind left him alone, Brock skirted around the groups of guests, his eyes seeking only one face within the crowd. He chanced running into Lennox and his friends by opening the door to the dining room. Several gentlemen, Lennox included, milled about a sideboard table, filling teacups. Brock stifled a snort. The small blue-and-white patterned cups in their hands looked ridiculous. Tea was fine enough, but Brock wouldn't be caught drinking from so dainty a cup, at least not here. He began to withdraw from the room after failing to spot Joanna, but someone called his name.

"Ah, Kincade," the Earl of Lonsdale said, humor glinting in the man's gray eyes. "If you feel the urge to smash some furniture, try to use the chairs in the kitchen. Lennox doesn't like them, and you'd be doing him a favor, old boy." The men all chuckled. Lonsdale crossed his arms over his chest, smirking in open challenge.

Poor bastard thinks he can rile me in front of the guests.

"As I recall, it was you who broke a chair...over *my* back, and it didna do much to stop me. In fact, I thought a barmaid had swatted me with a wet cloth until I turned around and saw it was you. I didna think the English were so weak, but...alas..." He trailed off, leaving the mild insult to fester in the air.

Lonsdale's grin faltered, and he glanced at his friends as though hoping one of them would defend him.

"Well, given what I've seen of barmaids in Scotland, that's a compliment, Charles. Some of those wenches look strong enough to toss a caber." The Duke of Essex snorted into his teacup.

Completely unperturbed, Brock chuckled. "Aye, our women have to be in order to serve us. I dinna have a problem with a strong lass. 'Tis your dainty English lassies I canna make sense of." If that didn't put any man off the scent of his plans for Joanna, he would be shocked.

"Kincade, come join us," Lennox offered, putting the barbed comments to an end. He nodded toward a teacup that had yet to be claimed on the sideboard.

"I thank you, but I'm afraid I'm looking for someone." Lennox's eyes narrowed, and Brock was hasty to add, "Aiden, my brother." Brock had no compunction about lying to Lennox.

"Ah…" Lennox's hawkish expression lightened. "He's outside in the gardens."

"Thank you." Brock left Lennox and the others to their tea and slipped back in the corridor again. He feared he would have to search the entire house to find Joanna. Just then, he saw a flutter of green fabric disappear into a room at the end of the corridor. He pursued the flash of color, opening the door a few moments later.

The library. Of course. She loved to read. Joanna was studying the shelves. The flare of her hips and the bright-green satin gown embroidered with wildflowers made her appear like a tempting garden nymph. Blonde curls danced down the slope of her swanlike neck, making his mouth run dry as he imagined placing soft, hot kisses on her skin as he held on to her waist from behind. Lord, the woman had a way of bewitching him.

He moved softly. Years of hunting deer in the sparsely wooded hills had trained him well. She was mere inches away when he reached out to touch her shoulder. Joanna screeched and leapt into the air.

"Hush, lass," he warned, instantly turning her around.

"Oh! It's you!" She placed a hand over her chest, breathing hard. The effort made her breasts swell against her tight bodice. "What are you doing here?" she demanded when she caught her breath.

Brock stared at her. "I came to see you...and Rosalind, of course."

"Of course. I meant, what are you doing in the *library*." She slid to the side, escaping him when he rested one palm on the shelf beside her.

"As I said, I came to see you." He didn't want her to escape. He reached out and caught the flow of her skirts, just above her bottom, pulling her to a stop. She turned, glancing down at his hand fisted in the fabric. She quirked a brow, challenging him, silently demanding that he let go.

He most certainly wouldn't do that. He gazed back into her blue eyes, watching a blush slowly unfurl on her cheeks as he moved closer and curled one arm around her waist.

"Is this your favorite color?" he asked, giving her green skirts a playful tug.

"What?" She looked up at him, and her lashes half lowered when she focused on his lips. He knew she was thinking about kissing him, and he wanted to grant that wish, but his sister was right—he needed to know more about her.

"Green, is that your favorite color?"

"I... No, not really."

"Then what is it?" He cupped her cheek and moved their bodies backward so he had her caged against the wall by the window.

"It's gold."

"Gold? Like this?" He slipped his fingers beneath the fine gold chain around her throat until the solitary blue sapphire stone pendant glinted in the light. Her skin felt warm beneath the backs of his knuckles, and for a moment he forgot what they were talking about.

Joanna's breath hitched a little. "No. Gold like the color of leaves in late October, or the way the sunlight illuminates the leaves just before they fall."

"Like glittering rain?" he added. He knew just the color she meant, and it was indeed spectacular.

Joanna nodded. "It's the most beautiful thing I've ever seen." She lowered her head, another blush flaming her face. "What about you? What's your favorite color?"

She placed a hand on his chest, her elegant fingers moving over the plain ruby-colored silk of his waistcoat.

For a moment he was ashamed that he was not dressed in finer clothes, like the other men here. She must expect a gentleman to look like a gentleman. Right now, he felt like a farmhand in his simple clothes. But he could not afford more. Back home he felt no embarrassment, but here in the fine trappings of Lennox's Bath house, he felt shame, though he had nothing to be ashamed of. He tensed, ready to step back, but she raised her eyes to his again.

"Brock?" His name upon her lips seemed to ring like a distant bell, giving him peace, clarity.

"Red, like the color of a fox's coat, that ruddy orange-red."

She tilted her head as though considering his words.

"That's a lovely color." She slid her hand up his chest to his shoulder, her fingers curled slightly, as though she hungered to hold him close. He echoed that need as he gripped her waist.

"I want to know you, Joanna. I want to learn all your secrets." Brock brushed the backs of his knuckles over her cheeks, and her lashes fluttered in response. His body burned for her in a way that made him unsteady, like he'd snuck a few too many sips of whiskey. A delicious shudder shot through him as he slowly pulled back the heavy blue curtain of the window and moved her behind it. Now they were shielded from the rest of the world, and it was only the two of them.

"What are we doing?" Joanna whispered.

"Learning each other, lass." He pulled the curtain closed around them. They faced the glass of the window and could see the thick blossoms of the rhododendrons that crowded the windowpanes with bursts of lavender amid the green leaves. No one could see them from the garden outside, except perhaps his head, but not Joanna's. They were safe in this private world.

"Do you like to ride?" Brock asked as he lifted one of her hands up, studying the blue veins that ran beneath her fair skin like lines on a map. He wanted to memorize the pattern, carve it into his mind because it was a part of her. His future wife.

"I do. I'm not particularly good, I suppose. Horses make me nervous if I ride alone, but if I'm with someone, I enjoy it." She was touching his shoulder again, exploring, her fingers caressing the muscles beneath the shirt he wore.

"I like to ride as well." Brock pressed his lips to her hand, against the entrancing pattern of those veins, and she trembled a little.

"And you read?" she asked.

He nodded. "Aye. Whenever possible. My mother loved books, as do I."

"That's good," Joanna murmured before her eyes strayed to his lips again.

"I have more questions," he promised. "But if I dinna kiss you right now, I may go mad."

He gave her time to resist, to push him away. When instead she curled her arms around his neck, he lowered his lips to hers, feeling a flood of victory within him that would have made his warrior ancestors proud.

My sweet little Sassenach *has surrendered to me.*

6

This was madness. Joanna knew she ought to protest, to push Brock away, but all she could hear was her mother and brother's conversation from the previous night, haunting her. Her melancholy thoughts soon faded beneath the hum of her blood under her skin as she surrendered to Brock's kiss.

She was not wanted, not desired...yet here was a man who *did* want her. He not only wanted her but he wanted to know her. And she wanted to know him, this quiet, brooding man who showed her a world of passion whenever he touched her. Perhaps lust could turn to love given enough time?

She closed her eyes as their mouths met in a soft, slow kiss. She gripped his massive shoulders, admiring the way he stretched the coat he wore. He towered over her and she couldn't help but feel small and delicate, in a purely feminine way that she liked immensely.

The gentlemen at the ball last night were nothing compared to him. He moved with a masculine, nonchalant grace that spoke of years of working every part of his body rather than lounging around card tables or billiard rooms. The outlines of his muscles strained against the fabric of his waistcoat, and she wondered if he had outgrown the garment over the last few years, becoming even more muscled. The thought sent a wild racing pulse straight to the core of her womanhood.

Brock moved his mouth expertly over hers, kissing her with great gentleness, which negated any fears she had about him using his strength to overwhelm her. She stroked a hand down the square line of his jaw, feeling the clean-shaven skin. Their mouths broke apart, and she was lost in his gaze, astonished by the inherent strength in his face and that sharp, assessing gaze that softened whenever he was close to her. She wondered if in some way she tempered the wild, feral man before her.

"Lass...what you do to me..." His voice was husky, and her skin broke out in goose bumps.

"What do I do to you?" she asked, her voice breathless as she craved to know his answer. Was he as affected by this wonderful madness as she was?

He stroked the pad of his thumb over her bottom lip. "You make me...forget," he said, his warm breath fanning her face. How could this feel so intimate? This closeness, the sharing of breath? He lowered his head again to kiss her.

"Forget what?" she asked between kisses.

"How to behave. I shouldna be doing this here, but I want you so much."

"I want you too." She tugged at his shoulders, wanting something more.

Brock's hand wandered up her leg, pulling her skirt up to her thigh, and she whimpered in delight, and with a little trepidation. His palm was rough and hot as a firebrand against her thigh. She'd never had a man touch her there before

The sound of the library door opening made them both freeze. Voices could be heard. Voices she recognized.

"Ash, what's wrong?" Charles asked.

Joanna shifted closer in Brock's arms at the same time he moved to shield her behind him. They were hidden by the fall of the curtain, so surely no one would see them. Especially, she hoped, her brother and his friend.

"Something is bothering me. I can't say what," Ashton said. His voice drew closer. Joanna could still feel Brock's hand on her thigh, his fingers digging into her skin as they both remained still.

"It's the Scots, isn't it? Ever since they came to Bath, you've been...twitching." Charles chuckled.

"I haven't." Ashton's voice was full of frustration.

There was another snort of laughter, but it cut off abruptly. "I say...are curtains supposed to have boots beneath them?"

Joanna had but an instant to look down and realize the curtain didn't cover Brock's feet and his boots were clearly visible. There was a wrenching of the fabric as it was flung aside.

"God's blood!" Ashton bellowed as he caught sight of them. A few feet behind him Charles stood, watching them, mouth agape. Joanna rushed to smooth out her mussed hair in panic.

"Ash" Joanna began, but her brother had already thrown a punch, catching Brock squarely on the jaw. He staggered but did not fall.

"No!" Joanna tried to get around Brock so she might step between him and her brother, but she couldn't. He threw an arm out, keeping her trapped behind him.

"I knew I couldn't trust you!" Ashton shouted and swung another fist. Brock dodged it. Joanna tried to grasp Brock, but her hands met thin air and she toppled to the ground, wincing as her hip and arms took the brunt of her weight on the hardwood floor. She scrambled to press herself flat against the wall by the window as Ashton dove at Brock, catching him around the waist. The pair stumbled back, knocking into a sturdy bookshelf, but the momentum made the shelf quake, and a number of books toppled to the ground.

Brock struggled to catch one of the books before it landed on the floor, but the effort only opened him up to a sharp jab of Ashton's fist straight into his stomach. He didn't drop the book, but he grunted with a look of pain.

Charles knelt beside her, offering her a hand, which she gratefully accepted. She got to her feet and tried to move toward the fighting men, but Charles caught her wrist.

"Wait a moment—you'll only get hit if you get too close. Let them sort it out themselves."

"But he's hurting Brock!" she cried and pulled free of Charles's hand. It was quite clear Ashton was the aggressor, and Brock was doing his best to fend off blows while not throwing any of his own.

"If you ever touch my sister again," Ashton shouted between each punch, "I'll bloody kill you!"

"Brock!" Joanna called his name, wanting him to defend himself, to fight back a little.

"Quiet, Joanna!" Ashton commanded, and she flinched. He'd never spoken to her like that before, with his tone so full of disappointment and annoyance.

"You willna not speak to her like that," Brock growled and threw a single punch to Ashton's stomach. It caught Ashton by surprise, and he stumbled back, sucking in pained breaths.

Joanna leapt forward to throw herself in front of Brock as Ashton tried to rally. Her brother skidded to a stop, his fist glancing off her cheek as he tried desperately to pull his punch back, but it was too late. He clipped Joanna, and she cried out in pain. Brock moved fast, lifting her gently into his arms and carrying her to a soft chair. She appreciated his gentleness more than she could say. The fall on the floor had left her shaken and bruised.

Brock stroked her cheek. "Does it hurt, lass?"

"Not much," she said, feeling oddly shy now that her brother was watching them.

Ashton walked over, his steps slow, cautious, his face pale.

"Joanna, I'm so sorry. I didn't mean to..." He scraped a hand over his jaw as he knelt by her. Brock never took his eyes off her as he stayed protectively close. He grasped one of her hands in his and didn't let go.

"Should we call the doctor?" Charles asked her as he hovered close by.

Her cheeks flamed in embarrassment. "I'm fine. Truly." She squeezed Brock's hand, and their gazes locked. She'd been having such a wonderful time with him until her brother had ruined everything. "Ashton, please go." She glanced toward her brother.

His worried expression turned to disapproval. "Joanna, I'm not going to leave you alone with him. You were just"

"Just what? If you say he compromised me, then think carefully about the consequences. Besides, *you* were the one who struck me." It was the first time she'd spoken so forcefully to her brother. She knew he hadn't meant to hit her, but she needed him to understand that only one man in this room had truly tried to protect her, and it wasn't Ashton.

Her brother's brow furrowed. "If I go, he goes as well. I'm not leaving him alone with you. That's final." Ashton's response was hard edged, and Joanna sensed she wouldn't win that battle. She squeezed Brock's hand again and gave him a small nod to let him know she was fine to be left alone.

"Come, Kincade. I'll see you out. I think it is best you go home today."

Brock rose, his gaze still on Joanna's face. "And the wedding?"

For a second Joanna thought he was speaking about her.

The two men stared at each other for a long moment, still breathing hard. Then Ashton's gaze softened.

"You'll still be there tomorrow to walk Rosalind down the aisle," Ashton conceded.

Brock nodded once at Ashton, and the two men left the library without a backward glance. Charles remained, his lips twitching.

"So, you and the Scot, eh?" He whistled softly, his gray eyes glinting.

Joanna stood from her chair, her hip twinging. "Yes... I mean no... No, I don't know."

"Jo, he had his hand up your skirts," Charles said more seriously.

She blushed again. It had been ages since Charles had called her Jo. She'd once believed herself in love with him, years ago, before she'd come to understand that loving Charles was like loving a distant god. He would never open his heart to any woman. Once she'd realized that, she let her girlish fantasies about him fade. But she was still mortified that he and Ashton had caught her kissing Brock.

"I don't have many options, Charles," she said quietly, her gaze fixed on the books that had fallen to the floor. She bent to pick up one, sighing at the way the pages were bent. She had not missed that Brock had done his best to catch the books, taking a few blows from her brother in the process.

Charles joined her, collecting a pair of books that had toppled on each other like wounded birds. "Of course you do."

"Do not try to spare my feelings, Charles. I know the truth. Ashton tried to find me a match. There is not a man in England who would offer for me. I don't under-stand why." She couldn't help the pathetic, forlorn tone to her voice, but after everything that had happened, she was ready to break down and cry. Or perhaps smash every bloody teacup in the house. But neither of those things would make her feel better.

"So you take up with the Scot instead?" Charles's lips

twitched. "Wonderful way to drive your brother mad with worry."

Joanna blew out a frustrated breath. "I haven't *taken up* with him." He had proposed, offhandedly, it was true. But that wasn't a *true* proposal, not to her.

"Hmm...you may not have taken up with him then, but I do believe you are *taken with* him."

She didn't miss the difference, and she had to agree, at least silently. She was indeed quite taken with the tall, brooding Scotsman. Joanna knew this topic was taking a dangerous turn. She didn't want Charles to tell her brother that she was ready to run off to Gretna Green with Brock.

"Once upon a time, I was taken with you."

Charles's eyes lit up. "Were you now?" He lounged arrogantly against the bookshelf, and she retrieved the last of the books from the floor.

"I was, and then I grew out of that infatuation. I'm sure it will be the same with Lord Kincade."

Charles laughed. "I'm not sure about that. That fellow seems to have had the good fortune of kissing you, where others have not." He winked at her and then left her alone.

Joanna stared around the library, feeling listless. Her sense of refuge in this room had been destroyed, for now at least. When she finally left the library, she could see the tea was well underway, but she did not wish to join them. Ashton had thrown Brock out, and she didn't want to sit in a room without him. She went upstairs to her bedchamber instead. After she closed the door, she threw herself rather indelicately onto the bed and buried her face in the mess of pillows. She was not a child. She would not cry, no matter how much she was hurting. She drifted off to sleep and was woken several hours later by a knock upon her door.

"Who is it?" She sat up and tried to compose the mess of her hair, which had partially come undone during her rest.

"Your brother."

Joanna stiffened. Ashton wanted to talk. Of course he did. No doubt he'd spent all bloody afternoon preparing some lecture or speech on her behavior. Before she could refuse him, he opened the door and stepped inside. He closed the door behind himself and leaned back against it.

"Joanna, about what happened today..."

She held up a hand. "No. You do not get to lecture me. Not after how you behaved. You threw Lord Kincade out."

Her brother bristled. She was one of the few people who could actually penetrate Ashton's naturally calm demeanor.

"He was *kissing* you! What if it had been our mother or one of the other guests? You would be ruined! You would have to marry him, and a cloud of shame would fall upon you, upon all of us, like"

"If you say like Father, I warn you" She was not like their father. He had gambled and lost their fortunes when she had been young. The shame and scandal had driven their father to an early grave. It'd taken years for their mother to piece their social lives back together, and Ashton had borne the duty of restoring their fortune by what means he could. It had made him somewhat ruthless in the world of business, and sometimes that ruthlessness followed him home.

"I know you aren't like Father, but Joanna, you must see it from my perspective. You were kissing a stranger, and his hand was up your skirts and..." Ashton's face turned red as he seemed to realize he was going into too much unnecessary detail about her encounter with Brock.

"I can do what I please." Ice dripped from Joanna's words, even though her whole body tensed with the thought of how ruined ladies had no real life. "It's not as though I have any real prospects for marriage, is it?"

"Why on earth would you say that?"

"Because it's the truth. You've been trying to bribe men from here to Paris with a hefty dowry, and it isn't enough, is it? I'm unmatchable." The words, despite calmly coming from her own lips, still stung. Ashton's echoing look of dread and regret sealed the coffin of her own dreams.

"That isn't true," he hedged.

"Isn't it? Three seasons, Ashton. *Three.*" She ticked them off on her fingers.

"So you'll turn into a petulant child because you haven't found a decent match?" he shot back, his control lost.

"Petulant child?" she hissed, and hopped off her bed so she could stand toe to toe with her brother.

"Yes. You're throwing a fit because you don't have a husband." His gaze narrowed. "Fine, why don't you marry him? Go home with him to his crumbling castle in the cold drafts and be used by that brute for your money."

Brute? The man who held her so tenderly, who kissed her like she was a delicate snow flower blooming in an early spring? That man was far from brutal.

"Just because he is larger than you"

"He's not *refined*, Joanna. You deserve a gentle husband."

Not refined? He'd danced with her more smoothly, more elegantly than any man she'd danced with before. His feet had seemed to float, and she had floated with him, spinning in dizzying circles and smiling as she truly enjoyed dancing for the first time in her life. He'd made her feel like herself, like she was worth something. That had meant *everything* to her. How Ashton could be so dismissive of him she couldn't understand.

"Get out of my room," she growled. "Out! Or I will not come to your wedding tomorrow."

Ashton stared at her, stunned. Joanna had never hated herself more than at that moment. She was indeed being a petulant child. But it was so unfair. A man kissed a woman and was praised for his seductive skills, but a woman was chastised for her sin of wanting passion, of wanting to be loved.

"I'm sorry," she whispered. "I didn't mean it."

Ashton cleared his throat. "I know. I couldn't get married if you weren't there to see it, little sister." He cupped her face and leaned in to press a kiss to her forehead. "We both let our tempers get the best of us. I only want to see you happy, and Kincade is not the answer. Give me more time to find you a good man here in England."

Joanna sniffed. That wave of helpless despair seemed to crash over her again, hard enough to knock her down. This time, when Ashton left, Joanna made up her mind.

He may not love me now, but Brock will grow to love me, with time. I'm sure of that.

Tomorrow, after the wedding in Hampshire, while everyone was celebrating and Ashton and Rosalind were in the midst of wedded bliss, she and Brock would race to Gretna Green.

❦ 7 ❧

Brock watched the rain droplets travel down the glass window of the coach as he and Rosalind rode toward the chapel in Hampshire. She looked resplendent in her fine gown as she laced and unlaced her fingers nervously. Brock reached over and covered her hands with one of his.

"You dinna have to do this, Rosalind. I can help you escape."

She laughed, her eyes suddenly brightening. "I want to do this, Brock. I have no doubts about marrying Ashton. I am feeling nervous, though. What if he changes his mind? What if he does not want me?"

"If he tries to flee the church, Brodie, Aiden, and I will hunt him down." He smiled as he said this, but he was completely serious. He'd be more than happy to drag that blond bastard down the aisle at pistol point to wed Rosalind if that's what she wanted.

"I'm sure that won't be necessary." Rosalind chuckled but then grew serious. "I heard you and Ashton quarreled yesterday during the tea. What did you fight about?"

Brock slid a finger under his collar, tugging on it as it felt suddenly tight.

"Er... Well... Joanna."

"Joanna? What did you do?" Rosalind demanded.

"I didn't do anything." Well, not anything worth confessing to his sister. She didn't need those kinds of details.

"Then why were you arguing?"

"Lennox wants me to leave Joanna be. He thinks of me as a brute and that I'm unworthy of her." Brock leaned back against the cushions of the couch, trying not to let his embarrassment show.

Rosalind's brow furrowed. "Surely not."

"Aye, he does."

"Well, I shall speak to him," she said.

"No, leave it alone," Brock warned. "You've other things to think about today, like marriage to that *Sassenach*."

Rosalind laughed at his scowl, but he didn't mind. He wanted her to be happy, and he wanted her not to worry about him or Joanna.

The coach stopped in front of the little church close

to Lennox House. The rain was still coming down as Brock exited the coach, borrowing an umbrella from the coach's attendant to shield Rosalind and her pretty wedding gown. Then they entered the church together arm in arm.

The pews were filled with people Brock recognized from the tea the day before. The wedding party and their guests had all traveled the previous evening from Bath to Hampshire. Brodie and Aiden were in the front pew on the left, smiling as he and Rosalind walked toward Ashton. Brock gave his sister's arm a gentle squeeze to reassure her that all was well. Lennox, damn his eyes, looked as pleased as a cat who'd recently fed on a bowl of cream.

Brock handed Rosalind over to Lennox and gave the man a small nod to show he was approving the marriage and then joined his brothers. Rafe, Joanna's other brother, stood in the front pew watching the proceedings. He and Brock shared an amiable nod. Unlike Ashton, Rafe and Brock got along rather well. A reckless Englishman always got along better with a wild Scot, at least in Brock's view.

Halfway through the ceremony, he caught sight of Joanna in the right-hand side of the pews. She wore a deep-gold gown, just like what she had described yesterday. His body hummed as his memories of those sweet stolen kisses flooded back to him. Yes, he had been "escorted" from Lennox's house yesterday over the matter, but it had been worth it to have had a few moments alone with Joanna.

She glanced over her shoulder at him, and their eyes met. Her face pinkened, accenting her delicately carved features, including the tempting curve of her mouth. Loose tendrils of pale-blonde hair teased her shoulders and neck in a careless way that made his blood hum at the thought of putting his lips to those same places.

She gave him a strange look, intense and focused, but he could not read her mind. Then she turned back to watch the rest of the ceremony, and Brock did the same.

After the wedded couple passed by the guests and climbed into their waiting coach, Brock lingered behind, sending his two brothers on ahead. Joanna was at her mother's side, but she slowly drifted toward him, casually greeting and thanking guests as they passed by her until she and Brock were among the last few people left in the church.

"Are you all right, lass?" he asked quietly when they were reasonably alone. "I didna want to leave you yesterday, but I didna have much of a choice."

"I know," she whispered. "I'm all right." She paused, her face turning red as she met his gaze. "I changed my mind, Lord Kincade. If the offer still stands...I would like to marry you."

Brock was nearly struck down by her unexpected words. It took him a moment to compose himself.

During that time, Joanna's eyes filled with tears, and she turned her face away.

"If you don't wish to marry me anymore, I understand," she said, her tone heavy with humiliation, and it burned him.

Didn't wish to? He wanted nothing more than to marry her.

"After what my brother did..."

He grasped her waist, pulling her to him and pressing his forehead to hers. "Lass, there is nothing that can stop me from making you my wife, so long as you wish it as well. I was merely surprised since you said no before."

Her lashes fluttered, and she trembled against him. "I do want to now."

He cupped her cheek and lifted her face so he could see her eyes. "You're sure?"

"Yes. I want to marry you, Lord Kincade."

"Brock," he corrected gently.

"Badger," she said, smiling and sniffling. He chuckled, remembering how when they'd first met she'd told him his name meant *badger*.

"Yes. *Your* badger," he vowed. What would she think when she learned that Aiden had a pet badger at the castle? It was one he had rescued as a young cub. The badger now trundled about the castle as if it were the true master of it, nesting in various rooms and becoming grumpy whenever disturbed. Aiden had tried several times to return it to the wild, but the stubborn creature had held its ground. Brock smiled, realizing he was much like his namesake. He would not let Lennox chase him away from Joanna.

"How do we do this?" she asked him. "Ashton won't give his permission. I suppose we must race to Gretna Green."

"Aye," Brock sighed. "It willna be easy, Joanna. We will have to travel light. No carriages, no servants. Once we are wed, we can send for your maid and your clothes."

"No coach?" Joanna's eyes grew wide, and he remembered what she had said about riding. She liked it, but being alone on a horse made her a little uneasy.

"I'll be with you every step of the way. Do you have a strong horse here? I have mine stabled, and we could take yours for you if you have a beast you trust to ride."

She bit her bottom lip. "I have a mare named Kaylee. She's a steady ride, and she's fast."

"Good." Brock could handle the care of two horses so long as Joanna could ride hers. "It will be two or three days on horseback, as long as the weather holds and we don't have much more of this rain."

He glanced out the front door of the church, wishing the clouds would disappear. The last thing he wanted was to put Joanna in harm's way by risking that she catch her death in the rain.

"He will come after us," Joanna said. "Once he realizes we are gone."

"I know. He's tenacious, that one, but if we leave tonight, while he's focused on Rosalind, he will not know we're missing until it's too late."

"Tonight? So soon?" Her voice rose in pitch, and he could feel her tremble in his arms again. The lass was frightened; he could see that now.

"We dinna have to go tonight, but it would be the easier way. Your brother is distracted with his new bride, which gives us only a short period of time."

"Yes, I see." Joanna burrowed into him, suddenly resting her body against his in the most wonderful way. He caught the scent of flowers when he pressed his lips to the crown of her head. Rubbing his palms down her back, he tried to offer her warmth and comfort.

"It will be all right," he whispered. "I'll take care of you."

She nodded against his chest and pulled away. "We should go. I'll need to prepare. There must be something I can bring?"

"Aye, you may bring a small sack, something I can tie to the saddles. When everyone is finishing up dinner, we should say our good nights. When they retire, we can slip away to the stables and go."

"Will your brothers come with us?" she asked.

"No, I'll leave them here. Brodie will tell anyone who asks that I came down with a cold."

"I'll tell my mother I'm having some female troubles. Ashton wouldn't bother me if he thought that was the case." Joanna's eyes were bright again as she eagerly schemed.

"That'll do just fine," Brock assured her. "Now let's return to the house before we're noticed." He led her down to the last remaining coach outside the church, which was thankfully empty of other guests.

When they reached Lennox's manor home, he watched Joanna rush up the stairs. She chanced a look back at him, smiling. It hit him in the stomach, sending a blast of butterflies up in its wake. What a beauty she was. And soon she would be his.

He went in search of his brothers, finding them in the billiard room with some of Ashton's companions.

"Kincade, there you are," Lonsdale said, his grin accompanied by an all-knowing smirk.

"Here I am," he echoed, smiling back at Lonsdale but not betraying anything to the English earl.

Brodie and Aiden met his gaze, and he flicked his eyes to the fireplace. They picked up on his silent message and continued to play their game of billiards while he poured himself a glass of whiskey and waited by the fire. Aiden came first, pretending to want a glass himself. They sipped quietly for a time before Brock spoke up.

"I'm leaving tonight and taking Joanna with me. You and Brodie must stay here. I'll tell Brodie to tell anyone who asks that I've come down with a cold and am staying in bed."

Aiden's eyes widened at Brock's whispered plans, but he only gave a tiny nod to show he understood. Aiden calmly walked over to the window, and a few minutes later Brodie joined Brock and was given the same instructions.

"That's quite a risk, brother," Brodie said. "Is the lass worth it? We both know Lennox would shoot you if he had half a chance."

"Aye, that he would, but 'tis only fair. He married our sister. I shall marry his."

Brodie chuckled. "I dinna think the English see it that way."

"Probably not. They're not as civilized as we are."

"You truly like the lass?" Brodie pressed. "We've barely seen her since we arrived."

"I've seen her plenty," Brock assured him. "She's perfect." Perfect in every way a man could ever hope for a woman to be. She was intelligent, amusing, tender, yet fierce and lovely. He cleared his throat, not wanting Brodie to see his weakness, and he added, "She has money, too. Money that's not simply a dowry—she has her own money in trust."

His brother narrowed his eyes. "Not thinking to marry her because of her money, are you?"

"No, I want *her*. But having a wealthy wife would be a good thing."

"Hmm." Brodie sipped his drink rather than argue.

Brock stayed in the billiard room, making small talk

with the men until dinner, and then he made his excuses, saying he felt unwell.

Joanna would attend dinner, while he saw that her clothes and her belongings were taken to the stables. It was important that she be seen with the guests while he was absent. It would strengthen their story and also keep at bay any suspicions off them running off together. If they were both missing from dinner, Lennox would notice and possibly guess their plan. But if he went to his marriage bed without any suspicions, being newly wed would certainly keep him occupied. It galled Brock to think of his sister sharing Lennox's bed, but he was relieved to have the man distracted.

As he left the billiard room, he went upstairs to find Joanna's room and take the bags if she had them ready. They were in for a long, cold, and rainy night.

❧ 8 ☙

Joanna stared at the bag on her bed. The leather had been oiled by one of the footmen so as to prevent rain from soaking into it and damaging any of the bag's contents.

"Will it do, miss?" her maid asked. Julia had talked discreetly to one of the footmen she knew, asking him for a bag that would travel well during poor weather. The young man had smartly insisted on preparing the bag for any rain, and Joanna had been incredibly grateful.

"I think so." Joanna's heart gave a nervous flip as she opened the bag's mouth wider so she could review the contents again. Three days' worth of dresses with ankle-length skirts to avoid mud and dust from the road, and one riding habit, which she'd wear tonight along with her best cloak. Even though it was a warm summer, rain could make anyone cold. Two pairs of sensible boots, one pair of black slippers, three fresh pairs of stockings, and two pairs of chemises and petticoats. She could survive with one set of stays until they reached Scotland and buy new ones once they were married. She also packed her pearl gilt hairbrush and comb, several ribbons, hair pins, and one book, *Lady Jade's Wild Lord*. It seemed fitting to take that book, the one that had led to such a wild and unexpected kiss in the library between her and Brock a month ago. She would finally have her own wild lord.

"Oh, miss, I can't believe we're doing this," Julia whispered.

Joanna smiled at the use of the word *we*. When she'd first confessed her plan to go to Gretna Green, she'd expected her young maid to try to stop her or disagree. Julia was only four years older than Joanna, after all. But Julia had all but swooned as she listened to Joanna's plan.

"I believe it's time for me to make my own fortunes, Julia. Ashton's had no luck finding me a husband, and I am tired of waiting for my future to come to me."

Julia grinned. "And you could not have chosen a more fitting man for a husband, if you don't mind me saying so. Such a handsome man."

Joanna agreed. Brock was indeed one of the most handsome men she'd ever seen. But perhaps what she loved most was the air of wildness about him, as though he were a warrior of old, one of those grand men who had fought for his way of life at Culloden.

Joanna's heart ached at the thought. She was sympathetic to the plight of the Scots—the family did have some Scottish blood in it, after all. How could she not feel pride and sorrow knowing that they had fought so valiantly? Brock made her think of those stories, of the men and women who'd bravely stood up for their way of life, their freedom. Just as she was doing.

She didn't want to be trapped in a loveless marriage to some country gentlemen her brother would have had to bribe into marriage. No, if she was going to be faced with being unloved, she would at least choose the man she married herself. And she hoped that with Brock she stood a chance of winning his love over time. At least in Scotland she would be free. She would be mistress of a castle and wife to a lord. She wouldn't have to endure the slights of London society or the merciless torture of endless balls where no one would dance with her.

"I shall leave after dinner. Once I'm at Castle Kincade, I will send for you and you may bring the rest of my wardrobe."

"Yes, miss." Julia helped her seal up the bag. They both stilled at the knock on her bedchamber door.

"Answer it," she whispered, and then carefully blocked her bag from view, lest whoever was there was not Brock. Julia opened the door, and Brock slipped inside.

"You have your bag, lass?" he asked quietly.

Joanna nodded and spun to pick up her bag. It was

fairly heavy given the tightly packed contents, but Brock took it from her with one hand easily. He winked at Joanna and quickly walked away without another word. They could not risk being seen together tonight. She dressed for dinner early, her nerves making her feel wild and on edge.

"Remember to breathe, miss," Julia reminded her as she styled Joanna's hair in a sensible chignon. It would suit her well for traveling.

Anxiety formed a tight knot in her belly, gnawing away at her confidence until it was time to go down to dinner. She sat at the table surrounded by friends and her family, all except for Rafe, who wasn't there. He'd left Hampshire to return to London. He'd left shortly after the wedding ceremony, riding north to heaven knows where. He was quite free to do anything he pleased, and when she thought of that it revived her determination to run away with Brock. She tried not to let herself be distracted by the romanticism of their plan.

He wants a wife; I need a husband. It's not about love. At least, not yet.

She looked down the length of the table, feeling a sudden surge of pride at keeping her plan a secret. No one knew that in three days' time she would be a bride herself. For a brief instant, melancholy struck her. She would be married all alone save for a few local witnesses in a faraway Scottish village. Her mother and brothers would not be there to see her, and Ashton would not be there to give her away.

But what choice did she have? She couldn't stay here any longer and let life pass her by.

She had to act, and she wanted Brock as a husband. If that meant sacrificing the wedding she'd always imagined she would have, then she would find a way to bear it. Brock would also be alone, his brothers and sister staying here. At least they would share their loneliness.

When dinner was over, Joanna lingered in the parlor with the ladies while the men went to drink port and smoke cigars. She glanced at the clock on the mantel of the fireplace and saw it was half past nine. Brock had said to be in the stables by ten o'clock. Joanna approached her mother, who was in an animated discussion with the lovely young Duchess of Essex and the Marchioness of Rochester.

"Mama," she interrupted gently when the conversation fell into a natural lull.

"Yes, dear?" Regina smiled at her. She was quite happy today, now that her eldest child was finally married.

What will she think when she discovers I am gone? That I married without her? She fought hard to keep the tears from coming.

"I'm afraid I'm not feeling well." She placed a hand to her lower abdomen, hoping her mother would make the assumption she was suggesting.

"Oh dear! Then you must go and rest." Her mother gently touched her shoulder and nodded.

Joanna started to leave, but she couldn't seem to go without one last embrace. She turned and hugged her mother fiercely.

"Goodness, what on earth...?"

"Have a good night," she murmured, wanting so much to say more but knowing she could not.

"Good night, my dear." Regina hugged her back and let her go. Joanna tried not to rush from the parlor. She was crying by the time she changed into her riding habit, but she wiped the tears away. She had to be brave now.

This is my choice, my future. It is time to grow up.

She waited in the shadows while Julia helped her sneak out of the house unseen by her family and the other wedding guests.

She reached the stables and panicked when she didn't see Brock. Had he changed his mind? Had he decided he didn't want her after all? Her heart splintered, and dizziness swamped her. She'd been abandoned?

"Brock!" she called out, her cloak wrapped tight around her, praying he would answer, that he hadn't just left her.

"Here, lass!" Brock stepped out of an empty stall, and she nearly collapsed with relief. Tears pricked her eyes as she tried to steady herself and focus on him. If she didn't, the world might start spinning again.

He wore dark clothes, a heavy greatcoat, and a hat, blending into the shadows of the stables. He walked up to her and reached for her hands, bringing them to his lips. Brock's tender touch nearly undid her in that moment. He hadn't left her.

"You've been crying," he said as he studied her beneath the lamplight.

"I'm fine," she lied. She did not want him to think she was some silly young girl who was afraid to leave home. He wrapped his muscled arms around her, holding her close as he had done earlier in the church.

"I'll ask one more time, lass. Are you sure you want to go with me?"

She studied the tall dark-haired man in front of her— eyes that promised understanding, hands that promised tenderness, and lips that promised wild passion. Yes, she was quite sure.

She stood up on her tiptoes and brushed her lips against his. A sinuous light passed between them, and a new urgency drove her to kiss him even more deeply, flicking her tongue against his. He moaned and pulled her tighter in his arms. She felt almost weightless when he held her, as though she might drift up to the heavens with pleasure if he wasn't holding her down. When their lips broke apart, she buried her face against his throat, inhaling the soft scents of the horses, the hay, and the scent of man, *her* man.

"I'm sure," she whispered.

"Thank the Lord," he said with a chuckle. "After a kiss like that, it wouldna be easy to let you go."

She smiled as they finally broke apart.

"The horses are ready. I have your bag strapped to mine." He led her to the horses outside. They were wet from the misting rain and shifted restlessly in the darkness. Joanna sucked in a breath as Brock grasped her waist and lifted her up into the saddle. She tried to settle herself to ride sidesaddle, but she realized there wasn't a proper saddle for it.

"You need to be steady and fast. You'll ride astride." He guided one of her legs over the horse's body so she could ride more steadily, and her skirts rose up to her knees.

"Oh…" She felt a flush of embarrassment and was relieved that it was too dark for him to see it. Shifting to get more comfortable, she did indeed feel steadier riding like this, with one leg on either side of her mount. She grasped the reins and waited for Brock to mount up in front of her. As he did, she caught sight of his broad back and muscled legs in his riding trousers, and her heart began to pound heavily with anticipation. This man, this powerful, beautiful man, was soon to be hers. Hers to share a bed with. Her entire body flushed with a sudden rush of heat.

"Stay close to me, lass. We want to put as much distance between us and your brother as we possibly can tonight."

"I understand." She guided her horse forward, and once she was alongside him, they broke into a fast trot until they were off Lennox's land to the main road leading north. They used the woods to shield them, keeping their mounts at the edge of the road where grass grew partially over the dirt, concealing their tracks a little.

When they were at the farthest point from her home where she could still look back and see the house, she did so. It was a distant pale stone shadow in the darkness with dotted gold lights of candles in the windows.

Regret pinched her heart, but she didn't hesitate in leaving with Brock. She wished she wasn't facing marriage alone in a Scottish town without her family. Brock slowed to ride alongside her. Their eyes met, and he tilted his head as though to silently ask if she was all right. She answered with a firm nod, and he smiled proudly back at her.

Then they broke into a fast trot. Joanna wound the reins around her gloved hands, holding on hard as she imitated Brock's natural horsemanship skills and leaned forward over the horse's neck. Her horse, Kaylee, kept pace with Brock's mount, and she felt a surge of pride that her English mare was as fast as his Scottish stallion.

Four hours later, her back was aching and her shoulders were rigid with tension. She felt a little dizzy, but she dared not call out to Brock. She had to prove she could keep up with him and not slow him down. Her fingers burned from gripping the leather reins too tightly. The rain continued to fall, making her clothes as heavy as lead, and her lashes collected droplets that constantly dripped into her eyes, but she couldn't risk wiping them away lest she lose hold of the reins.

Brock suddenly slowed his mount to walk, and she nearly cried in relief as she slowed Kaylee down beside him.

"We'll rest the horses. 'Tis well past midnight." He nodded to a grove of trees a small distance off the road. She followed him as they guided their horses in the direction of the grove.

Brock dismounted and then came over to her. He was dripping with rain, and his clothing was cold, but his face was sharp with a masculine vigor at defying nature. Their gazes locked, and she trembled with excitement as he gripped her waist and lowered her to the ground. They were alone, and no one would stop him now if he decided to kiss her. She certainly wouldn't have stopped him if he did. She almost moaned at the glorious feel of his large warm body close to hers.

"Will you be all right for a moment while I tend the horses?" he asked.

"Yes," she whispered, not sure why she felt she had to be quiet. Perhaps it was the nature of their flight, the danger, the excitement, but she didn't wish to speak too loudly.

He stepped back and led the horses deeper beneath the low-lying trees, tying their reins to a branch. He pulled two apples out of the pockets of his coat and quickly fed one to each. The horses munched on their treats, and then, after giving them each a quick pat, Brock returned to Joanna and guided her to a big tree. They eased down on the ground. He removed his greatcoat and pulled her against him as he stretched out near the grooves between the vast roots. His coat made for a decent blanket for them, yet Joanna shivered, pressing her face into his chest.

"It will be a rough night," he whispered. "I'm sorry for that. I wish I could give you a warm bed and a cozy fire."

"I'm all right," she insisted, but her chattering teeth made him laugh.

"I'll keep you warm." He rubbed one hand up and down her back in a soothing way. She didn't think she could fall asleep, not being so cold and uncomfortable, but soon she heard Brock humming a song, and the pleasant sound distracted her.

"What's that?" she asked drowsily.

"An old song. 'The Mist-Covered Mountains.' Would you like me to sing it?"

Joanna smiled. "You sing?" The thought of him doing so filled her with unexpected delight.

He laughed, the rich sound rolling through him as he answered. "Every good Scotsman sings."

"Yes, please sing to me." She hesitantly curled an arm around his waist as he held her closer still.

O chi, chi mi na morbheanna
O chi, chi mi na corrbheanna
O chi, chi mi na coireachan
Chi mi na sgoran fo cheo.

Chi mi gun dail an t-aite's an d'rugadh mi
Cuirear orm failt's a' chanain a thuigeas mi
Gheibh mi ann aoidh abus gradh 'n uair ruigeam
Nach reicinn air thunnaichean oir.

His Gaelic was sweet and melancholy.

"What does it mean?" she asked and yawned a little. His hand continued to rub her back, and his body heat seemed to spread through her own cold limbs. This time he sang the song again, only in English so she would understand.

Oh, roe, soon shall I see them, oh,
Hee-roe, see them, oh see them.
Oh, roe, soon shall I see them,
the mist-covered mountains of home!
There shall I visit the place of my birth.
They'll give me a welcome the warmest on earth.
So loving and kind, full of music and mirth,
the sweet-sounding language of home.
There shall I gaze on the mountains again.
On the fields, and the hills, and the birds in the glen.
With people of courage beyond human ken!
In the haunts of the deer I will roam.

Hail to the mountains with summits of blue!
To the glens with their meadows of sunshine and dew.
To the women and the men ever constant and true,
Ever ready to welcome one home!

His deep voice, the baritone that was as smooth as brandy, lulled her into a light sleep, dreaming of misty mountains and heather-covered fields.

My new home...

❦ 9 ❦

Brock woke just after dawn. He glanced down the length of his body with a slow smile. Joanna was pressed flush against him, her womanly curves fitting his body in a way that made him tighten with hunger, but he pushed aside the natural arousal that came from holding a beautiful woman in his arms. There would be plenty of time for that later, once they were married. She was still nervous, as was he. He vowed that when he took Joanna to his bed, they would be far more acquainted and comfortable with one another. Soon they would be tied together for the rest of their lives, yet they barely knew each other. Marriages like this were common enough, of course, but Rosalind had been right. He wanted to know his wife, wanted to truly understand her, and he hoped she felt the same about him.

He carefully slipped from her arms and wrapped her

up in the rest of his coat before he walked away to relieve himself. When he returned to the grove, he untied the horses and took them to the meadow to graze on the grass there. Once he was satisfied that the horses were fed, he tied them once more and dug through the saddlebag he'd packed the previous night until he found the flask of ale and the bit of bread and cheese he'd wrapped up in a cloth.

He kept an eye on his future bride, chuckling as she slept. Her nose wrinkled, and she murmured something in her sleep, her lips curving in a little smile. Whatever she was dreaming about must have been good. The thought filled him with relief. He hadn't wanted to force her to sleep on the cold, hard ground like this, but they had little choice. She was showing such bravery and courage, he could scarcely contain his pride.

He ate a little of his breakfast, trying to give Joanna as much time to rest as he could. Then when he felt he could wait no longer, he gently shook her arm, and she sighed, rolling onto her back, her lashes fluttering as she came awake. Damnation, he wanted to kiss her, wanted to feel her soften in his arms as he woke her the way a husband ought to wake his wife—with passion and ardor.

"Good morning," he greeted her softly, and held out the flask, cheese, and bread. If she was eating, it might get his mind off how much he wanted to roll her onto her back and kiss her. There wasn't time for that, not yet. They had to keep moving.

Joanna blinked owlishly against the morning sun as it crested the trees above them in bright-red shades. "Morning," she replied before she took the food and drink.

"Well, lass, you survived your first night beneath the stars," Brock said as he leaned back against the tree beside her.

"I did, didn't I?" She looked proud of herself, and her pride amused him.

He knew she was a gentle-born lady, not used to roughing it out on the ground like he and his brothers were. The fact that she'd made no complaints while trying to sleep beneath a tree in a light rain with no soft pillows or warm fire impressed him.

He stood, resting back against the tree as he let her finish her breakfast, but after a few moments she moved closer, leaning her shoulder against his leg where he stood, and he couldn't resist reaching down to stroke her hair. It seemed like such a luxury to touch her, to know that she soon would fully be his to cherish and protect. The thought filled him with a boyish giddiness he hadn't felt in years.

Brock stayed alert, his eyes on the road, making sure he did not see anyone. He could not guess how quickly Lennox would realize Joanna was gone. And once he did, it would then be a question of which route Lennox would assume they would take.

When he had taken Rosalind back to Scotland a month ago, he had not used the Great North Road, nor had he used this lesser-traveled road. He'd taken his sister overland, knowing she could handle sleeping on bedrolls on the ground for several days. But with Joanna he needed to stay on the actual road, because it would be safer for her as an inexperienced rider. As long as he could keep Lennox guessing as to their path, and if they managed to stay ahead of him, they might reach Gretna Green without any difficulty.

Joanna stood, offering him back his greatcoat. She straightened her own cloak before glancing about.

"Um... I need to..." She blushed, and he knew instantly what she needed.

"There's a thicket not too far off. You may go over and see to your needs. We'll be reaching a stream in a few hours where we can wash a bit and let the horses quench their thirst."

Joanna nodded and then rushed off in the direction he had pointed out to her. She returned a short while later, and he helped her mount her mare.

They rode for three hours, passing several farmers out in their fields while their cattle grazed. A flock of sheep crossed the road, and a farmer and his exuberant collie herded them onward to a pasture on the other side of the road. Joanna seemed to marvel at the sights, laughing as the collie nipped at the heels of the more stubborn sheep. Brock loved the way her smile seemed make her face glow. The shadows and the pain he'd glimpsed in her last night were not here today. She was bravely facing her new life with him, and he was damned proud that he would soon call this woman his wife.

They reached a small wooden bridge with a stream flowing beneath it. Brock led the way, guiding his horse over the bridge. They rode their horses through the shallows a quarter of a mile downstream where they could rest unseen from the road.

"I'll tend to the horses if you wish to bathe." Brock grabbed the reins of her horse and urged it along with his own to the stream bank. The two horses were grateful for the water, and he allowed them to have their fill. When he returned them to the shelter of the trees alongside the stream, he found Joanna had removed her boots and stockings and was wading knee-deep into the water. She kept careful hold of her skirts, and he caught a tantalizing view of not only her bare ankles but the curves of her calves. She had lovely legs. Brock drew in a measured breath as he imagined those legs wrapped around his waist.

"Brock, are you all right?" Joanna called out to him.

"Aye, I'm fine. Why?"

"Oh, it's just your jaw was clenched and" She didn't finish.

He dared not tell her the direction of his thoughts. It

would likely frighten her to learn the depths of his desire.

"I'm fine," he assured her again, forcing himself to relax.

She splashed about the shallows, kicking up water and dancing on the flat smooth rocks large enough to be stepping-stones. He had become so used to her as a fine, composed English lady that it was a surprising delight to see her act so playful now.

"There are tiny fish in here." She turned his way, a radiant expression of delight on her face as she pointed to the stream.

Unable to resist, Brock joined her in the shallows, his boots sturdy enough to resist a bit of water.

"Have you not seen fish before?" he teased, and caught her by the waist when she wobbled on an unsteady stone.

"I have, of course, but..." Her brow furrowed as she met his gaze. "It's just that...my mother never really let me go outside, not like this. I was only allowed to walk, sit, or ride. I was not permitted to swim, to run about, to fish—not like my brothers."

Brock's heart ached for her. Every child should be free to explore the world around them.

He cupped her face in his hands. "As my wife, and the lady of Castle Kincade, you may run about the woods and splash in our loch as much as you desire. I'll even show you how to fish." He could think of nothing more delightful than taking her out on the water in a small boat, the sun beaming brightly on the water as he showed her the pleasures of fishing.

"Would you really?" Her eyes widened, and her voice held a hint of shyness that made him want to tip her head up and kiss her senseless.

He stroked a fingertip down the line of her adorable nose. "Of course." His body hummed with arousal, but also with something softer, sweeter. He couldn't deny that he had a strong affection for his future wife.

"Ladies in Scotland have more freedom," he explained. "You may do anything you please. I want our marriage to be one of equals." It was vital that she understood that. He had no desire to order her about or lock her inside the castle and control her the way his father had controlled his mother. The very thought of it made his stomach knot with painful memories.

Her eyes darkened as she stood up on tiptoe, kissing him. It was not a kiss to inflame desire, nor did he wish for it to be. It was an expression of gratitude. Still, it flamed the desire within him, and he couldn't resist the temptation she presented. He caught her by the waist, lifting her out of the shallows and carrying her into the protection of the trees, where he pressed her against a sturdy ancient oak. Then he kissed her the way he wanted to, the way a man can when no one is watching. With fire and hunger and longing. He explored the delicate shape of her mouth, the shell of each ear, and the back of her neck, making her shiver and moan in his arms.

Before he could stop himself, he was sliding a hand up her thigh, questing eagerly for that sweet spot between her legs. When he found it, he slid a finger inside her. She jumped, digging her fingers into his shoulders. She was wet and hot and already unbearably tight.

She hissed and threw her head back in startled surprise as he gently thrust his finger in and out of her. He wanted her to know this, to feel him inside her, even in this limited fashion for now. This was how she would be, wild and wanton, clawing at him for more as her passion exploded.

"*Brock!*" She screamed his name in surprise and fright as her passion overtook her so abruptly that it caught them both off guard.

He kept her pinned to the tree, holding her steady, holding himself steady too. Her channel clamped down around his finger in little aftershocks, and she whimpered as he withdrew his finger and put it to his lips. He sucked it clean and moaned at the taste of her.

"My God, lassie," he uttered hoarsely. He shouldn't have done that. His body was rigid with need now, but he'd have to calm himself or else he'd be unable to ride today.

"That...you..." Her blue eyes were searching his, as though trying to comprehend what they'd just shared.

"That was us, together, lass. Soon it will be even better, I can promise you that." He kissed her then, soft and sweet, just as she had done to him moments ago, before he'd gotten carried away.

She and I will soon know each other in bed and outside of it. It was just as important to him as having a strong passion between them in bed.

She stepped back from him on trembling legs and returned to the grassy shore, where she dried her feet and put her stockings and boots back on.

He stood there, watching her. His blood hummed sweetly, and his hands ached to drag her back into his arms. But he had to resist. There would be time enough yet for all the things they could share.

"Ready to go?" he asked when she'd finished.

"Yes." She rubbed her neck while a wild blush stained her cheeks, but she made no protest as he helped her back onto her horse. They were making good time. As long as they didn't delay, they would reach Gretna Green in another day.

They rode several hours, taking only brief breaks to let the horses rest. As dusk fell, they entered more hilly countryside, and Brock kept a sharp eye out for a good place to find shelter for the night. He spotted some rocky outcroppings, and the two left the road and moved into the denser underbrush by the rocks. Brock dismounted and helped Joanna down.

"Stay here a minute." He left her holding the reins of

both horses while he did a quick investigation of the area. He found a small cave on the opposite side of the rocks, perfect for tonight. He returned to Joanna and showed her where the cave was. Then he tended to the horses while she saw to her personal needs. Then he broke the bread and cheese up between them, and they shared the flask of ale again. He could tell by her eyes and her face that she was weary from the travel, but she made no protest, not even a whimper.

Brock made a comfortable nest of his coat. He hadn't thought to bring extra blankets except for the ones to put over the horses after he had unsaddled them.

I'm a bloody fool for not thinking ahead. He'd been so focused on avoiding Ashton and getting safely away from the estate that he hadn't seen to his wife's basic needs. He vowed to find a way to do something special for her when they reached his home to make it up to her.

"Come and rest," he beckoned as the night closed in on them. Joanna could barely see him in the dark, but she managed to find him and lay down beside him. He wrapped the greatcoat over them and pulled her in tight. He'd never been more thankful to have a sunny day following the previous night of rain.

Joanna slid one hand over his shirt close to his throat, her fingers twirling the fabric of his shirt before she fell deep into slumber. Brock smiled in the darkness, unafraid to let his affection show given that the only witnesses were the stars and the two horses. He had grown protective of this woman in a way he never had about anyone else. It was frightening to care about her like this, but he knew he could never go back. He could not erase these feelings inside him.

He began to drift off to sleep himself, his mind settling into that hazy place between dreams and conscious thought.

Suddenly he was alert, his eyes flashing open. His heart beat fast, and he searched the darkness, trying to find what had disturbed him. A full moon cast its milky light over the trees outside their hiding spot. The silhouettes of the horses at the mouth of the cave were unchanged. What had woken him? Brock watched the trees, noting the shadowy sway of branches in the night breeze. He closed his eyes again.

His only fear was being caught by Lennox, and he was certain Lennox wouldn't leave the road to find them.

Snap! The distinct sound of a twig breaking had him sliding Joanna gently to the ground so that he could get up. He pressed his body flat against the wall of the cave, on the side that was darker with shadows. If anyone came inside, they would not easily see him, and it would give him a brief advantage if he had to fight.

An interminable silence passed before he heard a second snap and a soft whisper almost too quiet to be heard. A trio of figures moved into the mouth of the cave. They were decent-sized men, and any struggle with them would not be easy. He leapt at the man at the back, knocking him into the opposite wall of the cave. The man grunted and fought back, kicking Brock hard in the stomach. Air rushed from his lungs and he stumbled, fighting off a brief wave of pain. He had only a second before the other two men launched themselves at him. He bellowed and threw one of them off his back, but not before he heard Joanna's startled cry.

"Brock, help!" she screamed. The shout was cut short. Terror shot through his body, and he punched the man trying to choke him from behind.

"Hold him!" the first man hissed.

"Trying to!" the man behind Brock snarled, squeezing tighter. Brock clawed at his neck, his breathing dangerously shallow. He flung himself backward, ramming the man on his back against the cave wall. The man cursed in pain, and Brock repeated the move a second time. His vision was blurring now. Shadows darted across his eyes as he prepared to crush the man trying to choke him a third time.

Joanna needs me.

"Stop that right now or your woman dies." One of their attackers moved into view at the mouth of the cave. He held Joanna against his chest. Her mouth was gagged, and her wrists were pinned in the grasp of one hand while he pressed a knife's edge to the vulnerable column of her throat.

Joanna made no sound, no cry, no attempt at

pleading through the gag. Only her harsh breathing betrayed any fear. His lass was damned brave, but he had no choice but to surrender.

A sense of defeat hit him hard, and he forced himself to relax. He raised his hands in the air. The man holding his neck loosened his grip, but only so he could kick Brock behind the knees. Brock fell to a kneeling position, just feet from Joanna and her captor.

"Good. Obey me and she won't be harmed."

The man behind Brock grabbed his hands and tied them behind his back with rope, and then Joanna was released but only to have her wrists bound in front of her.

"Gather their things," the man who'd held Joanna ordered. The other men quickly picked up their saddlebags, throwing them over the horses' backs, and then the men began to walk the horses out of the cave.

"On your feet. Come with us," the leader ordered. He kept hold of Joanna by the shoulder and kept his knife out. They walked a mile or so deeper into the woods. Brock's fear that they would not survive this encounter increased with every step. If this was a simple robbery, it would be over and done with already. No, there was something more at play.

Lights suddenly blossomed in the darkness, illuminating a hunting lodge as they drew closer. Brock and Joanna were forced inside, their mounts taken to a small stable by one of the other men. Brock now had a better view of the two men holding them captive. They were tall, strong looking, and well dressed. They wore hats and black masks, hiding their faces.

Bloody highwaymen.

The man holding Joanna began to drag her back toward a room.

"Please..." Brock breathed. The second man pressed a pistol into his back between his shoulder blades, but Brock took another step toward Joanna. "Please, don't hurt the lass."

The man gripping Joanna frowned. "What is she to you?"

"She's my future wife." He hoped these blackguards would have some small piece of humanity still inside them.

Joanna made a soft sound, her eyes meeting his, and it broke his heart.

"Please," he tried again, his voice hoarse with fear. "I'll give you anything." He took a small step toward Joanna. The man holding her nodded at Brock, which confused him. A second later he realized the nod was not meant for him.

Pain exploded in the back of his skull, and the last sensation he felt was one of falling.

Joanna screamed and fought against her captor as Brock crumpled to the ground. The man who had struck him tucked his pistol back into his coat.

"I'm happy to admit I like this bloke better unconscious," the man grumbled, and then he glanced at Joanna, his dark-brown eyes curious.

"Pretty bird," he commented, still assessing Joanna. She shivered.

"And not for you." The man who held her now dragged her forcefully into the room behind them and slammed the door shut. She was shoved into a chair by the fire, and her wrists were freed from the rope. Then the man poured her a glass of wine and pushed it into her shaking hands. She took it, staring down at the contents, and started to raise it up to throw it back in his face, but then he spoke.

"Just drink, Joanna, for God's sake. You've put me through hell tonight."

She blinked, her gaze frozen in confusion as the man removed his hat and mask. Her mouth dropped open.

"Rafe?"

Her brother grinned as though a magician had conjured him out of thin air.

"What the devil were you thinking? You could have killed Brock and me!"

"Nonsense. Everything was quite under control. I'm actually rather disappointed that my lessons to you three years ago about defending yourself against a man didn't seem to stay with you. You've gotten soft on me, old gel." He flashed her that smug grin that had infuriated and charmed her as a child. It was quite a difficult thing growing up the younger sister to both Ashton and Rafe. They couldn't have been more different in manners and more similar in looks.

"I haven't gotten soft, I just didn't expect to be attacked in a cave! Why were you hiding in the woods?" she pressed, the tension in her body subsiding now that she realized she wasn't in mortal peril.

"It's a bit of a lark, really." He answered a little too quickly, and she knew he was avoiding the subject. "Now, how are you, sister?" He chuckled as he nodded at her glass. "Drink. You look like you might need it."

She raised the glass to her lips, her hand still trembling.

"But you left after Ashton's wedding. I thought you went back to London."

"I did leave, but not for London." He poured himself a glass of wine and took a long sip. "Now, what the devil are you doing here, and why were you with that damned Scot in a cave?"

"Well, we..." She debated whether to tell him the truth and decided she must. Rafe was not Ash. There was a chance he would understand her plight. "We are running away to Gretna Green." She took a drink and waited for him to react.

Rafe was quiet a long moment. "Mother and Ashton don't know?"

She shook her head. "No, but they will soon enough. If we can arrive in Scotland by tomorrow evening, we may be able to marry before they can stop us."

Her brother leaned back against the wall by the table where a few bottles of wine and some food were stored. She wondered if he came here often. Perhaps he lived here while he...

"Rafe... What are you doing here? Who are those men outside, and what is this place?" She waved a hand at the small bedchamber.

"I'm a highwayman, or hadn't you guessed?" he replied, his tone a little sarcastic.

She narrowed her eyes. "Yes, I gathered as much, but why?"

He shrugged one shoulder. "It's amusing, and it keeps

my pockets lined. Ash keeps a tight hold on the purse strings, as you well know."

"Only for you. I have a trust and a banker who sends me money whenever I require it." She had been trusted long ago with her own dowry funds as well as an annual income. Ash knew she was responsible. Of course, when she married, he would be furious that those funds would be used by her husband, but Brock would have to receive her consent to withdraw anything from the trust.

"Yes, well, dear Ash doesn't let me have any control, so I'm making my own way in the world."

"Mother and I thought you were trying your hand at speculating in the stock markets."

"Well, I am a speculator, somewhat. I merely speculate on which carriages have the most money. Now, why the devil are you and Kincade getting married? You scarcely know each other, and he's...well, he's a bloody Scot. Don't tell me you want to live in some dreary castle in the north?"

"And if I do?" she challenged archly.

Rafe laughed again and looked so amused that Joanna couldn't resist smiling as well.

"Then who am I to stop you?" Rafe took another drink of the wine. "If he's what you want, then off you go."

"You won't try to stop us?" She was used to Rafe being more relaxed than Ashton as far as protectiveness went, but this still surprised her. Lord knew Ashton was protective enough for a dozen brothers, but she thought Rafe still might protest. During her first season, Rafe had been even more protective of her than Ashton, and he'd even shown her some rudimentary ways to defend herself. Of course, tonight she hadn't been prepared, and she felt like a fool for not using the skills he'd taught her.

Rafe sighed and came over to sit beside her on the bed. "Joanna, if you want to run away with a man, I trust you know your own heart in the matter."

"I do know my own heart," she agreed. "It's been hard, Rafe. You haven't been home much in the last year. I've had no dances, no courting, no interest. I've been put firmly on the shelf. Ash has been reduced to trying to bribe men into marrying me, and even most desperate have refused. But not Brock—he wants me."

"Does he want your money, Joanna, or you? Have you talked with him?"

"I'm sure that has influenced him to some degree, but when he kisses me, it's as if—"

Rafe held up a hand. "Now wait a minute, I do not want to hear about you kissing anyone. Even I have my limits." He said this with a teasing smile.

She blushed. "I only meant that I feel wonderful, Rafe. I feel cared for and desired. It may not be a love match, but it's better than marrying someone Ash had to throw a fortune at to even consider me."

Rafe gazed into the distance. "Well...if it's what you

want, I will do what I can to help. You may both stay here tonight, warm up by the fire, and share our food."

"Thank you." She kissed her older brother's cheek. "I must see to Brock now. Your man hit him hard, and I want to be sure he's all right." Joanna left the bedchamber and found Brock still unconscious on the floor. The other two highwaymen jumped to their feet, masks still on. They moved to block her escape.

Rafe chuckled from the doorway of the bedroom. "Easy, men. This is my little sister, Joanna. I'm sorry I didn't tell you sooner. I wasn't sure why she was with this man and wanted to catch him unawares. Don't worry, she'll keep our secret." He leaned against the doorjamb with a devil-may-care grin. Joanna nearly rolled her eyes.

"Sister?" The one who'd called her a pretty bird looked down at Brock. "What about the Scot then? Who's he?"

"Her fiancé. It seems we've interrupted a race to Gretna Green. My older brother, Ashton, will soon be on their heels, or might be already. I've offered them shelter and food here tonight."

The other two men removed their masks, and Joanna gasped. She recognized the two men. Lord Falworth, a young viscount whose family was in need of money, and the other was a gentleman named William Amberly. She'd heard rumors about his home, Amberly Hall, being haunted, which was why he stayed in a bachelor residence in London much of the year. Many young ladies spoke in whispers about his beautiful home being left unattended and shared the ghost stories that accompanied the attractive man whenever he set foot in a ballroom. Both men were close to Rafe in age and had gone to school with him at Eton and Cambridge.

"It is a pleasure to meet you, Miss Lennox," they said, bowing in a courtly manner. Nearly all traces of their highwayman personas vanished now that their identities had been revealed.

On the floor, Brock groaned softly. Joanna knelt beside him and held out a hand to her brother.

"Your knife, please." She wanted to cut Brock free of his bindings.

Rafe removed the blade from his coat but didn't give it to her. "I will free him once he's calm and knows we mean you no harm. He's liable to kill us if he wakes up angry and afraid for you. I don't suppose there's any chance we could convince him some *other* band of highwaymen attacked him?" her brother teased.

Joanna brushed her fingers over her fiancé's face. "Brock, please, wake up."

His dark lashes, ones she envied, fluttered before he finally blinked and gazed around.

"Joanna," he murmured. Then in a flash, he struggled violently, trying to free himself and get to his feet. "Get behind me, lass!"

"I'm fine! Please, calm yourself. Look around. The men from the cave are Rafe and two of his friends."

Brock's gaze darted from Rafe to the other men before returning to Joanna.

"They didn't hurt you?" he asked.

"No," she promised him.

"Lennox? What the bloody hell were you doing, attacking us in the dark?" Brock spoke to Rafe, looking more clearly around at the room.

"My apologies, Kincade. I didn't know why you had my sister. I thought it best to take control so I could talk to her without you around in case she needed rescuing."

Brock glared at him. "You shouldna have put a blade to her throat. She could've been hurt."

Rafe swirled his wine, chuckling. "She's not the first lady I've held like that. I knew exactly what I was doing. The angle of the blade was down, and it would have pushed into her cloak if you'd tried to fight me. Also, it was not a sharp blade." He held out the blade and dragged the edge on his palm, showing how it couldn't cut him.

"It is indeed dull," Brock muttered.

"Now this"—Rafe slipped a second dagger out of his coat and knelt by Brock, easily cutting the ropes—"is my dangerous one." He then held out a hand to Brock and lifted him up on his feet.

"And these men?" Brock nodded at Falworth and Amberly.

"This is Viscount Falworth and Mr. Amberly." He

jerked his head at his two friends, who kept a smart distance away from Brock.

"Friends of yours?" Brock asked.

"Yes, since we were lads. Gentlemen, this is Lord Kincade. He has one of the Scottish earldoms," Rafe explained.

Brock nodded at them.

"Sorry about all this. Rafe didn't tell us he knew either of you until a moment ago," Falworth said.

Brock ran a hand behind his head and winced.

"As I was telling Joanna, you may both stay here tonight. Your horses are safe in our stables. We have plenty of food and drink."

"Thank you." Brock glanced to Joanna, and she nodded in encouragement as he accepted a flask from Falworth. Brock took a drink. "Fine whiskey."

Falworth grinned. "Took it off some gentleman we stopped on the road a few weeks ago. Nasty brute, but he does know his liquor."

Brock chuckled, but he carefully examined the hunting lodge.

"We have two bedchambers. Joanna, you may have my room." Rafe pointed to the room where she'd been moments ago. "I'll sleep on a bedroll out here."

"Did Joanna tell you why we were in" Brock stopped himself, a concerned look in his eyes.

"She did. And you won't find any resistance from me.

But you *will* sleep out here with me tonight. I may not be the best brother, but I insist on her sleeping alone."

Brock laughed, beginning to relax. "I agree to those terms."

Joanna rolled her eyes and sighed. "You know that I am right here. What if I don't wish to sleep alone?"

Falworth and Amberly fixed their gazes elsewhere, and Amberly whistled softly.

"No," Rafe said at the same time as Brock said, "Not tonight, lass."

Joanna glowered. "You're not my favorite brother anymore, Rafe." She wanted Brock to be with her. Was it possible after only two nights to need a man so fiercely, the way she needed him?

Rafe snorted. "I shall always be your favorite brother because I'm the one who let you run away to Scotland. Remember that."

Brock laughed again, even though it made his head ache. "We appreciate the help. I dinna want to risk taking her down the Great North Road. Your brother would expect me to take her to the inns along the way. We've been bedding down beneath the stars instead."

"Joanna? Sleeping outside?" Rafe suddenly laughed. "I can't believe it, but I suppose we did find you in a cave."

Joanna bristled, hating that Rafe was making her out to be such a delicate creature.

"She's a strong lass. She's made not a single complaint

since we left." Brock smiled at her with such pride that a wave of heat flooded her body, and she had to shyly look away.

"Well, do you wish to eat? Or sleep?"

"I'm fine for now. Joanna?" Brock asked.

She'd had plenty to eat earlier with Brock and didn't want him to think he hadn't given her enough. Men could be quite silly when it came to matters of pride.

"I'm ready to go to retire for the evening."

"Then take my room whenever you like." Rafe retrieved several bedrolls and put them on the floor. Falworth and Amberly tossed dice to see who would take the other bedchamber. Falworth won, and Amberly stalked over to his bedroll, muttering. Then Brock and Rafe arranged their sleeping places, with Rafe closest to Joanna's door. She longed to speak to Brock, to say something to him, but all she dared to whisper was a good night.

She turned to the small bed in the bedchamber and removed her cloak. With no maid to assist her, she would sleep in her gown yet again. She was too tired to care tonight, but tomorrow she would be rather cantankerous if she didn't have a chance for a bath and a change of clothes.

She pulled the bedclothes up around her and collapsed on the feather tick mattress, uncaring that the fire in the bedchamber was dying out. She had only to face one more night, and then she and Brock would be husband and wife. They would be free to stay in a cozy inn without fear of being stopped by Ashton. She burrowed deep into the blankets, her eyelids too heavy to resist sleep.

Just outside she could hear the murmur of masculine voices, Brock's seductive brogue among them. Strangely, in a hunting lodge full of highwaymen, she felt incredibly safe. Safe enough to quickly fall into a dreamless sleep.

11

Brock took a small bite of mutton from a plate on the table. He had decided to eat a little once he and Rafe started talking. He was still too wound up to sleep right away, even though he knew he needed his rest if they were to finish their mad dash to Gretna Green.

"You'll have to move fast tomorrow," Rafe said as though reading his mind.

Brock leaned back in his chair. "Aye. I'm planning on your brother being right on our heels. If we'd had a coach, I would've changed horses every four hours the entire way without stopping, but I couldna risk taking the main road."

Rafe chuckled. "You're smarter than I would've expected." Brock was struck by the similarities between Rafe and Ashton. In looks alone, the two men were close enough to be twins, yet despite the years between them, they couldn't have been more different in their manners and thoughts.

"I'll take that as a compliment, Lennox." Brock smiled at Rafe, and they shared another bit of the fine whiskey Falworth had acquired.

Rafe nudged his glass on the rough-hewn wood of the table with a single finger, seeming to be deep in contemplation before he spoke.

"You do have an affection for her, don't you? I need to know this isn't just about money."

Brock knew the truth mattered, and he was not about to lie.

"I admit, knowing she has money helps. Men in our position canna help but consider that sort of thing. But when I first laid eyes upon her, all I could think was that she was the bonniest lass I'd ever seen." He thought back to that first night with her and smiled. "I was there to rescue Rosalind, before we realized she didn't need rescuing, but instead I find this wee blonde angel with a book, wearing a tartan shawl and sitting rosy-cheeked by the fire. It made my heart soar at the sight of her. I didna know she was your sister—I only knew I wanted her. That didna change when I learned who she was."

"So it's her looks that matter to you? Looks fade, old boy," Rafe pointed out shrewdly.

"They do, but kindness of the heart doesna fade. She offered me her book, wanted to know if I was hungry and if I needed a bedchamber prepared. She didna know who I was or why I was there, only that I was Rosalind's brother. Such kindness, such an open heart. I want that in a wife." As he spoke, he came to a sudden realization. What had drawn him to Joanna was indeed her heart, her kindness, which was so like his own mother's.

"Joanna is sweet. She's always been that way. But she can have a temper when pressed." Rafe chuckled. "Be wary of that. Push her too far and you will pay."

"Aye. I've seen her get a wee bit riled." He thought of the night of the ball and how she'd struck him, but that anger had been justly deserved. He'd pushed her, hurt her. He vowed he would never do such a thing again.

"As long as you care for her and treat her with respect and honor, I'll be happy to welcome you to the family. I cannot say Ashton will be as understanding, but between our father and yours, you can imagine why he is so protective of her."

"I can," Brock agreed solemnly. The dirt upon his father's grave was still fresh, and the memories of those years of pain at his father's hands would take far longer to heal. He never wanted to be like that man. Never wanted to strike down those he loved with fists or cruel words.

"What of your father? Joanna hasn't spoken much about him."

"He was kind enough, I suppose," Rafe said. "But he didn't care about us the way he should have. He gambled away our fortunes, broke our mother's heart, and left Ashton with the responsibility to rebuild our family and fortune. This burden on my brother makes him distant and controlling."

"I had wondered why he was that way," Brock mused, but he could see it now. Joanna's eldest brother kept a hold on anything that was within his power to control because it made him feel safe. He didn't need to control Joanna. Brock would protect her now, the way a husband should.

"We should get to bed," Rafe said. "You'll need to leave early."

"Aye," Brock sighed and finished his whiskey before he headed for his bedroll. He was asleep long before the candles burned low and were extinguished.

IT WAS CLOSE TO MIDNIGHT WHEN ASHTON WOKE from slumber by his mother's frantic pounding on the door. He kissed his wife's forehead and grabbed his dressing gown from his chair and wrapped it around his body. When he cracked open the door, he found her looming before him like a specter, holding a candle aloft, illuminating her white cap over her hair.

"I'm so sorry, Ashton, but I must speak to you."

"It's all right, Mother. What's the matter?" He raked

a hand through his hair, getting it out of his eyes as he stepped into the hall with her.

"Joanna wasn't feeling well two nights ago. She went to bed, and her maid told me she wished to stay in bed all of yesterday. I went to look in on her tonight but when I did, her room was empty."

Ashton's blood ran cold. "Empty?"

"Yes. I woke her maid, and after threatening to let her go, I learned the truth."

Ashton's heart stuttered in fear. Surely his enemy, Hugo Waverly, wouldn't go after Joanna. But of course he would. Nothing was beneath that man.

"She's run away with Lord Kincade," his mother hissed. "They are fleeing to Gretna Green as we speak, and they have at least a two-day head start."

Ashton wouldn't say he felt any relief at this news, only that his fears shifted from one ill fate to another.

"Are you sure she ran away with Kincade?"

"I'm certain. I went straight to his room after I spoke with Julia. He is gone as well. His brother, Brodie, said Lord Kincade had a cold the last two days, but it was a ruse. Lord Kincade's room is empty like hers. Ash, you must go after them!"

"I will." He opened his bedroom door again and glanced back at his mother. "I'll ride with the League as soon as they are ready." He slid back into his room and started to dress by the light of the dying fire.

Rosalind stirred as he was donning his boots. "Ashton? What's the matter?" She brushed her hair back from her face. His heart turned over in his chest at the beautiful sight of his new wife. He didn't want to worry her, but they had vowed to have no more secrets between them.

"Joanna has run away with your brother."

"Brock?" She shoved the bedclothes back and started to climb out of bed. "Oh dear..."

"Stay in bed." He came over and cupped her face in his hands so he could steal a lingering kiss.

"But shouldn't I come with you? He is my brother, after all."

Ashton shook his head. "I need to know you are safe here. Hugo is still plotting moves against us, and I need you here, where I trust you will be safe. Also, I cannot be entirely certain Hugo doesn't have his hand in this."

Rosalind blanched. "You wouldn't think Brock would—?"

Ashton shook his head. "No. Hugo is as much his enemy as ours. But I've wondered of late as to why no man has been interested in Joanna, and I'm beginning to see Hugo's hand at play there. I wonder if in some way he might have driven her into your brother's arms. And if he did, then it was not with the best of intentions."

"I still think I should come."

"No, love. The odds of reaching Brock and Joanna in time are slim, and there is still the matter of settling the situation. Mother will be terribly upset if she missed her youngest child's wedding. You are the only person I trust to comfort her."

Rosalind smiled a little. "I suspect it's also because you'll likely fight with Brock again, and you don't want me to see it."

"Smart wife." He chuckled as he retrieved his greatcoat.

"No dueling. That's all I ask."

"Yes, darling." They laughed together for a moment before she grew serious and so did he.

"I warned him, Ashton. I knew he had an interest in her, but I thought that he would court her properly if he was serious." Rosalind sighed heavily.

"I know you did. I'm afraid it may be my fault. Joanna has been desperate to prove that society has no cause to laugh at her for failing to find a husband. She has more pride than I realized. She's more like Rafe than she is like me."

Rosalind chuckled. "Husband dear, you suffer from pride as well, or need I remind you how we ended up being wed?"

"I certainly don't need any reminding." He knew his own pride has caused many a problem over the years, especially when he had first met Rosalind.

"Take care when you find them. Brock is a good man. He won't hurt Joanna."

Ashton didn't tell her that he was worried for other reasons. What if Brock later became the monster his father had been? He couldn't let his sister marry a man who may someday lose his charms and turn on her. He gave Rosalind one more kiss before he left their bedchamber and went to rouse his friends. They would ride at once, take the Great North Road to Gretna Green. Joanna was not a natural horsewoman which would slow Brock down. They would most likely take a coach and change horses every four hours.

One by one he woke his friends, Godric, Lucien, Cedric, Jonathan, and finally Charles, who grumbled as they met Ashton out in the stables.

"We're leaving in the middle of the night to chase down a bloody Scot?" Lucien scowled sleepily.

"Yes," Ashton snapped. "He has my sister."

Charles glanced at the others. Godric stifled a yawn, and Cedric rubbed his eyes wearily. "Ash, if Joanna went with him, maybe she"

"Maybe nothing." Ashton pulled on his riding gloves as a groom brought round the horses they needed. "She's my sister, and she's under twenty-one. The Hardwicke Act won't let her marry without permission in England for another year. She is most likely doing something foolish that she will regret, and I at least want to have a chance to talk to her before she ties herself forever to that damned Scot."

Cedric chuckled behind a gloved hand. "Isn't that what you just did? Tie yourself to a Scot?"

Ashton clenched his jaw. "I ask that each of you take this seriously."

His friends sobered and nodded to show they would. Then he led them to their horses. It would be a long night for all of them.

12

Joanna stretched languidly in bed, forgetting for a brief moment where she was and how she'd come to be there. She opened her eyes at the sound of a rumbling male voice nearby and bolted upright, staring about the sparsely furnished bedroom in the little hunting lodge. The events of the night before came back to her. Someone knocked on her door.

"Time to wake up, Joanna," Rafe called. "Kincade is seeing to your horses. You have time to eat some breakfast, and then you must leave."

"I'm awake," she called and climbed out of bed. For the first time in two days her body wasn't stiff, and for that she was grateful, yet she felt a twinge of disappointment in not being able to sleep out-of-doors with more ease.

Perhaps I am too soft. What if Brock married her and

later decided he wanted a stronger, more hardy Scottish lady, someone who could sleep with him outside beneath the stars without complaint?

No, don't think like that. He chose you; he wants you.

She cleaned her teeth, washed her face, and saw to her needs before joining the men in the common room. Rafe had prepared a plate of apple slices and cheese along with a bit of cold cuts. She ate quickly, licking her fingers clean since there were no cloth napkins with which to wipe her hands. Rafe watched her, a smug smile on his lips.

"What?" She didn't like that he found such amusement in her situation.

"You really intend to go through with this, don't you?" But it wasn't asked like a question.

"I do. I'm tired of not having a choice in my fate. I chose Brock, and he chose me."

"I believe you. I don't think I've ever seen you serious about anything before. I just want you to be happy."

She squeezed his hand lightly. "I will be happy, and I hope someday you find your own happiness." She wanted Rafe to be happy, to have a life of joy and to put the darkness in him away. But she feared it may be years before that happened.

The hunting lodge door opened, and Brock strode in. His coat swirled around his knees, and the breeze played with his hair. He smiled when he saw her. That smile removed any doubt she had about her choice to be here with him. His smile knocked her knees together and made her feel like she could fly all at the same time. It made her feel like she was the only woman in the entire world and she was the only thing that mattered to him.

"Lass, you do look bonny in the morning." He strode toward her, heat burning in his eyes, but he slowed when he saw Rafe cross his arms, a slight frown upon his lips. Joanna shoved an elbow into her brother's ribs and rose from the table. It would have been lovely to have another kiss with Brock, but Rafe might change his mind about approving their plans. Rafe and his friends outnumbered her and Brock.

"I'm ready to leave." She checked to make sure her cloak was secure and removed her riding gloves from her pockets, tugging them on.

"Be careful, Joanna." Rafe embraced her tightly, and for a moment she didn't want to let go. She was not weak, and she would not let childish fears to stop her. She released Rafe, blinking rapidly to hide the burn of tears, and turned to face Brock. He was studying her closely, worry knitting his brows.

"Are you all right?"

She nodded and accepted the hand he held out to her. She waved goodbye to Rafe as he followed them out of the hunting lodge. She let Brock help her up onto her horse, and she winced at the soreness as she took her seat in the saddle.

Brock placed a hand on her thigh, the touch sweet rather than seductive. "It's not far now. Can you make it a few more hours?"

"I can," she assured him. Even if she couldn't sit down for several days afterward, she would do anything to make it to Gretna Green before Ashton caught up with them.

As they left the hunting lodge behind them, Joanna grew more rigid as her nerves took over. With each passing minute they were closer to Scotland, and she would soon be married. She glanced at Brock, the impressive man who rode slightly ahead of her, leading the way. She trembled a little at the thought of what would follow, for she knew the rumors about what followed these hasty weddings. They had to be consummated immediately, to avoid a male relative challenging the marriage's validity and try to have it annulled. Ashton would challenge her wedding, which meant she and Brock would do more than share a bed this evening. They would... She blushed at the thought and was so relieved he could not see her face while he rode ahead of her.

They stopped to rest the horses two hours later.

"We'll soon be at Headless Cross," Brock said.

"Headless Cross?" Joanna leaned against her mare as her horse drank from the small stream Brock had led them to.

"'Tis the place where five coaching roads meet and is

also the heart of the village of Gretna Green. The black-smith shop is the first place you'll see when we arrive. 'Tis why couples tend to marry there. They dinna always have time to go farther into the village."

"Is that where we will be married?" Joanna asked.

He nodded and held up a few slices of apple to each horse before he clicked his tongue, catching both horses' attention and pulling them away from the stream.

"There is a man there, David Lang, who will wed us." He helped Joanna up, and once more they were riding quickly. "Then we must consummate the marriage at one of the inns so your brother canna challenge it with an annulment."

When they reached the main road on the southern border between Scotland and England, they passed through Longtown, the last English town before the border to Scotland. Brock didn't slow his horse, but sped up a little as they trotted down the street. Joanna noticed the townsfolk kept well out of the way, no doubt used to the road being trafficked by madly dashing coaches.

Another short half hour passed, and Brock slowed as a village came into view. Joanna pulled up a little on her reins, patting Kaylee's neck and getting a better look at what had to be Gretna Green. It was a very small village, filled with only a few clay houses. The quaint parish kirk was in the distance. Old stones had been cobbled together into a respectable church. A minister's house was close to the kirk, and puffs of smoke curled up from the chimney while someone cooked dinner. Joanna's stomach grumbled. There was a rather large inn that she knew from its position offered a fine view of Solway, past Carlisle and the Cumberland hills. But the building immediately present was a brick structure with an open forge at the front.

The blacksmith's shop.

"Wait here, lass." Brock stopped at the hitching post outside the shop before he entered the back door. A moment later he returned with a tall man in black breeches and a black waistcoat. He looked to be in his midsixties, and there was a shrewd, businesslike manner to him.

"Joanna, this is Mr. Lang. He has consented to marry us."

She greeted Lang with a smile, despite the flutter of nerves inside her.

"Come with me," Lang said, and waved for Joanna and Brock to follow him into the back of the shop. They entered a surprisingly tidy room. The walls were freshly painted white, and several windows let in sunlight, making it feel rather cheery. There were two chairs in the room. One was occupied by an elderly man who smiled at them and the other by a middle-aged woman who was knitting a shawl. She stood when she saw Brock and Joanna.

"These are your witnesses, Mr. Gregory and Mrs. Wilcox."

Joanna and Brock shook hands with both of them, and then Mrs. Wilcox pulled Joanna aside into a small room away from Brock to speak privately with her.

"Are ye here of yer own free will, lassie?" Mrs. Wilcox's role here must be to rescue any young lady who might have been kidnapped or coerced into an anvil marriage.

"Yes."

"And ye want to marry, er... What's his name?"

"Brock Kincade."

"Kincade?" Mrs. Wilcox blinked. "I didna catch his name at first. Child, we know the Kincades here." Mrs. Wilcox put a gentle hand on Joanna's shoulder. "Ye sure ye wish to marry him? They say his father was quite a brute."

"I'm quite sure. Lord Kincade takes after his mother, not his father." At least she believed he did. She didn't know much about his mother, but the Brock she had known for the last few days was anything but a monster.

"Very well, if yer quite sure."

"I am quite sure." Joanna and Mrs. Wilcox returned to the main room, and Joanna looked at Brock who stood near a black anvil on a pedestal. He produced a length of pink ribbon from his pocket that looked suspiciously like one of her hair ribbons from her bag. It brought back a wave of heated memories of that first night they had met, when he had bound her hands with her sash and used a hair ribbon to gag her. Though that had been a frightening moment, he had been gentle, kind, and, in hindsight, only trying to protect his sister.

"We are ready," Mrs. Wilcox announced, and she escorted Joanna up to the anvil.

Joanna had a moment of despair and heartache for the loneliness of this moment. Only strangers were here to witness one of the most important moments in her life. Her mother and brothers, her older sister, her friends...not one of them would see this.

She looked to her future husband. Brock's eyes were solemn. Perhaps she saw the same sorrow in his eyes, that his siblings were far away during such a momentous occasion.

"I wish our families were here," she whispered. He reached up to cup her cheek, brushing the pad of his thumb over her lips.

His gray-blue eyes softened on her face. "As do I, but we dinna have another way."

No, they didn't.

"Are you ready, Joanna?" He said her name so sweetly that she fought off tears and nodded.

"I am."

Mr. Lang cleared his throat as he stood in front of them. "What are your names?"

"Brock Kincade."

"Joanna Lennox."

"Where do you reside currently?" Lang asked.

They each answered, and then Lang inquired if they were both single persons.

"Aye," Brock said at the same time Joanna replied, "Yes."

"An' did you come here of your own free will and accord?" Lang waited for the answer in the affirmative, and then he produced a printed marriage certificate, filling in their names on a part of the page with the pen provided by Mr. Gregory.

"Lord Kincade, do you take this woman to be your lawfully wedded wife, forsaking all others, keep to her as long as you both shall live?"

Brock smiled at Joanna. "I do."

"Miss Lennox, do you take this man to be your lawfully wedded husband, forsaking all others, keep to him as long as you both shall live?"

Joanna stared into Brock's stormy eyes, seeing the hope and the longing there, and her heart fluttered wildly.

"Yes, I do."

Mr. Lang held out a ring to Brock, who took it. It was a silver band, simple in design.

"Put it on her fourth finger of her left hand and repeat after me. 'With this ring, I thee wed. With my body, I thee worship. With all my worldly goods, I thee endow. In the name of the father, son, and Holy Ghost, amen.'"

Brock slid the ring onto her finger and spoke the words, his voice strong and his brogue thick as he stared at her intensely.

"Now hold hands." Lang took the ribbon from Brock. Once they joined hands, he made a small cut on their palms with a blade. Joanna winced at the sting of the cut, but she pressed her palm together with Brock's. Lang banded the ribbon to their wrists in a hand fasting. She knew it wasn't necessary, that their wedding was already legal, but Brock had seemed to want to have an older custom to represent their joining. She rather liked that.

"Now, Miss Lennox, repeat after me. 'What God has joined together, let no man put asunder.'"

Joanna spoke the words, and something deep inside her changed. She felt connected to him, bound by an ancient magic that could never be undone, nor did she want it to be.

Lang spoke more loudly. "For as much as this man and this woman have consented to go together by giving and receiving a ring, I, therefore, declare them to be man and wife before God and these witnesses, in the name of the father, son, and Holy Ghost, amen."

Brock's smile grew into a wide grin, and he leaned over the anvil, pressing his lips to hers. A sudden clang startled them both, and they jumped apart as much as their bound hands would allow. Lang chuckled and put away his heavy blacksmith hammer.

"We just need to complete your certificate, and then you are free to leave." Lang motioned the two witnesses over, and they signed after Brock and Joanna. Lang rolled a sheet of blank paper over the wet ink on their certificate to help it dry, then bound the certificate with a black ribbon and handed it to Brock.

"Congratulations, my lord. I suggest you rent a room at the Queen's Head Inn, have your horses seen to, and then...your bride seen to." He winked at Brock, who chuckled. When Joanna and Brock left the blacksmith shop, she paused.

"What did he mean when he said I needed seeing to?"

Her husband—how strange and exciting it was to think of him like that—laughed and swept her into his arms, kissing her.

"He means the consummation, lass. We have a long night ahead, but don't worry, I will be a good and caring husband."

Before she could respond, he was tugging her along, their bound hands still clasped together as they took their horses to the stables next to the inn. Brock handed the waiting groom a handful of coins, and once they left the horses, they walked around to the front of the inn.

The Queen's Head was a large inn, and the common room was bustling. Joanna expected to be stared at because of their newly married state, but the crowd dining there must have been well acquainted

with the sight of new couples because they were prac-
tically ignored. Brock rented a room and ordered some
food to be sent up. He hurried Joanna upstairs and she
ran into Brock's back when they halted at the door to
their room. He opened the door and ushered her
inside, and she swallowed hard as she tried to stay
calm.

"I'll have our bags brought up from the stables and a
hot bath readied for you," Brock said. "I know you've
worn the same dress for three days."

Joanna blushed with mortification. She must look
and smell dreadful by now. She'd been so focused on
racing to Gretna Green that she had been able to think
of little else.

"Thank you. I would like that."

He reached between them, gently pulling at the
bonds of the pink satin ribbon until it loosened, then
released its hold over their bound wrists. Blood smeared
both of their palms, and Brock examined her hand.

"When I return, I'll see to your hand." He brought it
to his lips, kissing her knuckles tenderly. "My brave
bonnie lass." He quickly exited the room to see to their
bags.

Joanna stood in the center of the room, trembling
despite the warm weather.

I am married. It is done.

Ashton had not reached them in time. She hadn't
wanted him to, but she felt a twinge of guilt knowing he

would soon be here, and he would be furious when he found them.

While Brock was gone, she removed her cloak and examined her appearance in the small mirror on the washstand. Her hair was a tangled mess. With a sigh, she began removing pins and combing her fingers through the strands. She was still plucking pins from her hair when Brock returned and set their leather bags on the floor. He knelt by Joanna, and she recognized the bag he dug through as hers. He found her silver-and-pearl-handled hairbrush and held it out to her.

"Thank you." She took the brush, holding it against her chest for a moment, feeling shy now that she was alone in a bedroom with him.

"A lad is on the way up with buckets of hot water for the bath." He pointed toward a copper tub in the corner. He then stood and came over to the washstand and poured water into the porcelain basin. "Let me see to your hand."

Joanna held out her injured palm, and he carefully washed the blood away. Then he pulled a small flask from his coat pocket and looked at her.

"This will sting a wee bit," he warned before he poured whiskey over the cut. Joanna bit her lip hard, but she refused to make a noise. Then he dabbed the cut and returned to his bag, where he retrieved a small black glass jar. He opened it and dipped a finger into the white substance and rubbed it over the cut.

"This will help you heal." Then he ripped up a bit of a white handkerchief from his pocket and bound it tight around her palm.

"What about you?" She caught the wrist of his own injured hand.

He shrugged. "I'll tend to it later."

"No, please, let me help you. I'm your wife now. We did pledge to care for each other, didn't we?" Her heart pounded hard as she waited for him to respond.

Brock's lips curved in a teasing smile. "Aye, we did." He extended his cut palm over the basin. She cleansed his wound, poured whiskey over it, dried it, and rubbed the cut with his salve, and then she wrapped it securely with the remainder of the handkerchief. She held his hand in her own injured palm, a further bond between them. She met his gaze, and she saw an invitation in the burning depths of his eyes.

"Joanna," he whispered, the single word betraying his ardor, and she trembled as he reached for her.

Someone knocked on the door. With a curse, Brock stepped back and opened the door. Three lads came in, each carrying a pair of buckets. They poured the water into the tub and exited after Brock slipped them some coins.

"Bathe now, and I'll see that we have a fire lit so you willna catch cold."

She nodded, her body still humming with the excitement of what had almost happened. She turned her back on him and began to undress. She'd worn a gown that buttoned down the front, and her stays were a little loose, so she could undo them herself if necessary.

Brock worked on the fire, keeping his back to her until she'd slipped completely naked into the tub. She dipped her head below the surface, scrubbing her hair. When she surfaced, Brock was still on the opposite side of the room, but she saw he'd left a bottle of rose oil by the tub. He must have found it in her bag and put it there in case she wanted it.

For a Highland brute, he was strangely caring and thoughtful. She lifted the rose oil to her nose and breathed in the sweet floral scent, not too strong, not too weak. Perfect. Just like him.

Everyone is wrong about him. But not me. I know what kind of man I married.

13

"**D**o you wish to bathe, Brock?" she asked. "The water is still warm." She had taken care to wash quickly so he could have warm water if he wanted it. She already dreaded getting out, knowing her damp skin would turn cold. She'd soon be able to put on a dressing gown and perhaps feel the heat of her husband's body when he held her against him.

Brock's eyes locked on hers as he picked up her dressing gown and came over. Her senses came alive as she realized she was about to stand up from the bathtub completely naked before him.

"Er...yes. Thank you," he replied. He held the gown for her and then turned his head. She climbed out of the tub and slipped into the gown, then moved around him carefully, toward the heat of the fire and away from the very different heat between them. As she started to comb through her hair, she listened for his every movement, keeping her face turned away out of respect for the privacy he'd shown her. But oh how she longed to have a peek.

He splashed around a bit, and she smiled when she heard him humming a song to himself. Her husband liked music. She bit her lip, trying to contain a giddy laugh. It would take a while still for her to become accustomed to being married.

He belongs to me, and I to him. The thought was a welcome one, however strange it seemed. She finished combing her hair and then spoke.

"Where is your dressing gown? I shall fetch it for you."

"In the large bag by the door. 'Tis dark red," he said.

She carefully dug through his clothing, feeling strangely excited about touching the soft buckskin trousers, the embroidered waistcoats and even his stockings. She almost giggled at the silly thought that she was fetching her husband's clothes, such a domestic, intimate task. Joanna soon found it and lifted the heavy red dressing gown out of the bag.

She turned back to him and stopped, frozen in place. She did her best not to stare, but he was so tall that he was almost folded in half in the small tub. His long, muscular legs stuck out of the water where he bent his knees like two mountainous islands. Unable to stop herself, her eyes moved over the rest of him. His chest was smooth except for a patch of dark hair that covered the center. She gazed at him, fascinated. She had known that men were different than women, but to see it so clearly, knowing that Brock was her husband, that his body was hers to explore... She swallowed hard as she realized the same was true for him. He could look his fill of her and explore her body just as well.

A flash of fear filled her. He had said he would be gentle, but she had heard that being with a man could hurt, and that men often took their pleasure sooner than women and left the bed the moment they were done. She had heard such whispers over the years, sometimes having to read between the lines of such talk.

What would Brock be like in bed? Would he use her, even gently so, and then abandon her? Surely he wouldn't. They had one bed to share, at least here. What would happen when they reached his castle? For the first time since she had left home, she was assailed with doubts.

"Are you all right?" Brock asked. His eyes had widened with concern.

"Yes." She set his dressing gown by the tub and fled to her chair by the fire. There was another knock on the door, and she stiffened.

"It will be the lad with food. My coin purse is by the

washbasin. Can you give him a shilling, love?" Brock
asked. Joanna averted her gaze and hastily opened the
door, just enough to take the tray of food and bottle of
wine and glasses before she handed the boy his money.
The lad smirked when he saw her clutch her dressing
gown closed at her neck. She scowled at him to send him
running.

Brock splashed behind her, getting up, as she placed
the food by the fireplace. Her hands jangled the tray as
the image of him standing there naked and glorious just
behind her overpowered her good sense. Lord, she could
almost picture it, the water dripping down his muscular
body, but she didn't dare look. Not yet.

"Brock, would you like a late luncheon now or..." She
swallowed hard and tried to rearrange the plates on the
tray, her fingers clumsy and her skin hot.

Then she felt him right behind her, the heat of his
body close against her barely clothed skin. "Aye. We
should eat a bit before..." Brock cleared his throat but
didn't finish.

"Yes," she agreed, her body shaking. "Oh!" She
knocked over the bottle of wine on the table, but he
reached around her, catching it before it could fall. His
clean male scent enveloped her, and she wanted to purr
like a contented cat.

"Easy, lass, I know you're a wee bit nervous. Allow
me." He moved beside her and poured the wine into two

glasses. Joanna was envious of how calm he seemed to be, his hands steady whilst hers wouldn't stop shaking. She took a seat in the chair while they split the food between them. She was too nervous to be truly hungry, but she needed to eat or else she would be too faint to deal with what would come next.

They ate in silence, and Joanna poured herself a second glass of wine, drinking it hastily. Brock watched but said nothing. Still, she felt compelled to explain.

"I'm sorry. I just want to be calmer before we..." How silly she must look, stammering and shaking like a bloody virgin. Well, she was one, but she wanted to appear more worldly, more self-assured for him, and she was letting herself down.

"It's all right, Joanna. We dinna have to do this now if you dinna wish to—"

"Yes, we do. Ashton could arrive at any moment, and I don't want him to have a reason to annul our marriage." She paused, summoning her courage to tell him the truth. "And I do want to be with you. It's merely unnerving to think of one's first time. I know so little about all of this. Mama never spoke to me, and my older sister, Thomasina, was busy raising children and having a life of her own. Rafe and Ashton were simply out of the question when it came to getting answers." She hoped he wouldn't find her silly.

Brock laughed, the rich sound putting her at ease. "I

can only imagine, lass. Rafe would tell you far too much, and Ashton would tell you nothing at all."

"Exactly," she said, joining in with a chuckle. But he looked at her more seriously then.

"It can be frightening. The first time I lay with a woman, I thought I was about to die—it felt good and terrible all at once. That passes. You won't be afraid the next time."

She placed her hand in his as he drew her up from the chair and pulled her into his arms, simply holding her to him, embracing her.

"Lovemaking should be tender and gentle the first time. Later, when a man and woman feel comfortable and know each other better, it can be wild, fierce, *powerful*." He coiled his hand into her damp hair, pulling lightly at the base of her neck so that she tilted her head back to look up at him.

"Forget what you've heard from other ladies. When you and I share a bed, it will be about mutual pleasure." His voice was deep and hypnotic, lulling her into a sensual trance. "You understand, lass?"

Joanna nodded, spellbound by the soft allure of his gaze and his rich, rumbling voice.

"Good." He lowered his head, and just as his lips touched hers, her heart throbbed in her ears and her pulse quickened into an erratic rhythm. Her soft curves molded into the hard lines of his body as she sank into his arms. His mouth covered hers hungrily, his lips persuasive and seductive, setting her body aflame. She was only barely aware of his hands removing her dressing gown and the sensation of cool air caressing her bare skin before she was consumed again by the tender ravishment of his mouth. The fabric of his dressing gown was soft and ticklish against her. She almost sighed in disappointment when it fell to the floor, but then the searing heat of their naked bodies touching sent shock-waves through her. He showered her with kisses along her lips and jaw as he lifted her up and carried her to the bed.

Brock laid her on her back, and she shivered as he gazed down upon her naked body. She wanted to cover herself, to hide from him, but she worried that if she did he would stop, and she didn't want that, no matter how nervous she was.

"Lass," he whispered hoarsely. "You're beautiful. So much it near hurts me to look at you." He cupped her face and trailed one hand down her body, a fingertip exploring her nipples, then her navel before pausing above her mound.

Joanna's breath caught in her throat as he knelt down by the foot of the bed and gently nudged her legs apart. "Brock, wha—"

He placed a kiss upon her mound, and she gasped. The sensation of his warm breath down there was...*shocking*.

"Did I hurt you?" he asked. She propped herself up

on her elbows to watch him do whatever it was he was going to do.

"No, it's just... I didn't know that men did that."

Brock's chuckle made her blush. "Not all men, but the best lovers do. 'Tis a pleasurable spot for a woman." He placed another kiss, this one closer to her sensitive bud, and she wriggled, trying to escape and yet get closer at the same time. He gripped her thighs, pressing them open as he moved his mouth lower still. Joanna nearly shot off the bed when his tongue flicked against her sensitive folds. Sheer exquisite pleasure rippled through her, making her legs shake. She had never felt anything like this before.

"That feels...*good*," she gasped, starting to lose some of her shyness as the sensations began to overwhelm her. Brock licked her again, then sucked the pearl of her bud between his lips, and she cried out as sharp pleasure exploded within her. Every muscle inside her tightened and then went completely lax, and she sank deep into the bed, strangely euphoric. Her husband was gifted with a magical mouth.

"How was that?" Brock asked with a chuckle as he stood up between her thighs.

"Wonderful," she sighed, and then she gasped as she felt him push her thighs wide again. She opened her eyes and watched as he gripped his shaft and nudged her entrance. She didn't mean to tense, but the sight of him, massive, erect, was daunting to say the least.

"Try to be calm," he murmured as he leaned over the bed, bracing one arm by her head so he could kiss her. She fisted the sheets by her thighs, instinctively trying to close her legs against him, but all she could do was squeeze his hips with her knees. He pressed deep, shaft penetrating hard, and something sharp stung her inside. She whimpered against his lips as he moved out a little and rocked back in, and then she cried at the new flash of pain as he sank fully into her. Their bodies were pressed tight, and she wriggled beneath him, trying to escape the uncomfortable pain he caused.

"Kiss me, Joanna," he whispered gently and feathered his lips over hers.

She did kiss him, because she was desperate to be distracted by his intoxicating kisses. She uncurled her fingers from the sheets and slowly wrapped her arms around his neck. Their breath mingled as she opened her lips for his questing tongue, and the panic from before softened. The pain receded after a moment, and when he moved, withdrawing slightly before sliding back, it felt better. She was still sore, but there were new sensations now. The pleasure from before was coming back, yet it felt strange, more intense somehow, now that it was combined with the power of being filled by him. The sensation of being connected to him, she a part of him and he a part of her was something she never could have imagined possible. Their kisses grew slightly rougher, and it was exciting, wicked, and wonderful.

She shifted her legs higher on Brock's body, the heels of her feet pressing into his lower back. Their mouths broke apart as he strengthened his thrusts. Their eyes locked as he gripped her hip with one hand, holding her still so she did not slide up the bed. Brock grunted, and Joanna found the primal sound both exciting and erotic.

They didn't speak—she merely clung to him, her fingers digging into his bare shoulders as he thrust over and over into her, owning her body, claiming her as his wife in the most ancient way a man could. His eyes devoured her, and she felt as if she couldn't hold on to her body anymore. She came apart, her eyes temporarily blinded by a flash of sparks as a fresh wave of pleasure raced through her.

He murmured something soft and seductive in Gaelic, thrust twice more, and went still, his body pressing heavily onto hers. She didn't mind his weight on her, but she knew he was still standing, awkwardly bent over the bed which could not be comfortable. Joanna stroked his face, smiling in a daze.

"Can you move, Brock?"

He lifted his head, still breathing hard. "Am I too heavy?"

She shook her head. "No, but it must be uncomfortable for you to stand there. Why don't we pull the covers back and get into bed?"

"I like that idea." He pushed off her, and she winced a little as he withdrew from her body. His shaft was streaked with blood, hers. She was a little embarrassed, but she was also glad it was over. She had consummated her marriage with her husband. They were truly married now.

Brock wet a cloth from the basin and cleaned himself. He returned to the bed and kissed her as he gently wiped her thighs. Then he helped pull back the covers, and they slid under the sheets together. The feather tick mattress was little old and lumpy. Once his bigger body settled in beside her, she rolled into him with a startled gasp. He caught her by the waist, laughing softly. She laughed as well, then ducked her head shyly.

"Still all right?" he asked.

"Yes. It came as a shock at first, but there at the end..." She couldn't finish, but instead pressed her lips to his throat. He was so deliciously warm.

"It was nice, I hope?" He sounded a little vulnerable, which seemed so unlike the Brock she was used to. The one who was usually so full of quiet confidence.

"Yes," she assured him. She brushed her fingertips over the patch of dark hair on his chest, again fascinated by his body. He in turn curled a lock of her hair around his finger.

"Do you need to rest? We can sleep here if you like. The room is paid for the night."

She was about to say no but then yawned and burrowed deeper into him.

"Rest," he commanded with a gentle chuckle. "We'll eat again when you wake."

She didn't think it would be possible to sleep, not lying naked in her husband's arms after what they had just done, but somehow she simply slipped off to sleep without even realizing it.

14

Brock held his new wife in his arms, a quiet peace filling him. They had managed to enjoy a peaceful night's sleep at the inn as man and wife. Late morning sun boldly illuminated the room. Brock knew he should have gotten up and roused Joanna from her slumber, but they'd traveled so hard the last few days that she deserved to rest. And he couldn't resist enjoying her like this.

She was nestled against him, his arms around her, pulling her tighter to him. Having been inside her, sharing himself with her and she with him, the idea of putting any distance between them now was unfathomable. Merely *holding* her while his lips occasionally dropped kisses onto the damp curls of her head, filled him with a peace he'd never before experienced and never imagined he would feel.

The scars left behind from his father's violence were still there, marring him inside and out. He still feared, deep down, that he would end up like his father, that he also held that cruelty within him. He feared what would happen if he ever lowered his guard, if he stopped holding those feelings at bay. Yet somehow, when he was with Joanna, he wasn't afraid of himself anymore.

The anger that had always simmered beneath the surface faded when she was near, leaving behind only a faint prickling sense of something poisonous being removed. She was, in her own way, a kind of magic, one that leeched away the darkness within him. He would never hurt her—it was impossible now for him to do so. The rightness of being with her, protecting and caring for her, was there, buried deep in his bones, deeper than any anger and violence could reach.

He studied her face, the way her dark-gold brows softened when she was relaxed, and yet he remembered how they could arch imperiously when she wished to challenge someone. Her lips were not too full, nor were they the desired Cupid's bow pout that many men deemed pretty. They were simply kissable lips, ones that curved into a breathtaking smile whenever she was happy. Her eyes, though hidden from him now, were twin pools that he wanted to bathe in, to dive deep and explore the depths of her soul, if she would let him. He could've stared at her sleeping form for centuries. She brought him out of the darkness he felt so trapped in.

He dreaded what would happen when her brother caught up with them. Brock did not want to fight Lennox again, especially when he knew it would upset Joanna. What if he lost control when he took one punch too many from the Englishman? He'd lost his temper before, years ago when he'd fought the Earl of Lonsdale and the Duke of Essex over a barmaid who'd fancied Brodie. They'd destroyed the inn, but thankfully not each other.

He kissed Joanna's forehead and slid out of bed before he tucked the bedsheets securely around her. He dressed in fresh clothes from one of the saddlebags and shaved himself before he left Joanna alone in the room. He wished to check on the horses and acquire some more wine. Joanna would need to lunch, and he wanted to make sure she had a full belly. Castle Kincade was more than a full day's ride from Gretna Green but they wouldn't reach it until dinner the following day. They would hire a coach for the rest of the journey and tie their horses to the back of it.

He found their horses in good shape in the stables and took care to search their extra saddlebags for blankets. Then he groomed each, chuckling as Joanna's horse, Kaylee, nibbled on his shoulder while he flicked the brush against her coat, making it shine.

"You've done well," he praised her. "You've brought your mistress safely to Gretna Green, and you need not worry about another wild race." He brushed out her mane, removing the tangles caused by the winds blowing down the northern English roads. Then he saw to his own horse, who was far more used to mad dashes like this. All the while, Brock felt a warmth stir in his chest as he realized how much his life had changed. He would soon return to his rooms and find his wife waiting for him, warm and sweet in their bed.

I'm a lucky man to be gifted with her as my wife.

He exited the stables and stood there for a moment, taking in the bustle of the village, the carriages lining up at the smithy across the street. Mr. Lang stood outside the forge, welcoming a new couple inside. When he saw Brock, he gave a wave and a nod, which Brock returned. The smells coming from the meat and spices inside the inn, made his stomach growl. It would soon be time for lunch, and they could both use another meal after eating so thinly the last two days.

He was returning from the stables when the thunder of hooves drew his focus. It was unusual to have so many riders grouped together. Gretna usually had single riders or coaches. Brock brushed off his trousers and risked a glance toward the men.

Bloody hell! There was Lennox, a thunderous expression on his face. Five of his companions rode behind in a phalanx formation. Brock frowned, worry knotting his insides. He'd hoped for more time with Joanna before having to face her brother. He wondered if the damned *Sassenachs* had slept at all the last couple of days.

Lennox slid off his horse and headed straight into the blacksmith's shop. The others dismounted and waited nearby. Brock watched them unseen from his vantage point at the door of the stables. He was tempted to rouse Joanna and get her dressed and bundled into the nearest available coach, but that would not stop the coming storm, only delay it. He would have to face Lennox. Best if he spared her the pain of witnessing it.

Lennox stormed out of the blacksmith shop, clearly aware that he was too late. Brock stepped out of the doorway of the stables. Jonathan St. Laurent, one of Lennox's friends, was the first to see him. He whistled sharply with his fingers, drawing the attention of the others. Within seconds, Brock was surrounded by the League of Rogues.

"You...bloody *bastard!*" Lennox bellowed and dove at Brock, slamming him against the outside wall of the stable. He grunted as the air was forced from his lungs. Brock was beginning to wonder if every encounter with Lennox was going to end in a fight from now on.

"Where is she?" Lennox demanded, delivering a right hook that hit him hard in the eye. It was going to bruise, he could feel it.

He growled, shoving hard at Lennox's shoulder, sending him stumbling back. "She's safe."

"Married to you? Safe? I don't think so."

That set Brock's anger ablaze, but he summoned his control, refusing to fight back. When he looked at the man's face, he saw Joanna's bright-blue eyes burning into his. Punching Lennox would be like hitting his own wife. *Impossible.*

"Where is she? I want to see her!" Lennox demanded.

"Calm yourself first. I'll not have you upsetting my wife." The moment the word left his lips, he knew it was a mistake. But he accepted the blows that would come because he deserved to let Lennox strike him. He had stolen the man's sister away without his blessing.

"Don't you *dare* call her that!" Lennox hit him again, this time on the jaw. He tasted blood when his teeth sank into his cheek.

"I assume since you visited the blacksmith shop that you know we were married yesterday," Brock said as he wiped blood from his mouth with the back of his hand.

"Ash, calm down," Godric, the Duke of Essex, said. "You knew we not likely to reach them in time. There's nothing to be done now."

"Isn't there?" Lennox snapped. "If we take Joanna home now, we can still annul the marriage."

"You can't," Brock said. "We are fully man and wife now." He couldn't deny the relief he felt in that moment. He hadn't wanted to rush Joanna into consummation, but this was the very reason why they had. Thank God their passion had swept over them so quickly.

"Oh Lord," Lucien, the Marquess of Rochester, muttered. "You consummated it, didn't you?"

Brock answered with a nod.

Lennox, rather than throwing another punch, went very still. "I ought to shoot you." The cold menace in his tone would strike fear in any other man, but not Brock. He had grown up with an abusive father. There was very little Lennox could do or say that would frighten him.

"I swear to you, I will be a good husband to her," Brock replied quietly. "She'll want for nothing."

"Because you'll use her fortune," Lennox said. "Does she know you married her for her money?"

"It wasn't about the money," Brock assured him. "I wanted her for her."

Lennox harrumphed. "Of course you would say that."

Anger rose within Brock, despite himself. "Are you calling me a liar?"

"Time will tell. When she comes home with a broken heart..."

"She won't." If anyone risked a broken heart, it was him. Joanna could decide he and his home weren't enough, and she might go back to England. It was why he was so determined not to love her. He would care for her, but never love her. She would break his very soul if he dared to give her his heart.

"I want to see her. Now."

There was no winning that argument. Brock sighed and walked back to the inn, Lennox and his friends following once they put their horses in the stables.

"Wait here. I'll bring her down. You'll only upset her

if you go barging in." He nodded to a large empty table in the common room. The men all took their seats except for Lennox, who stood, arms crossed, at the base of the stairs to await his sister.

Brock climbed the steps, heart heavy as he ran to the room he'd shared with Joanna. She'd rolled onto her back in the time that he'd been gone, and he couldn't resist walking over to the bed and leaning over to kiss her. She sighed dreamily, kissing him back before she opened her eyes and stretched out like a contented cat. Lord, why did he have to ruin this moment by telling her Lennox had caught up with them? If he'd had the ability to stop time, freeze it to just this moment, where he held his wife in his arms and kissed her...

But he was no sorcerer, no keeper of time, and he was powerless to stop whatever would come next.

She looked over his clothed body. "You left?"

"Yes, I went to check on the horses."

"What happened? Your eye's red, and your mouth... Is that blood?" She bolted up in bed, briefly aware that she exposed her perfect breasts to him when the blankets dropped to her waist. "He's here, isn't he?"

"Aye. Lennox and his friends are downstairs. You should get dressed and go speak with him."

"Oh Lord..." She leapt out of bed, rushing to her saddlebag and retrieving a clean set of clothes.

"Did he hurt you?" she asked while changing.

"I've had worse." He couldn't help but watch the

adorable sway of her rounded bottom as she hopped into her petticoats and pulled on her stockings. He assisted her with her stays and gown, although he was a bit clumsy with the buttons on the dress. She dragged a comb through her hair and used one of the pink hair ribbons that had handfasted them to tie her hair back at the base of her neck. It made her look young and vulnerable in a way that tore at him. Brock's heart ached at the thought of what she must be feeling, knowing she was soon going to face a very angry brother.

"He is down in the common room," Brock said when she turned to him, ready to leave. She followed him downstairs and clutched his arm when she saw Lennox and his gang waiting for her.

"Joanna, are you all right?" her brother asked in a rigid voice that matched his posture.

"Of course I am." She let go of Brock's arm and moved to stand in front of him like a shield. Warmth filled him as he noticed her protectiveness, not that he needed it. Or perhaps he did, just not in the way she imagined.

"I would like to speak with you *alone*," Lennox said.

"Whatever you wish to say, my husband can hear as well."

Lennox shot him a look, then focused back on his sister. "Very well. So you married him, and from what I understand it cannot be annulled."

"No, it can't." She did not wilt under Ashton's disapproving gaze this time. She seemed different. Not because she had slept with Brock, but because she had taken her destiny into her own hands and had done what she wanted. Brock imagined it must have felt empowering for her. At least, he hoped she felt empowered.

Lennox was still scowling at her. "And you won't come home, even if I beg?"

"No, and I know you wouldn't beg—you'd simply command me. But you can't now. I'm a married woman, like Thomasina."

"Thomasina chose a safer husband than you did."

Brock tried not to scowl at Lennox. The man seemed to have no problem insulting him. It was a very good thing he could control his temper, because by his count he owed Lennox a couple of good punches.

"Who I married was always my choice, Ashton. I'm quite content with my decision. If you cannot accept it, then perhaps you should leave." Joanna raised her chin, not in a silly childish way, but in a womanly way that told Lennox he no longer held any power over her. Brock had to bite his lip to keep from grinning. He had married a warrior, and she was battling her brother quite well.

"Jo...I don't want to leave." Lennox's tone softened. "I want to make sure you're happy, that you're well. I don't want you to end up brokenhearted when you learn Kincade only married you for your money."

Joanna's spine stiffened. Brock could see it in the sudden rigid posture of her body.

"How *dare* you," she warned in a soft tone. "That is no longer your business. It is a matter between me and my husband." She looked over at Brock. "I'm going back to our room to pack our things. We shall not stay the night after all. I want to leave at once and see my new home." She stomped past him, as fierce as a warrior queen of old dismissing her unruly generals.

Brock tugged on his waistcoat and then met Lennox's pointed stare.

"If you'll excuse me, I must go hire a coach." He paused, clearing his throat. "Please don't make her sad, Lennox. Go make amends with her. She's in the last room on the left." Then he walked past the League and headed toward the stables again.

No one tried to stop him.

15

Joanna was so angry and upset that she was shaking. This was her wedding day! She should have been enraptured, wrapped in her husband's arms, relishing the intimacy of their bed, the feel of the fire from the fireplace and the wine sweetening Brock's lips as they kissed. She was not supposed to be dealing with her bloody stubborn brother and his nonsensical ideas about what was best for her.

When she heard the knock, she thought it was Brock and hastily opened the door. Ashton stood there, one hand flat on the doorjamb. She was half tempted to slam the door on his fingers. They shared a long look, a flurry of emotions passing between them.

This should have been a happy reunion, Ashton hugging her tight and accepting her kiss on his cheek while she told him how happy she was. But that was never going to be the case. Instead, there was anger, sorrow, and distrust between them, clouding over the sunny memories of their youth together. She'd often heard that siblings could grow apart over time, but she'd never believed it would happen to them. As she looked upon him now, she wanted him to be gone from here, gone from her life. The realization left a bitter taste in her mouth, and she suddenly wanted to cry.

"I'm sorry, Joanna." He choked on the words, but then he wrapped his arms around her before she could stop him.

She fought against his hold for a minute, not wanting to find any comfort in his arms, but it was impossible. Ashton had always been the big brother who was there for her. Rafe, as loving as he was, was rarely around and couldn't be counted on for any kind of support. She shuddered, a wave of emotions pulling at her heart. Ashton was safe, he was family, and she was leaving him behind. She had married and lain with a man, a near stranger, and was now mistress of his castle. It was her new life, and she had to face it with an open mind and an open heart.

"I can still take you home. You have but to say the word," Ashton murmured, holding her tighter.

"No. Please understand, I *want* to stay with him. I chose him." She couldn't explain the complexity of her feelings, how she would miss her old life, her friends, everything, but she needed to see this through. She wanted to learn to be brave, to explore the wilds of Scotland with her husband, and to win his heart, even if it took a lifetime. It was frightening, though, to know she had many battles ahead of her.

"He will be a good husband, Ash. He already is. He's been so gentle, so caring." She pulled away from her brother so she could look up into his eyes.

"Bu—"

"I know you're worried he will change, but I see kindness in his eyes. He cares, he's kind. There is no cruelty in him. Even when we..." She blushed and skipped over the embarrassing words. "He could have been harsh and cold, but it was quite the opposite. I loved being with him and was cherished. He makes me feel so protected. I *want* to stay with him."

Ashton sighed. For a long moment he said nothing, and then nodded, accepting her decision at last. "Very well. Mother will be upset she missed your wedding. Shall I bring her to visit soon?" He spoke casually, but she didn't miss the regret and sorrow in his eyes.

Joanna nodded. "Please. You should all come. Give me a month to get settled with Brock at the castle and then bring her, Rafe, and Thomasina, if she has time to visit."

"I can do that." Ashton pulled her into another hug, and Joanna could feel his hesitancy to let go.

"It's all right to let go, Ash. You have a wife now, and

I have a husband. We aren't children anymore. It's time we grew up."

He chuckled, though his smile was sad as he released her. "When did you become so wise?"

"A few days ago," Joanna said, laughing. She already felt so changed from since Ashton's wedding day. It felt like a lifetime ago.

"You don't have to leave the inn," Ashton said. "You can stay here with…" Ashton seemed to choke on the next words. "Your husband."

"We should go. I believe Brock has much at the castle to tend to, and I am looking forward to helping him."

Ashton nodded. "I am proud of you, Jo. You are making your own way in the world. I just wish you could have done it in a less…dramatic fashion."

"Drama would seem to run in our veins, wouldn't you say? Haven't you forgotten that your own wife showed up on your doorstep in the middle of a rainstorm because you'd bankrupted her? I daresay a race to Gretna Green was far less dramatic."

"You are right." He kissed her forehead and smiled. "Let me chase down Kincade and tell him all is well."

Joanna watched her brother leave and bit her lip, holding back the tears that stung at her eyes. All would be well; she had to believe that. She packed the rest of her belongings in her saddlebag and waited for Brock to return. When he did, he raked a hand through his hair, watching her carefully.

"You and Lennox sort things out?" he asked.

"Yes, I believe so."

"But you still wish to leave?" She didn't miss the apparent disappointment on his face. Did he think she didn't want to spend another night with him?

"I'm nervous about your home, and my brothers always taught me to face my fears. I think we should go straight to Castle Kincade."

"You fear my home?" The disappointment in his eyes deepened into concern.

"No!" She rushed over to him but stopped just inches away. She wanted to hold him, to feel his heartbeat against her ear, but how could she? They were still so new to each other in so many ways that she wasn't sure what else to do. She reached up to his face, gently touching his bruised jaw. It was already swelling.

"I don't fear your home. It's just unknown to me." She traced her fingers over his lips, and he caught her wrist, holding her fingers to his mouth. He kissed the pads of her fingers, and she shivered as a slow, delicious wave of arousal moved through her.

"I don't want you to fear anything." Brock curled an arm around her waist, pulling her flush against him. She wanted him again, but she was a little afraid. She was still sore from the first time.

"I know. You are wonderful. Did you know that?" She smiled up at him and stood on tiptoes to kiss him. She could feel his lips curve against hers, and for some reason she was deliriously happy. Their closeness was like a drug, lulling her into a sweet euphoria that she didn't want to end. He suddenly lifted her up in his arms and carried her to the bed. He sat down on it and cradled her in his lap. She loved feeling like this, warm and safe in his arms while he kissed her. He reclaimed her lips, crushing her to him. She returned his kisses with a hunger that belied her outward calm. Perhaps she wasn't too sore to—

"We should go, lass. If I hold you much longer like this, I will not be able to stop myself from claiming you again, and I know you must be hurting." He nuzzled her neck, and she clutched his shoulders, sighing.

"I suppose. Let's go and find our coach."

He stood and set her down gently on her feet. They gathered their belongings and walked back down to the common room of the inn. Ashton and his friends were drinking at one of the tables, and a barmaid was bringing them plates of food.

"Care to have lunch with us before you go?" Ashton asked as they paused by the table.

Brock looked to Joanna uncertainly. "I will be happy to dine with them if you wish to."

Joanna decided she would, as she would not see Ashton again for at least a month. "Yes, if you don't mind, I would like that."

"Very well. I'll take our bags to the coach and tell the driver we will depart after lunch."

The men stood as Joanna joined them. Charles winked as she looked at her brother and his friends. "Married at last, are we? Well, it suits you, Jo." Cedric elbowed Charles in the ribs, and he grunted before muttering an apology.

"Lady Kincade, lovely for you to join us," Godric, the Duke of Essex, bowed and she blushed. In just two days she'd gone from Ashton's little sister to *Lady* Kincade. She had to admit, she rather liked the sound of that, especially if such a title made it easier to keep men like these in line.

Ashton pulled out a chair for her, and the other men waited for her to sit before they resumed their seats. Ashton gave her his plate, smiling in a way that reminded her so much of their childhood. When Brock returned, they shared a meal, the mood much more relaxed.

An hour later, she hugged Ashton again and with a falsely cheery smile waved goodbye and climbed into the coach with Brock. It stung to leave her brother behind, as well as her past. There was a tightness in her chest that only seemed to ease when she cuddled next to Brock. She sat beside him, leaning against his side, and he didn't seem to mind.

She was happy to be with him, she didn't doubt that, but it was sad to know that she was never truly going to go home to Lennox House again. She'd visit from time to time, but only visit. There was something undeniably sad to know that a person would never be a child in their childhood home again, that they'd left that part of their life behind. She reminded herself that she had a new home now, one she would fill with merriment and love with Brock.

16

Joanna and Brock rode in silence for a long while before she spoke.

"What is Castle Kincade like?"

Brock grinned, his mood beginning to brighten. "It sits upon a hill, not a big one, mind, but below it is a loch, with waters as blue as the summer sky. My mother had some gardens built, but they've fallen into disrepair in the years since she died. I have no talent for them, but perhaps you could set them straight."

"I would like that very much," Joanna agreed. The prospect of restoring the gardens his mother had once created seemed like a lovely idea. She was also relieved that she would have something to occupy her there. Joanna had never been the sort of woman to sit idly by when she could take charge of something.

"What was she like? Your mother, I mean."

Brock stiffened slightly, and for a long moment Joanna wondered if he would even answer.

"My mother was tenderhearted. There wasn't an injured animal or wounded person that she didn't try to heal or help. There was a light in her eyes, one that I can see in you. It reminds me so much of her." His voice roughened, and Joanna squeezed his arm, wanting to show him her support. Brock drew in a steadying breath before he continued.

"Brodie called her an angel when we were little. He thought she came down from the clouds to be our mother. And Aiden...he is so like her in spirit—loving and easily hurt."

"Are you like your mother?" she asked.

Brock shook his head. "I know I am not."

Joanna was worried he'd say he was like his father, but thankfully he didn't.

"I think you are," Joanna said quietly. Sometimes speaking the truth, one that someone needed to hear more than they could ever admit, was a way of showing love. And she wanted Brock to feel her desire to love him. She didn't yet, but she would love him someday soon. It was like the way she could always sense a coming storm—she could tell that she would love this man more than her own life. She hoped that when that day came, she would find he had come to love her too.

They dissolved into another silence, this one longer,

more contemplative, but no less peaceful. She liked that about him. Being with him was restful, at least when they weren't kissing. He was so different from the men in London and Bath, who were desperate for conversation, but the depth and value of that conversation was often shallow. When Brock spoke it was to make a difference, to share part of himself with her.

"Would you sing me another song?" she asked, closing her eyes.

Brock chuckled. "Am I to be your Scottish songbird, lass?"

"Yes," she giggled. She laid her head on his shoulder as he started to sing sweetly in her ear.

Frae that sweet hour her name I'd breathe.
Wi' nocht but clouds and hills to hear me,
And when the world to rest was laid
I'd watch for dawn and wish her near me,
Till one by one the stars were gone,
The moor-cock to his mate called clearly,
And daylight glinted on the burn
Where red-deer cross at mornin' early.

The sweet, almost mournful tone tugged at Joanna's heart.

The years are long, the work is sair,
And life is aftimes wae and wearie,
Yet Foyer's flood shall cease to fall
Ere my love fail until my dearie.
I'd loved her then, I loved her now,

And could the world wad be without her.

The notes trailed off into silence, yet Joanna felt the tune hum deep beneath her skin in the most wonderful way. She'd never been talented when it came to music; she'd been more proficient at sketches and watercolors, one of the many interests and talents young ladies were expected to focus on rather than the interests that truly called to her. She'd been fortunate Ashton was her brother, because he had encouraged her to learn about economics and business as well as managing investments. She wasn't as gifted as he was, but she did have a knack for it.

"Brock?" she whispered.

"Hmm?" His reply felt intimate in a way that made her blush.

"I love when you sing to me."

His arms tightened around her body as he pulled her closer.

"Then I shall sing often," he promised.

They passed the remaining evening and the following day inside the coach. They paused for breaks to rest the horses, to see to their needs and to take quick meals. When the coach stopped for a final time Joanna awoke from a light sleep that she hadn't even been aware she'd drifted into. Brock opened the coach door and offered her his hands, helping her down. She looked up, gaping at the stone edifice towering above her. It was breathtaking. The fierce gray stones in the jagged edges of the parapets along the roof were like a wolf baring its teeth. Yet there was a softness to it, the way the stones were smoothed from years of rain rather than pitted and craggy. Whoever had built this castle had built it with love and thought, not in haste to defend against enemies.

"What do you think?" Brock asked, shifting on his feet.

"It is wonderful," she exclaimed, her gaze sweeping over her new home.

This is my world now. The sweeping clouds and the still waters of the lake beyond the solitary castle, standing like an ancient ring of stones amidst the distant hills.

"Come, let me show you inside." Brock offered her his arm, and she lifted her skirts as they crossed the gravel carved road and reached the tall semicircular arched doorway.

The sturdy oak was intricately carved and weathered by centuries of harsh Scottish winters. Brock pushed on the rusted latch, and the heavy door swung open on its ancient hinges. She stepped into the dim interior with Brock, feeling like a woman being taken into a dark fairy realm. She caught sight of curving stairs, tapestries hanging against the stones while shafts of light pierced the darkness from tall windows. The dusty, old feel of the castle would have scared away any number of new English brides, but not her. Joanna was instantly bewitched with the cobwebs clinging to the chandeliers that glinted like gossamer in the sunlight. It was rather how she'd envisioned the castles in her Gothic novels, but at least here there would be no lurking ghouls or terrifying specters to send her fleeing onto the moors at midnight.

Brock smiled nervously as he waved a hand about the entryway. "Welcome to Castle Kincade. Such as it is."

"Oh, Brock," she said with a sigh and ran to him, hugging him. "It's magnificent."

"You mean that?" He tilted her chin up, studying her closely, as if trying to find some sign of deception. But he wouldn't find any. This was a place of magic, a place she felt drawn to, connected to in a way that defied any explanation she could give.

"You truly like it?" Brock asked.

"I do. Now, show me *everything*."

Brock led her through a corridor that contained a dozen or more bedrooms, then the courtyard, which held a small herb garden and a rose garden. He took her to the windows of the tower, where he pointed to the outside gardens. They reminded her a little of Vauxhall in London, but he was right, they would require a lot of attention. Then he took her down to the large kitchens. They were dark, only firelit. A squat, red-faced woman sat by the fire, roasting a pot of potatoes over the flames.

The woman leapt to her feet when she saw Brock. "My lord!"

"Mrs. Tate, this is my wife, Joanna, the new mistress of Castle Kincade."

Mrs. Tate's eyes widened as she took in Joanna and dipped into a hasty curtsy.

"It's a pleasure to meet you, Mrs. Tate." Joanna smiled at the woman, but she saw a flash of dislike in the woman's eyes when she heard Joanna's English accent, before the dark look was buried beneath a polite mask.

"Congratulations on your nuptials, my lord," the cook said. "I hope you will be as happy as the great master was with your mother."

Brock tensed at the mention of his parents, and Joanna squeezed his arm gently in silent support.

"Thank you," Brock murmured. "I'm sure you and Lady Kincade will have much to discuss regarding the running of the kitchens, the menus for dinner, as well as the other household accounts. Joanna, her brother has seen to much of the work as well while I've been focused on the tenant farms and animal husbandry. I'm sure he'll be glad to divide the work between you and himself. It's time we changed from how my father ran things. Don't you agree, Mrs. Tate?"

"I thought the great master ran things just fine," she muttered, arching a brow in skeptical challenge. Joanna swallowed back a bitter taste. This was not going to be easy; she would have to convince the cook to trust her.

"Mrs. Tate, have you seen Mr. Tate? He did not greet us when we arrived," Brock asked in a low voice.

"Oh! Mr. Tate was seeing to the books in your study, my lord."

"Ach, good." Brock escorted Joanna from the kitchens. As they left, she glanced over her shoulder one more time and saw Mrs. Tate still frowning.

Oh dear. She wasn't looking forward to dealing with Mrs. Tate, but she suspected it was due to the fact that she was English. The Battle of Culloden was still fresh in the minds of many, especially the Scots.

She and Brock returned to the main hall, and he took her down a narrow corridor.

"This is my study. You may visit me anytime here. Unlike some men, I will not bar any of my home from you. Every room is as much yours as it is mine." He opened the door, and she followed him into the study. A man sat at the large desk, poring over account books.

"Ah, Tate, there you are. Allow me to introduce you to Joanna, my wife."

"Wife?" Tate rose from his chair, frowning slightly at Joanna. "You have married, my lord? I received no letter about such a thing."

Joanna stared at Mr. Tate, shocked that the steward of the estate had taken such a tone with his master.

"I'm sorry, I didn't have time to inform you." Brock stared at Tate. "Joanna is Rosalind's sister-in-law by marriage, and now she is my wife. Joanna, Mr. Tate is the brother to the cook, Mrs. Tate. Mrs. Tate isn't married, but we've always called her missus for as long as I can remember," he explained to Joanna before turning back to his steward. "Mr. Tate, please make sure Joanna has everything she needs."

Tate closed the account books and bowed formally to Joanna.

"I apologize, my lady. I was shocked to hear of the sudden wedding, that is all." He offered her a smile, but it wasn't as warm as she'd hoped.

"Thank you, Mr. Tate." Joanna smiled at him, trying to be cordial.

"Why don't I show you to your rooms," Brock said, and then they left Mr. Tate to his business in Brock's study.

They went up the elegant winding staircase and down one of the corridors. Joanna stared at the lovely tapestries lining the walls. One depicted a unicorn trapped in a small circular fence. There was something about the scene, the tranquil immortal creature allowing itself to be captive while flowers bloomed around it and the animals in the woods looked upon the snowy-white beast in fascination and awe.

"My mother loved this tapestry." Brock's rich voice rumbled from behind her, pulling her out of the spell of the intricately woven tapestry for a moment.

"It's beautiful." Joanna gazed at the almost shimmering strands of the white thread. The unicorn almost seemed to breathe in the light coming from the windows opposite. She wasn't sure why, but she felt a sudden mix of joy and sorrow at the sight.

Brock placed a hand on her waist, and the comforting touch sent a bolt of excitement through her. She turned so she could see his face. His dark brows arched over his storm cloud–colored eyes. They made her think of the summer storms that swept over fields of bending trees and bursting with lightning. Beautiful, frightening, and yet so full of life and energy.

She reached up, gripping his waistcoat at the neck and tugging his head down to hers. She needed to kiss him. In a strange way, it seemed that she could express herself with small, little things like kisses when words failed her.

He returned the kiss, his tongue slipping between her lips as he moved her backward, pressing her against the unicorn tapestry. The sun-warmed cloth heated her back, and she felt cocooned between it and Brock's body. He mastered her mouth with wicked kisses that flushed her with heat and hunger in equal measure. It never seemed like enough. One kiss from him was a spark inside a tinderbox. She lit up, as though lightning was surging through her in violent, powerful explosions. All from one kiss.

When they broke apart long minutes later, Brock was breathing hard. He closed his eyes as their faces touched. His fingers held on to her hips, digging in as he recovered his breath.

"Is it always like this?" she asked, still clutching his waistcoat collar.

"I..." He hesitated. "I've been with a few women before—not many, mind, but a few—and it has never come close to this, lass. Not like it is with you." His lips softened into a seductive smile that seemed almost boyish in its charm. Her heart skittered in her chest.

"Truly?" She felt foolish for wanting him to reassure her, but she was falling in love with him bit by bit, like sliding down a rain-slicked hill in the spring. Soon she would be hopelessly in love with him, and it terrified her to think she would be the only one who felt that way.

"Aye. You are different from all the rest." He nuzzled her before stealing another faint kiss, and the ghostly press of his mouth to hers was felt down to her core. It was not a kiss to seduce nor to inflame desire. It was one that expressed affection, to linger like a sweet dream.

"Come." He led her down the corridor and stopped in front of a closed door.

"These will be your private chambers for when you wish to be alone. I understand that gentle ladies need their private sanctuaries." He opened the door for her and showed her inside. The room was circular and very unusual. A fireplace was to the right and a four-poster bed to the left. There were two large windows, one close to the fireplace and one closer to the bed.

"Are we in the tower?" she asked, trying to make sense of the large circular space.

"Aye. There are a few large spaces such as these. My mother converted them into guest chambers when she reminded my father that we were no longer fighting the English and had no need for armories and such."

Joanna gazed at the room in wonder. Perhaps it'd once been a medieval armory, but all she saw now was a place of peace, decorated with feminine touches. The bed coverlet was a pretty shade of emerald with gold fringe, and the vanity was made of a beautiful rosewood with a mirror inlaid into it. Everything in the room was elegant.

"What do you think? Will it do?" Brock asked, his hopeful tone so endearing that she turned to look at him, her fingertips still trailing along the dusty surface of the vanity.

"It's perfect, but..." She felt a blush rise up in her cheeks.

"But?" He hung up on the word, worry clouding his eyes.

"But I do not share a chamber with you?" she asked. It was well known that most husbands and wives did not share bedchambers, except in rare circumstances. Those couples who were deeply in love often shared one chamber. Joanna desperately wanted that, to feel him beside her each night. She craved that quiet intimacy of two people sleeping close enough to share their dreams in the dark.

"You wish to share a chamber with me?" Brock asked uncertainly.

She nodded. "I would. That is, if you do. If you do not, I—"

He crossed the room before she could speak further, and he kissed her hard, that rush of passion exploding between them again.

She chuckled as they broke apart. "Is that a yes?"

He grinned. "It is. I didna think you would want to, so I didna think to ask."

"Never be afraid to ask, Brock," she said softly. "I want us to be open with each other, unafraid to speak on such things."

He rubbed his hands up and down her back, sighing. "I'm so used to keeping my thoughts to myself. My father..." Brock's gaze turned distant. "He never wanted to talk, and when he did, I didn't usually wish to hear what he had to say. The man was cruel. It made for a lonely childhood, even with my brothers and my sister."

"You were all trapped by pain. I understand that." She and her siblings had grown up in a similar way, but at least they'd always had their mother.

"Never give up on me, lass. Don't let me shut you out." Brock's voice was rough with emotion.

"I won't," she promised.

Then she squealed as something moved under the covers of the bed beside them.

Brock spun and grasped the edge of the coverlet, pulling the green fabric back. A gray-bodied beast the size of a small dog trundled toward them. Its face was black with a large and snowy-white stripe down the center.

"Ach, Freya! What are you doing here, wee one?" Brock picked up the creature and set her down on the ground.

"Is that...a badger?" Joanna stared down at the beast, knowing it was indeed a badger, but she couldn't believe she was watching one inside the castle, in *her* bed.

"Shoo! Go on with you, Freya." Brock nudged the badger into the corridor with his boot. The badger huffed, lifted her head, and trotted with surprising speed down the hall and out of sight.

"She is one of Aiden's. You will find wee beasties all through the house, I'm afraid. We have owls nesting in the roof of the library, a fox in the kitchens, and at least half a dozen other creatures roaming the corridors. I hope that willna upset you."

"No," Joanna said with a smile. "I think it's charming. She just frightened me. One doesn't expect a badger in one's bed."

At this Brock laughed heartily. "Ach, lass, but you *do* have a badger in your bed. Or are you forgetting?" He snapped his teeth at her playfully like a badger, and she burst into giggles and lightly shoved his chest. He caught her by the waist.

"I love your home," she said when she finally stopped laughing.

"*Our* home. 'Tis yours as well now."

"Our home," she echoed, her face heating again. "Why don't you show me your room?"

"I'd be happy to." He escorted her from the tower, and they headed toward his chambers. Joanna couldn't stop smiling.

I suppose I do have a badger in my bed.

17

Brock held his breath as he led Joanna into his bedchamber. It was not the official room of the laird of Castle Kinkade. That had been his father's chamber, and Brock would never sleep in that room. It was as though his father's presence still lingered there. But this chamber, the one that had two large windows facing the lake, was his favorite. It had high vaulted ceilings and a large four-poster bed with dark-blue bed hangings. Two overstuffed armchairs faced the fireplace. Joanna moved straight to them, touching the warm fabric with a smile.

"It's very inviting," she said, glancing over her shoulder at him. Lord, he was having trouble keeping his hands off her, but he needed to. He needed to give her time to heal from the first time they were together.

"I'm glad you like it. If you ever wish to, you may

sleep in the other room, although I hope you will stay here with me each night. Would you care to go riding before dinner?" he offered. If they were riding and touring the countryside, he would not be easily tempted to take her back to bed. He held out his hand to her.

"I would like that very much." When she placed her hand in his and smiled up at him, arousal hit him hard. Perhaps he had been too hasty in his reasoning to avoid bedding her again so soon. Brusquely, he led her down to the castle courtyard, pointing out various niches of the grounds that reminded him of the better parts of his youth. He fought valiantly to resist the sweet warmth of her skin and his together as they held hands. For the first time in his life, he was viewing his lands as a means of seduction rather than a source of shame for the condition they were in. Which hedgerow could he press her into? Which garden path could he lead her to and be certain they would be alone?

Before they entered the stables, he pulled her close, slipping his other arm around her, enclosing her within his embrace so that he could kiss her soundly. The sweetness of her settled in against his soul and hummed through his blood, giving him the strength to pull away from her and guide her toward the fresh horses that had been readied for them, while their other horses rested from the journey.

"Oh, Joanna." Brock smiled suddenly, his hands around her waist as he prepared to lift her onto her mount. "I'm afraid I dinna have a sidesaddle here, love." And with that warning, he lifted her high and placed her gently onto the horse. The skirts of her carriage dress rode up over her knees, and she blushed as he placed a small kiss above her stocking.

"I'll have to order new riding gowns from London or Edinburgh, I suppose," she reasoned, eyes following Brock to his own horse. "Ones that would be suitable for riding astride."

Brock sighed at the unfairness of hiding those knees, but he nodded. "Aye, ye will. Or you could wear breeches."

"Breeches?" she gasped, the scandal of such an idea heating her face. "Wouldn't you be furious? Forbid it? I cannot imagine any man would let his woman go about in a man's clothes."

Her husband chuckled. "Those men would be fools. I'd love nothing more than to see your bonny bottom in tight breeches." He eyed her bottom as he said this, and a new flush of heat, this time from desire rather than embarrassment, rolled through her.

"Perhaps...perhaps I will have some breeches made." She grinned at him.

He mounted his horse, and they rode through the bailey and under the open portcullis farther down from the main door. Then he kicked his horse's flanks, and they raced down the sloping hill toward the still waters of the loch.

It felt good to be home, to feel the wind upon his face, to see the heather upon the hills and the sun bathing the tops of the forests with gold. He hadn't minded Bath, but the ballrooms and townhouses were confining in a way that his castle and the hills could never be.

"Brock, this place is beautiful." Joanna sighed wistfully, her gaze sweeping over the countryside.

"These lands have been in my family for more than four hundred years," he told her with pride.

The breeze played with Joanna's hair, tugging it loose, and she looked more like she belonged here than any other person he'd ever seen. She fit into the land the way a dryad would fit in the shadowed glens.

"May we see the loch?" she asked, her blue eyes bright with fire. The excitement and wonder in her voice woke a sense of longing inside him that he'd been afraid of for far too long. The longer he spent with her, the more he believed he might yet fall in love with her. But could he love someone the way his mother had loved? Loved beyond all doubt, reason, and good sense? Loved through the end of his days and even longer? Did he dare to? It had done his mother no good in the end. But then, Joanna was no monster. She wouldn't treat him the way his father had treated his mother. But the thought of letting that stone wall around his heart come down was too terrifying.

"Aye, we can." He wanted to show her everything,

and the lake was by far one of the best parts of the Kincade lands. She grinned at him, and this time he saw less of Ashton in her and more of Rafe's mischievous temperament. That was a side he was interested in exploring. A playful wife was a happy wife, and he wanted Joanna to always be happy.

He led her down past the lake, through the forest that bordered his lands, and they stopped deep in the woods. The clearing had been made thousands of years ago by the men and women who had lived on this land before it had become Scotland. A group of gray stones formed a strange pattern that pointed to a pile of stones in the center. During the summer months, the sunlight cut through the trees in streaks of light that illuminated the patches where the stones stood, making the site even more mystical.

His mother had told him that the pile of stones was possibly a burial chamber for an ancient chieftain. Whenever Brock visited this place, he felt as though he could hear the stones of the burial chamber breathing, in that way things in nature often can. A delicate but somehow deep inhalation that went straight to the core of itself. His mother used to tell him and his siblings that magic, *old* magic, resided here, deep in the circle of these stones that guarded the eternal rest of an ancient chieftain who'd perished defending these lands.

"What is this place?" Joanna whispered as they slid off their horses. He took her hand again as they passed through the muted gold beams of light. They paused before one of the taller stones, which stood like a flat rectangle pointing up to the sky.

"These are the stones of Kincade, but many call these tall pieces *fir bhreige*, or false men." He pulled her closer, embracing her from behind so she leaned back against him as he whispered his family's stories in her ear.

"When the trees were younger, the stones pointed to the sun and moon. It also showed the men the way home during the seasons. They would travel far from home to hunt, and seeing these stones upon distant hilltops was the only way in which they could find their way back to their tribes."

They walked up to the tallest stone nearest them. He placed his palm on the tall flat stone. The rock was rough. Brock swore that if he closed his eyes, he could feel the people of the past—his past—humming just beneath his fingertips, like the murmur of a thousand whispering souls.

Joanna placed her palm over his.

"It's so peaceful here."

"It is," he agreed.

Scotland was a place of deep peace and beauty, a land God made to be perfect. He could never live anywhere else but here. His blood would always yearn to be on Scottish soil. He wondered if Joanna would someday feel the same. What if she changed her mind, decided she missed England, her friends and family and the life she'd had there? He wouldn't want her to be unhappy or to force her to stay here. The thought made a sharp pain knife in his chest.

"Will you miss England?" he asked, forcing his voice to sound calm so she didn't hear the concern in his words.

She was quiet a long moment as she circled the stones. Again he couldn't help but picture her as a dryad, tempting a man into the woods so he might catch and kiss her, only to find she'd turned into a beautiful tree. She peered around the edge of one of the stones to look at him. The wind tugged her unbound hair playfully, the blonde strands dancing across the roughhewn rocks.

"I suppose I will, but this...I can't quite explain it, but I feel as though I was destined to be here." She shook her head. "I know it sounds silly."

"No, it doesn't." He circled around the stone, catching her waist from behind and pulling her back against him as he breathed in the floral scent of her hair. He laced the fingers of his hands over her stomach, holding her to him. She covered his hands with hers, leaning back against him as they watched the light and shadows dance through the stones the way they had done for thousands of years. For the first time in his life, the quiet around him was a peaceful one, not an awful, foreboding one that filled him with dread. Holding his wife and standing among the stones, he felt his soul, which had been so often wounded, begin to heal. This moment with this woman was a gift he'd never fully deserve.

He brushed his lips against her ear. "Thank you for marrying me, Joanna," he whispered. "I know you gave up everything to be here."

She turned in his arms, her eyes filled with hope.

"I thought I was running away from England and the disappointments there, but now..." She shivered and leaned closer to him. "Now I know I was running toward something better."

Brock leaned down, stealing a slow, sweet kiss that sent flames up the stone wall around his heart, challenging it to crumble. That aching in his chest began again as her gaze searched his for answers, and he knew before she spoke what she was about to ask, only he was too terrified to answer truthfully.

"Do you love me?" she asked.

Love? He dared not love. He slowly let go of her and stepped away, hating the distance but needing some clarity to think before he responded. It also gave him time to strengthen his defenses against her sweetness.

"I care for you, lass," he finally replied. The look of hurt was so strong on her that it hit him as though he'd actually been punched.

"I knew it would take time for us to fall in love. I just had hoped it would be sooner." She let out a breath and turned away from him. Not even the spell of the stones could bring her back to him. She walked away, back to where they had left their horses. She waited without a word as he joined her and helped her up in the saddle.

He wanted to take his words back, to explain himself. But what could a man say? *"You're a bonny lass and the greatest thing in my life, but I'm not capable of love, and I'm bloody terrified of it?"* No, that wouldn't go over well with her at all. Best he distract her from it instead.

"Would you like to meet some of my tenants on the land before we return to the castle?"

"If it pleases you, then I would be happy to." Her tone was soft but also a little flat, as though she wasn't fully paying attention to him anymore, like she'd locked herself away inside her own thoughts.

Brock frowned at her complacent, almost absent answer. He didn't want a complacent, obedient wife. He would rather have her spitting mad as a polecat than quiet and withdrawn. He resolved that he would find a way to show her he cared, even if in the end he could not love her. He couldn't lie to himself—if he were brave enough, he would love her like mad, but he was a coward for fearing what love would cost him.

They took the road back to the castle, and he guided her around the edges of his lands to where his tenants lived. These people raised sheep, and much of his exports were lamb-based products sent to the south of England. His father, as with some other lairds, had seen the tenants as mere cogs in a great wheel of forging a profit from the lands, but Brock refused to see his people that way. Now that they were his responsibility, he wanted things to change. He wanted to make sure they had the means to feed their families well and live in good homes. Many lairds in the Lowlands encouraged their tenants to abandon Gaelic, but Brock had removed any such restrictions after his father had passed a over a month ago.

His gaze swept the distant hills that were slowly being swallowed by the rising shadows of dusk. So much had changed in Scotland after the English had destroyed their spirit and broken their land apart by bankrupting many of the chieftains. Those men had sold their homes, their castles, all of it. His father had been one of the few men able to keep his lands intact.

Of course, now Brock knew the darker truth as to why, that his father had sold out his countrymen to an English spy, and he'd been rewarded for it. The thought turned Brock's stomach and filled his mouth with a foul taste.

There had been rumors when he was growing up that his father had been a traitor. The men he'd claimed had been his closest friends from the other Scottish clans— the Campbells, the MacLeods, the Stewarts, the MacKenzies—had all lost fathers and brothers years ago in an attempted uprising. Just days before they'd planned to go to Edinburgh to rally support for their cause, they'd vanished in the night, every one of them. Only his father had survived, and finding himself alone, he soon abandoned his fight.

Brock sighed and looked out over his lands. Englishmen were happily buying up the land and building new castles. He didn't want the Kincade lands to fall to the English like that. Better if the place were burned down than strangled by purse strings. Part of Brock's desperation to marry had been with that in mind. He had to put the lives of his tenants first above his own interests.

But he would not force Joanna to part with her fortune, not unless she wished to do so. His hope was that once she saw his people, saw the needs they had, her heart would open and she would agree to help. Most of the Scots here lived in comparative poverty, eking out a living from the thin soil in a harsh and challenging climate.

Every day his heart weighed heavily with the duties he owed to the men and women who worked on his land. As in Ireland, potatoes were a mainstay of the diet of the less fortunate, but disease and famine were frequent and devastating when they struck. He'd seen far too many die from starvation. Last year alone, his tenants had lost wee bairns in the winter months from being unable to feed them enough. The wailing of those mothers holding their children in their arms before having to put them in wee caskets had broken Brock's heart. He wouldn't let that happen again, not on his lands.

Brock wanted Joanna to help secure new farm equipment so they could raise better crops to give his tenants
a chance to not only survive, but thrive.

"We are here," he told Joanna as they rode into a
small village. There were two rows of old black houses.
Their dark interiors were less pleasant than the more
recent structures called white houses that many tenants
were building on other estates. He halted his horse by
the first dwelling and slid to the ground. Then he helped
Joanna down and escorted her to the door. It opened
before he could knock.

"My lord!" one of his best farmers greeted him.
Dougal Ramsey was a tall, thin, but strong man in his
forties with piercing blue eyes. His young wife, Annis,
stood behind him, one hand resting on her lower back as
she bent over a pot hanging above a fire in the hearth,
her pregnant belly preventing her from reaching easily
into the recesses of the fireplace.

"Evening, Mr. Ramsey. I returned from Bath and
brought my new wife to meet you and the other
tenants."

"Married? My hearty congratulations to ye!" Ramsey
grinned and waved them both inside. "Annis, put the
kettle on for his lordship."

Annis blushed shyly at Brock and Joanna as they
stepped inside. Two small barefooted children scam-
pered around, the girl holding a doll made of straw and

the older boy holding a wooden sword, swinging it at invisible opponents.

"Elsbeth, Camden, his lordship is here. Go an' wash up," Annis commanded, then set about putting the kettle on. Brock shot a glance at Joanna, wondering what she thought of all this. It had to be so different from what she was used to. These cottages were bare inside, and the floors were simply the earth that the walls were built upon. The dark stone walls were grim and dark in color, and the thatched roofs offered dreary comfort in the winter and the rainy season.

Brock had spent a few nights in these cottages in the winter when the icy winds of the Atlantic dragged its claws across the hills and valleys of most of Scotland. The dilapidated state of many of these black houses was further darkened by the fact that the only source of light came from the doorway and the small hole in the chimney. It wasn't an easy way to live.

Joanna's stare moved about the gloomy home of Dougal and Annis, and he saw sorrow flash in her eyes.

"'Tis wonderful to meet yer bonnie bride, my lord." Dougal bowed to Joanna, and Annis did her best to curtsy.

"Please, call me Joanna. Are these your lovely children?" She nodded at Camden and Elsbeth, who had stopped playing and were now standing solemnly by their parents' sides, the doll and the wooden sword hanging limply from their hands.

"This is Camden. He's eight. And Elsbeth here is five."

Joanna bent down, a warm smile lighting up her face as she looked at the children.

"That's a lovely doll you have."

Elsbeth blushed shyly and held out the doll as though she was expected to give it up to please Joanna. It was something Brock suspected his father would have taught the tenants at a young age. He'd never let Brock spend much time around the tenants; he'd kept his sons busy with other things, like riding to Edinburgh to try to find markets to export the lamb they produced. Joanna took the doll from the little girl, gave it a hug, and passed it back to the child.

"Thank you for sharing her with me. She's lovely." Joanna beamed at the girl, and the child smiled back hesitantly.

"Tea's ready." Annis retrieved four plain white pottery cups and poured everyone tea. Brock and Joanna took their cups and sipped.

"So, Dougal, how is everything for the tenants? I hope to make some changes here soon."

Dougal looked uncertainly at his wife. "Changes, my lord?"

Brock set his cup down on the table. "Yes, I want to raise the wages you are paid for labor, and I'd like to explore building better housing for everyone."

Dougal blinked, and Annis's eyes were suddenly overbright.

"I believe we'd like that, my lord." Dougal's smile grew broader again.

Brock felt suddenly bashful. After his father died, Brock enjoyed having the freedom to spend time among his tenants when he could, but he was aware that he would always be a laird to them. Bringing an English wife into their midst, he feared that they might be upset. But seeing Joanna's easy and gentle nature with the tenants had filled him with hope. She wasn't as distant with him now as she had been after they'd visited the stones. Coming here had been a good distraction from that upsetting conversation.

"Well, I promised I'd see my wife home for dinner. I'll be back in a few days to discuss the particulars of my plans."

Brock stood, and Joanna thanked Annis for the tea and waved to the children before she followed him outside. Her gaze swept over the other black houses, seeing the *gille-wee-foots*, the barefoot children running about while their parents toiled in the fields.

Joanna drew close to him after she mounted her horse. "Brock, those houses must be so cold in the winter. How do they stay warm?"

"Well, the houses are built on slopes, you see? And they keep cows at the bottom of the lower end of the homes on the back side where there is a partition. It makes it easy to remove waste, and the cows do provide some heat, because it warms the peat and the stones that make up the cottage walls."

"But the kitchen was bare. What do they eat?" Joanna's eyes were wide with concern. *Lord, she does have a big heart.*

"When times are thin, they can bleed the cattle. Not kill them, mind, but they can cut a flank or side and catch blood in bowls. It mixes well with oatmeal and milk to make cakes. Tastes terrible, but it does provide some nourishment."

"Blood? Oh, Brock, there has to be a better way."

"Scotland is a beautiful land, but she can also be harsh. We've learned how to survive any hardship. It has made us who we are. But as I told Mr. Ramsey, I'd like to explore better options. We must move with the times or risk those times leaving us behind." That seemed to put Joanna's mind at ease somewhat. Brock supposed this was as good a time as any to broach the subject of money. He cleared his throat. "In fact, that is something you and I must speak about."

"What do you mean?" She studied him in the growing darkness.

"'Tis your money, lass. I wouldna command it to any purpose, not without your consent, no matter what your brother may have told you. I willna use you in that way. But if you did have a mind to help the estate, I would suggest you put your efforts toward helping the tenants first. The castle can wait." He'd only hoped, desperately, that she would wish to use it herself to help his people.

"Oh..." She was quiet a long moment. "And if I do want to help them, we could?"

"Aye. Very much so. We can start with food, buying crops that they can grow, and then we can build new homes—proper sturdy cabins, not these black houses."

"And the children? Can we buy them things too? Toys and proper shoes..." Joanna trailed off in embarrassment.

"We can," he assured her. "So long as you wish to."

They rode the rest of the way in silence, and when they reached the castle, they parted with their horses as the groom took them to the stables.

"We'll also need more staff," Joanna said quietly. "Could we arrange for that in the village? I also must post a letter to send for Julia, my maid."

"Aye, we can go tomorrow. I suspect our larder needs filling as well. The kitchens looked bare." He noticed that the cook hadn't stocked it very well since he had left with his brothers for Bath. He gestured to the bottom of the stairs. "Why don't you meet me here, and I'll escort you to dinner in half an hour?"

"All right."

He watched her ascend the stairs, and it made his chest ache. He wanted to give her everything she had ever dreamed of, and right now it must seem like he wanted her only for her money, despite all that he'd said. And all she wanted was his heart.

But he couldn't give it to her. He didn't trust himself to love. Perhaps he was like his father after all. It was possible that he was the villain for denying her the love she so desperately needed all because he was afraid. The thought filled him with dread and horror. His desire to protect himself had left him trapped and his own wife suffering—just like his mother.

I am like him. A monster.

Part of him reasoned that if Joanna didn't have his love, she could always leave, return to her family and be safe. But if they fell in love and he turned cruel someday, she would not leave him. Her heart was too open, too trusting. The thing he admired most about her would seal her fate. The same fate as his mother—the fate he'd feared he would suffer.

His shoulders drooped as he ascended the stairs and entered the western wing of the castle. He stopped in front of his mother's room. It had been locked ever since her death. It was only after his father had died that he, Brodie, and Aiden had found the key and seen their mother's chamber for the first time in years.

It had become a lovely tomb, missing only their mother's body lying nobly on the bed in a state of eternal repose. The wide windows allowed moonlight to fill the room, washing the soft colors of the robin's-egg blue walls almost white. The birch carved four-poster bed was still there, and motes of dust swirled in eddies in the moonlight. He trod lightly and respectfully into the room. It felt almost as though his mother were still there, a hint of her perfume, the echo of a lighthearted laugh, as though she had merely stepped out of the chamber for but a moment and would soon return.

Brock swallowed thickly as he approached her tall wardrobe in the corner, but he didn't open it. Instead, he reached up on tiptoe and ran his hand over the edges of its top. His fingers trailed through a thick layer of dust before bumping against a small wooden box.

He grasped it carefully and brought it down to inspect. The box was carved with vines that had been painted green. The craftsmanship of the box was so well done that he half expected the vines to curl up and twist around his fingers. He had seen it often as a boy when his mother had been preparing for a fine night out at a ball or a dinner with guests here at the castle.

He set the box down on his mother's vanity and opened the lid. The inside of the box held a dozen pieces of jewelry. He sifted through the various bits inside. A strand of pearls, each one gleaming like a drop of condensed moonlight, the intense glittering diamond ring she'd so often worn, the pair of sapphire earrings, and finally, the piece he'd been searching for. A simple gold band with a turquoise gem.

It was his mother's engagement ring. The turquoise was supposed to bring good luck; the pharaohs of Egypt had believed that and had filled their tombs with it. His father had actually been to Egypt when he was younger, which was where he'd acquired the ring. Brock wouldn't ordinarily want to touch anything his father had acquired, but this ring carried his mother's spirit. When she had fallen ill, she'd instructed Brock to collect her jewelry and place the pieces in this box and hide it on the top of the wardrobe. Thankfully, his father had never found it.

Brock wanted Joanna to have something of his mother's. The turquoise almost matched her eyes. It would look beautiful upon her finger. He closed the box and set it safely back on top of the wardrobe. Then he looked over the room once more and left, keeping the door open. The room, like any other part of the castle, needed to breathe. It would take a long time for him to learn to trust that the castle was safe from his father, but this was a start. No more locked doors, no more treasures hidden.

৩৯৩

JOANNA RETURNED TO BROCK'S STUDY BEFORE DINNER and found Mr. Tate thankfully absent. She'd sensed he was not at all pleased that she was here. Perhaps he didn't like that she was English, or maybe he feared that she was going to reduce some of his responsibilities in the castle. Many men would have jumped at the option to be paid the same for less work, but perhaps it was a matter of pride. Or maybe he saw his duties going to a woman as an insult. She would endeavor to do her best to put him at ease and let him know he was not going to be replaced.

I want to help, that is all, and a good lady knows how to run a large household.

Her mother had trained her to run a household, and her brother had taught her how to run a business, how to analyze investments, and other important financial matters. Brock's sister, Rosalind, had become a banker, which was rare, though not unheard of. Joanna rather hoped she might do the same once she and Brock had settled into married life.

She examined the study, the large oak desk littered with papers and the fireplace with a cozy-looking over-stuffed chair nearby. Joanna smiled and stroked finger-tips over the faded fabric of the chair, as she imagined nights where she would come in here and bring Brock hot tea and she would curl up with a book and read while he reviewed her work on the household accounts. Then he could sit here in the chair, and she might...

Joanna blushed at the wicked thought. She imagined herself sitting upon his lap, and after a lively discussion, Brock would silence her with a kiss, or she would silence him—whoever needed it most. Lord knew she wanted him as much as he did her, and she felt brazen enough to show him her desire.

Yes, spending the evenings here with her husband would be a delight. Joanna approached the desk and sat down in the chair. The papers rustled as she began to sort the documents. She couldn't find the account books, but these papers were at least a start.

Most of them were statements from banks, letters from creditors, along with the occasional document regarding payments to the tenants for their work and their animal husbandry efforts. It seemed quite normal, only it wasn't. The amounts paid to tenants were smaller than expected, and the creditor debt was substantial but by no means enough to put Brock's estate in such dire straits. Had he lied to her?

No. She refused to believe that. She puzzled over the statements for almost half an hour before her eyes were tired and she had to go change for dinner. Perhaps Mr. Tate was not talented with accounting. If that was the case, then she would be happy to take over that duty.

She was adept at mathematics—Ashton had seen to that. He had told Joanna long ago that a woman could dress prettily all she liked, but if she truly wished to be noticed and respected, then she would do well to educate herself in matters of business, politics, and literature. When she was thirteen, she hadn't wanted to sit in a dusty old schoolroom while her governess droned on, but she had done it, and now it would pay off.

Brock had chosen well in a wife—he simply had no idea yet. She smiled to herself, thinking of how pleased he would be once she made his estate profitable, not only through her funds, but through her management.

Joanna arranged the papers on the desk, making the chaos more organized. Tomorrow she would find Mr. Tate, and they would sort out her duties. She would ask him where he had placed the account books, since she hadn't seen them among the stacks of papers.

When she felt the study was in decent shape, she blew out the candles by the desk and headed for her bedchamber. But as she left the room she froze. The unsettling feeling of being watched raised the fine hairs on the back of her neck. She studied the corridor and saw no one, yet the feeling of being watched followed her all the way back to her rooms.

❦

BROCK HEADED FOR HIS CHAMBERS AND WASHED HIS face. He tried on one of his more colorful waistcoats, a burgundy one embroidered with a pattern of gold diamonds. Then he carefully folded his cravat. He had learned to do it himself years ago when their father had sent away most of the staff. He had to admit, though, he liked having a valet to help him, even though it went against his nature to rely upon others for anything. The castle needed more servants, and he needed help. Mr. Tate was juggling responsibilities both as steward and butler since their previous butler had left along with most of the staff long ago.

He finished dressing and picked up the ring, feeling a

little foolish for hoping that Joanna would like it, as though he were trying to impress a maid for the very first time. He waited at the base of the stairs and turned when he heard steps. Joanna stood at the top, her evening gown a striking bishop's blue. It was the only evening gown her maid had put into her leather traveling bag. The light from the wall sconces gave it a slight purple tint when she moved. It was almost iridescent, and it highlighted the cornflower blue of her eyes.

She stared at him with longing as she came down the stairs, and he felt that same pull toward her. She paused on the bottom step, which brought her almost level with his face. Her breath raised her breasts up and down in her tight bodice, and he couldn't resist peeking at the low neckline, praying for a glimpse of a rosy nipple. But the gown was just modest enough to leave him wanting.

"I have a gift for you," he said. "I wish I could have given it to you on our wedding day." He removed the ring from his pocket and held it up to her.

She blinked, startled, and extended her hand to him as he slipped the ring onto her finger. It rested against the simple silver band that he had given her at the blacksmith's shop, a perfect fit.

"It belonged to my mother. Her engagement ring." He held on to her hand for a little longer, not wanting to let go. Something intense and powerful flared between them.

Joanna looked to him, her eyes soft as a caress. "It's beautiful, Brock. I shall treasure it always."

He brushed his fingers along her wrist, needing to touch her, to connect with her. "They say turquoise brings good luck."

"Then I hope it brings me the kind of luck I'm thinking of." The smile she gave him left little doubt as to what that was.

He wasn't blind to his desires. He had wanted and craved Joanna from the moment he'd stolen that first kiss more than a month ago, but he wrestled now with the problem of how to make love to his wife without *falling* in love.

"I wish I had something to give you in return." She bit her bottom lip, and his body burned with arousal.

He cupped her cheek. "You have, lass. You've given me *you*."

Her cheeks pinkened, and she shyly lowered her head. He raised her gaze back up, and she smiled at him. It was like watching the sunrise over the Torrington hills in the middle of spring.

"Let's go to dinner."

"Yes. I'd like that."

He offered her his arm and escorted her to the dining hall. Tonight he would take her to bed. She was simply too irresistible.

18

Joanna felt the weight of the engagement ring on her finger, but it was not unwelcome. Rather, it was comforting to feel the press of the gold circlet beside her wedding band. She could not believe he had given her a ring that had belonged to his mother. Joy bubbled up inside her as she considered what it meant. He could try to stay distant, but she saw the heat and the longing in his eyes. It wasn't simply physical for him—at least, she sensed it wasn't. She had to have faith that she could win his heart, help him realize that he wasn't like his father.

We will have a happy marriage, a happy life. I refuse to believe anything else.

They entered the dining room, and she gasped. It was stunning. Red satin wallpaper covered the top of the room, and the bottom half was dark with oak paneling.

Portraits of noblemen in kilts and women in tartan dresses were interspersed between mounted deer heads and elk antlers. It looked in equal parts a hunting lodge and an elegant dining room, the type that she might see in England.

"I do like this room." He grinned and pointed at a large beautiful buck head. "I do not hunt for sport, mind you, but I was proud when I caught him last fall. He fed a number of families last year, including Dougal and Annis. I hunt when the herds grow too large during the lean winter months. Sometimes there is not enough vegetation to feed them all once the snow falls."

He escorted her to a chair close to the large fireplace. It was almost as tall she was. She wondered if this might have been part of the great hall a few hundred years before. Brock pushed her chair in, and when she sat down he waved to a footman who'd been standing politely in the corner of the room.

The young man retrieved a tureen and came forward, ladling soup into each of their bowls before returning to his position in the corner.

"Turtle soup," Brock said. "One of my favorites. We never eat it. Mrs. Tate must have gone to great effort for us tonight."

"I must remember to thank her. I like this soup too," she admitted with a grin, and dipped her spoon into the bowl. They ate quietly, the fire crackling behind them. Even in the summer it was noticeably cooler in Scotland than it was in Bath. Once they finished, the footman brought out a platter of salmon and then roast beef. They then shared a tart with meringue, laughing when their forks both collided as they reached for the same piece.

But they didn't speak much, except to discuss the tenants and what books they had read as children. She was delighted to discover that they both enjoyed reading many of the same kinds of stories. Books with adventures, books that discussed history and philosophy. Brock was well read, far more so than she'd expected. That left her feeling a bit silly, having assumed he was more of a barbarian. It was the sort of thing Ashton would have assumed about him, and she hated herself for that.

"Tomorrow we will ride into town and inquire after some new servants. I shall post your letter to your maid, and we will have you fitted for more gowns, unless you wish to have your maid bring your old ones?" Brock asked.

"I might order a gown or two in the Scottish style, but Julia can bring more of mine with her. Do you..." She paused, choosing her words carefully. "Do you wish me to have new clothes?"

Brock toyed with the stem of his wineglass, considering her question. "I would, yes, but not yet. There are more important things needed, such as seeds for crops and farming equipment for the tenants."

"Yes," she agreed. "But do you think we might upset them? How would they respond to our generosity? I do not wish to insult anyone's pride."

"Aye, that's a fair point. I will raise payments to them first, and then we will hire an architect from Edinburgh to draw up plans for some better housing and see what the cost will be. I would like to have a few houses constructed before winter, if possible."

"That would be good. I cannot stop thinking about those people living in those bleak houses during the dark days of winter."

"I fear my father did not care about such things, but we will help them." He reached across the table and covered her hand with his. She almost pulled away, not because she didn't want him to touch her, but because it felt wonderful and she feared it didn't mean the same to him as it did to her.

"I think it's time for me to retire. It's been a long day." She rose from the table, and Brock got his feet as well. They didn't speak as he escorted her to the stairs.

"Joanna, I assumed you might wish to sleep apart tonight, but..." Brock caught her by the waist. "May I come to your bed tonight?" The question was a soft, husky whisper in that heavy brogue that always made her feel weak.

Yes. The word was on the tip of her tongue, but she didn't dare say it. Until she could find a way to make him fall in love with her, she wasn't sure she could risk her own heart like that. When they were together, it was as though everything fell away and it was only the two of them together in a world of heat and pleasure.

"I...I don't know if I'm ready for that again." She choked on the words as she fled upstairs. She'd imagined her marriage so differently, at least when it came to her husband. She had thought they would be madly in love with each other, that nothing would come between them, least of all their own hearts.

I'm afraid to love the man who is afraid to love me.

There was a cruel irony to their fears, but she knew she was closer than he was to love. She could feel it fluttering around her heart like doves searching for a place to nest.

As she stepped into her room, the one that Brock had said could be her quiet refuge, she paused, noting the fire in the hearth and the pot of tea on a tray left on the side table by her bed. The young maid Maura, who had helped her dress tonight, must have brought it up for her. She poured herself a cup, and when she started to sit down in the armchair by the fire, she jumped as something moved.

She stared down at the badger who'd been curled up in the chair asleep. "Freya?"

The badger raised her head and blinked sleepily at her. So much for sitting by the fire. She was not silly enough to try to dislodge a badger when it was happily settled somewhere, and the room had only one chair.

She finished her tea and then headed back down-stairs, hoping to find the library. Given how Brock loved books, she rather hoped he would have an extensive collection. Joanna tiptoed down the hall and began to open doors one after another. Most were drawing rooms or parlors. Finally, a door she tried opened to reveal the library.

Two-story bookshelves covered the walls, reaching up to the ceiling. Several tall windows allowed moonlight in, and she gasped when she saw that most of the shelves were tragically empty. Only a few books remained. She moved deeper into the library, her heart sinking to the floor. There were barely any books, perhaps only a dozen, in a room that could have held thousands. She spied a tall figure standing before the fire, one hand resting on the mantel as he gazed into the flames. Brock. Joanna debated trying to slip back out of the room, but he must've heard her because he spoke.

"I wasna planning to show you the library until I had a chance to buy more books." Shame colored his tone, and her heart ached for him.

Joanna sighed and walked up behind him, wrapping her arms around him from behind. She rested her cheek against the back of his shoulder. His warmth seeped into her, and she could feel the strong muscles of his abdomen clench beneath her hands even though he still wore a shirt and waistcoat. He turned his head to look over his shoulder at her.

He nodded at the skeletal shelves. "I'm sorry you had to see this, lass."

"I'm not," she replied. "Do you want to know why?"

He nodded.

"Because it means that you and I will have the pleasure of visiting bookstores together, choosing every title we wish to read and bringing them home with us. This will be *our* library, one we'll build together." She rubbed her cheek against his shoulder, hoping she could offer him some comfort.

"The shelves were once so full. Each and every book contained the magic my mother taught me and my siblings to cherish. She loved to read and would spend the nicer days out by the lake reading in the shade of an old tree. On days when it was cold or rainy, she would sit here by the fire, spellbound by each book that came into her hands. She taught me the power of words, how to transport oneself far away from one's troubles." Brock placed his hands over hers. "When my father turned cruel, these books helped me forget the bruises, the lingering pains." His misery was so acute it caused her throat to ache with grief, thinking of what he must have suffered.

"When she died, he began to sell things—the furniture, the jewelry. And then I started to notice the books disappearing from the bottoms of the shelves, where they'd be less likely to be missed. The house seemed to grow thinner with every passing day, and then one day I caught him here in the library. Half the books were packed in wooden crates." His voice was low, tormented, each word full of utter agony. "I asked him what he was doing, and he struck me, *hard*, with his cane. I fell, right there." He pointed to a place by the fireplace. "There was a fire poker there, and I hit my head against it. I passed out on the floor. He left me there, bleeding and unconscious. Rosalind was the one who found me and helped me." Brock reach to touch his temple. "I still have a wee scar there."

Her growing sorrow for him finally shattered her fragile self-control. "Oh, Brock, I'm so sorry." She came around to stand in front of him and hugged him again, burying her face against his hard, muscled chest. He clasped her body tightly to his, his hands gripping her lower back. As she held him, her Highland warrior with a broken heart, she realized it was impossible for her not to fall in love with him. She wanted to give him all the love he had been denied since his mother died.

I am lost to him.

She reached up to the buttons of his waistcoat, slipping them free one by one. He didn't stop her, nor did he interfere or try to take over. When she was finished, she pushed his waistcoat off his shoulders and let it fall to the floor. When she tugged his shirt out from his trousers, he finished by pulling it off. He stayed still while she placed her palms on his chest, exploring his smooth skin and the patch of dark hair in the center of his chest. She then discovered the thin line of dark hair from his navel down beneath his trousers. She hadn't noticed it the first time they had come together.

She trailed a fingertip around his flat nipple, and his breath caught. Were men as sensitive here as women? She felt no shame for being wanton as she leaned forward and kissed him there, flicking her tongue against his nipple. He sucked in a harsh breath, and she smiled in silent triumph as she moved to the other side, repeating the wicked little kiss. He stayed still and silent, except for his responses and the sound of his breath as she explored him.

If she stopped, turned away, and went to bed now, what would he do? She wasn't cruel, so she wouldn't do that to him, but she wanted to know what it would take to shatter the control inside him. She reached for the buttons on her garments, staying close to him as she loosened the bodice, then shrugged out of her evening gown. It gleamed in the moonlight at her feet like a fairy pool. She began to unfasten the ties of her stays, and he watched, silent, hungry, unmoving. There was a brooding look in his eyes, but he made no move as she let the stays fall to the ground. She then removed her petti-coats. Would it take her being completely naked to make him let go? She loosened the ties at the front of her chemise, then slid off first one shoulder and then the other before it to fluttered to the ground. She now stood completely bare before him.

"I thought you didn't want me to come to your bed tonight, lass." The words were low and husky, and they sent a shivering thrill through her.

"This isn't my bed...and I changed my mind." She licked her lips, feeling wild and wanton as she challenged him. She'd promised to share his bed, but after feeling so vulnerable that afternoon, she'd longed for the privacy of her separate bed chamber. But again, she'd changed her mind, her desire burning too hot to keep her away from him. "Now, what are you going to do, husband?"

His fingers curled into fists at his side, and his nostrils flared. "I'm worried I can't be gentle, lass. Not when I feel so..." He didn't finish. "I dinna want to hurt you."

She tilted her head. "Can't a man and woman make love roughly without pain?"

"Aye, 'tis possible."

"Then let's try." She pressed her body to his, her nipples scraping against his muscular chest felt so good. She moaned as he cupped her bottom, his large hands always so capable in any situation.

"Lass, you are—" The rest of his words disappeared as she kissed him. His lips opened in surprise, and she slipped her tongue inside. The excitement of being the aggressor was new and arousing for her.

"Take me. Make me yours," she whispered. "We both need this." Only rough pleasure would sate them both now. She hungered for it as much as he did.

He lifted her up, and her legs wrapped around his waist as he carried her over to the nearest reading bookshelf that had a ledge. He sat her down on it and fumbled with his trousers. She placed kisses on his chest and throat as he freed his cock. She had but a moment to prepare as he spread her thighs with his palms and then thrust inside. The tenderness was there, but she was wet and ready, and he pushed mercilessly into her with little effort. Her breasts bounced as he rammed deep into her, and then he paused, watching her face. She knew he needed to see that she wanted it like this. She met his gaze and nodded. Whatever resolve he had been holding on to seemed to disintegrate. The savage, wild Highland lord she'd envisioned in her darkest fantasies was finally here.

Their breath mixed, and his eyes were now blind with the same desire she felt. There was nothing outside the fusing of their bodies, the ancient rhythm of flesh, breath, and pleasure, dancing like leaves on the fall wind. Endless, natural.

He curled his fingers into a fist in her hair, pulling her head back as she leaned against the wood of the shelves. The wood dug into her, but the pain was eclipsed by the exquisite earthshattering thrusts he made into her body. Brock made love like a firestorm, all wind and flames, completely consuming. She throbbed around him, welcoming him inside her with a sharp pang of need. Joanna dug her nails into his shoulders, urging him on, deeper and harder.

Let go of your fear, she tried to say with her eyes. *Let go and be who you truly are. You won't hurt me.*

He plunged into her over and over, his shaft huge, but she craved the slight edge of pain it gave, knowing that if she could take this and enjoy it, then she would never fear that he would hurt her. Brock was not his father. He spoke kindly, touched kindly, and even this savage lovemaking still held some tenderness to it that she felt deeply without being able to fully explain it. White-hot pleasure exploded through her, and she screamed. Brock covered her mouth with his, stifling the sound. She went limp, bone-tingling pleasure reverberating through her. Brock, still alive with savage energy, kept thrusting while kissing her. His hands tightened in her hair and on her hip until at last he groaned low and deep as he went rigid.

Joanna was vaguely aware of his release, of him giving up part of himself to her, and she gave it back in sweet kisses as he panted for breath. He stayed inside her, their bodies still joined. It was the most intimate thing she could have ever imagined and so wonderful.

"Ach, lass," he sighed, his gaze heavy as he brushed the backs of his knuckles over her cheek. "Did I hurt you?"

"You didn't," she replied, leaning into him to nuzzle

his chest. She hoped he'd found some peace in this, the way she had.

He slowly pulled out, and her face burned with embarrassment at the sight of him, but he merely chuckled and fixed his trousers. Then he retrieved her chemise, and she stood so she could slide it down her body. But before she could pick up the rest of her clothes, he caught her and gathered her up into his arms.

"Leave it, lass. I want to take you to my bed and hold you."

"I won't argue with that. Freya may well be in my bed by now. And I'd much rather cuddle with you than her." She couldn't say that she'd felt foolish for going back on her desire to share his bed every night. But perhaps he'd understand now that she was recommitting to her desire to keep one shared marriage bed and not two.

He chuckled and kissed her as he began to carry her back to his chambers.

"I can walk."

"I know. But let a man feel like a conqueror, lass. Sometimes it's nice to carry one's woman about, especially when he's headed to bed."

She definitely wouldn't argue with that.

They entered his bedchamber, and he set her down on her feet before he pulled back the covers so she could crawl beneath them. She rolled onto her back, closing her eyes as she listened to him remove the rest of his clothes. She smiled at the sound of his boots hitting the ground. She felt the bed dip, and then she was cocooned by his large, warm body. He kissed the shell of her ear as she spooned back against him on her side.

"I truly didn't hurt you?" he asked in a whisper.

"No, it's was spectacular." She rolled over to face him. They shared a pillow as she tucked her head under his chin. She'd had plenty of rest in the last two days while they'd taken the coach to his castle and she'd felt relaxed and ready for him this time. And the pain of losing her maidenhead hadn't been present this time. There had only been intense pleasure.

This was going to be one of her favorite parts of being married. Sleeping beside Brock, feeling his breath stir the fine hairs above her forehead and the way their legs twined and his arms curled around her, holding her close. It was impossible not to feel cherished...*loved* in a moment like this.

If Brock did not feel anything, she reasoned, he wouldn't be doing this. That was the hope she clung to as sleep crept in upon her. She would find a way to make him fall in love with her.

She fell asleep to the sensation of him stroking her hair back from her face as moonlight and shadows rippled across the room. This was sweet married bliss.

19

I t was still hours before dawn when something jolted Brock from his sleep. He struggled for a moment, the dream of riding through the forests with Joanna at his side still lingering in his mind, before a strangled panting sound caught his attention and drove him fully awake.

Joanna!

He turned toward his wife, and panic seized him. She was writhing in pain. Beads of sweat dewed on her forehead, and she clutched her stomach as she curled in around herself.

"Lass, what's wrong?" He pulled the bedclothes back, afraid he would see blood or some evidence that he had harmed her during their lovemaking, but he saw nothing save her legs, which were bent up in a state of agony. He tried to catch his breath as his heart beat a visible pulse under his skin as loud as thunder. She couldn't be ill. No, she couldn't be.

"I...feel quite...wretched." She leaned over the side of the bed and suddenly vomited. Brock held her, letting her heave as he pulled her hair back from her face and rubbed her back as his thoughts raced wildly. What was happening? Why?

"Breathe, Joanna. You must calm your body or else you will never stop."

She sucked in a whimpering, anguished breath and started to cry.

It shattered his heart and terrified him. He needed to send for the doctor, but he couldn't leave Joanna until she calmed a little.

It took nearly ten minutes before she stopped heaving and lay limp and exhausted on the bed, her head dangling off to the side a bit. He gingerly moved her back a little to try to make her more comfortable.

"Will you be all right alone for a minute, lass? I need to wake Tate and send for the doctor."

"Yes. I don't think...I have anything else left in me to..." She winced and placed a hand over her stomach. Brock stroked her hair, murmuring an apology before he threw his trousers and boots on and ran from the room. He headed to the east wing where the servants' quarters were and pounded on Tate's door.

"Tate!" he bellowed and pounded again. "Tate, wake up! Joanna is ill."

A moment later, Tate opened his door and blinked owlishly up at him. "The lady is ill?"

"Yes. It's very bad. I need you to fetch Dr. McKenzie straightaway."

Tate grabbed his housecoat and pulled on his boots. Brock went to wake the cook, Mrs. Tate. She was not all amused to be dragged from her bed, and she grumbled about delicate English females as she headed to the kitchens to make some tea. Brock rushed back up to his room and found Joanna in the same position, lying on the edge of the bed.

"Mr. Tate is off to fetch Dr. McKenzie, and Mrs. Tate is bringing you some tea. How is your stomach?"

"I...I'm better, I think. My stomach is still cramping, but I don't feel like I'm going to be sick anymore." She tried to sit up but collapsed back down. Her face was ashen and her lips were pale, almost white. Fear dug into Brock's chest as he carefully guided her back up to the head of the bed. He propped several pillows behind her.

"Does that feel all right?" he asked, tucking her hair behind her ears.

"Yes, thank you." She reached for his hand, but her arm wavered and dropped. "Lord," she whispered. "I feel as weak as a newborn kitten."

"Perhaps you caught an illness when we visited the tenants. I heard from my footman that the grippe has been going around."

Joanna whimpered a little, her body tensing as she almost heaved again. "Perhaps," she finally whispered.

"Stay and rest. Do you want to try some water? A bit of tea?" He fetched a cloth and wiped cleaned the floor beside the bed.

"Perhaps some water," Joanna finally said. Her voice was so weak, each word a struggle. He took a pitcher of water and poured it into a glass and brought it to Joanna. He held it up to her lips, and she swallowed down a few precious gulps, which filled him with relief. He set the glass down on the side table and joined her on the bed, holding her hand.

"I'm so sorry, Brock," she murmured, her eyes closing. His heart stopped as he frantically checked her pulse. She was still alive. His muscles relaxed but only just. She had fallen asleep. He hummed an old nameless tune as he waited, hoping she could hear it through her sleep and that it soothed her. It seemed to take hours for Tate to return, but the clock on the mantel of his fireplace said only an hour had passed. When Tate arrived, Dr. McKenzie on his heels, Brock could have hugged them both.

"My lord," Dr. McKenzie greeted solemnly. "I am told the new Countess of Kincade isn't feeling well?"

"Aye, she's very unwell." Brock waved him over to the bed, and the doctor, a man in his late forties, frowned as he placed his spectacles on. He lifted Joanna's head and examined her face. The doctor took hold of her wrist and removed his pocket watch from his waistcoat. He remained silent, holding on to the watch and her wrist. Then he pursed his lips.

"Her heartbeat is slow, far too slow for someone so young. Is she sickly by nature, my lord?"

"No, she was a strong and healthy lass until we went to bed an hour ago." What had changed? What had happened to her tonight to cause such an illness? Maybe she got the grippe from one of the tenants? But Annis, Dougal, and the children had looked healthy. So what had happened?

"Ah..." Dr. McKenzie pursed his lips thoughtfully. "Has she changed any habits, done anything new?"

Brock rubbed the back of his neck as his face flushed. "Well, we're newly married, and..."

"You've been seeing to your marital duties?" The doctor's eyes twinkled a little.

"Aye, exactly."

"Well, that sort of activity wouldn't cause this, unless...you haven't been seeing to your duties for a few months? She could be with child. In some cases, a woman can grow faint in the early months."

"No, she was a virgin until a few days ago."

"Well, we'll rule out a child then. Has she changed her diet drastically or eaten anything unusual?"

"No, not that I can think of. She ate the same dinner as I did."

The footman, Duncan, who had been lingering near

the door spoke up. "She had some tea after dinner in her chamber, my lord."

"Tea?" Brock couldn't see what that had to do with anything.

Dr. McKenzie was quiet a long moment, and he stroked his chin, frowning before he spoke.

"Lad, could you bring me her cup, if it hasn't been washed yet?" the doctor asked.

Duncan looked stricken. "I'm sorry, Doctor, it's already been sent to the kitchen."

The doctor turned back to Joanna and produced a small dark-blue bottle with smelling salts, which he uncorked and waved under her nose. She jerked awake and stared up at them with tired eyes.

"My lady, I'm Dr. Joseph McKenzie. I need to ask you some questions. Is your mouth numb? Do you experience any burning or tingling?"

"My mouth feels a bit numb. It's been tingling for a few hours, since before Lord Kincade and I fell asleep."

"What?" Brock gasped. "Why did you not say anything, lass?"

"I don't know," she said evasively. He realized she did not want to admit that she'd been focused on him and their lovemaking while in the presence of several men.

Dr. McKenzie was quiet for a long moment before he motioned for Brock to follow him to the window where they could speak privately.

"My lord, when I came to the house, I saw some

plants growing by the entryway, plants which should not be there."

"Plants?" Brock couldn't fathom what the doctor was getting at.

"Wolfsbane."

"What?" He didn't recognize the plant, but he did know it was a dangerous one to have about.

"Aye, wolfsbane or monkshood. I saw it in clusters by the castle doors. I hesitate to suggest it, but someone in this castle might have tried to poison your wife."

Brock's throat tightened. He could feel the gazes of Mr. Tate and young Duncan upon his back, but he kept his voice low. Who would have tried to poison her?

"Can you help her?" That was the thing that mattered most. He could find the person who had tried to hurt Joanna after he knew she was safe.

"She may not have had a strong enough dose to kill her. Some intelligent would-be murderers start with smaller doses to avoid suspicion. If this is her first reaction, she's come around now well enough." McKenzie glanced toward the bed, as did Brock. Joanna was watching them quite clearly now, although still tired.

"Aye?" Brock urged the doctor to continue.

"I can administer atropine and digitalis. That might counteract the poison."

Brock dragged his fingers through his hair. "Let's try it."

The doctor nodded, and they returned to Joanna. Dr.

McKenzie opened his black leather bag and pulled out two vials and needles. He filled each with a large dose, one of atropine and one of digitalis. Then he looked at Joanna.

"My lady, I must inject this into your stomach. I will need to lift your chemise."

Brock lifted the bedclothes, shielding her modesty even though Tate and Duncan had stepped into the hall. The doctor looked at her waist. He pinched her stomach gently and injected the needle. Joanna closed her eyes, wincing, but made no sound. Then the doctor injected the second needle. She was so brave, his little lass.

The doctor lowered her chemise and tucked her beneath the bedclothes again. "She must have water. Boil it first, and prepare it yourself." The doctor whispered the last bit under his breath. "She should eat chicken broth and toast." The doctor looked at Brock. "No strenuous activities for at least a week, unless she's feeling completely well. I would like to check on her in a few days. And you must send for me immediately if she worsens."

"Thank you, Doctor." Brock shook McKenzie's hand and nodded to Tate, who'd stepped into the room again. "Please see the doctor out."

"Of course, my lord." Tate's gaze shot to Joanna in the bed, his face twisted in worry. The doctor left, and Brock shot a glance at Duncan and waved him over.

"My lord?" The young man's brows rose.

He could trust Duncan. The lad was an innocent babe, and he was one of the sons of a tenant that Brock trusted. "Only you and I will see to my wife's needs from now on. The doctor suspects she was poisoned."

"Poisoned?" Joanna and Duncan both gasped.

"Wolfsbane," Brock explained. "Duncan, I want you to keep an eye on the others in this house. I want to know when that tea was prepared and who took it to her room."

"I did, my lord. But..." A shadow passed over Duncan's face.

"But what?" Brock pressed.

"But I passed Mr. Tate in the hall on the way back after I left the tea in her bedchamber."

"He was going into my wife's room?" His suspicions deepened, as did his fury. If Mr. Tate was set on harming Joanna, he'd have to face the wrath of the laird of the Kincades.

Duncan nodded.

"Why would Tate want to hurt her? Has he said anything to you, lad?" Brock stroked his jaw and glanced at his wife. She was drifting back to sleep, and he didn't have the heart to wake her.

"No, my lord. I heard him grumble about her snooping around in your study, but other than that, no."

His study? Why would Tate be upset about that? Many wives of great houses were heavily involved in the running of the accounts. That was nothing out of the ordinary. Unless...

Unless Tate had something to hide.

Brock stopped himself from growling and curling his hands into fists. "Duncan, you are to forget your other duties until my wife is better. You and I will take shifts to watch over her for the next few days. She must never be alone."

"I understand, my lord." Duncan straightened his shoulders, and Brock nodded in approval.

"Now, off you go. Bring me some chicken broth and boiled water. Keep a watch on Mrs. Tate. If she challenges you, say it was my orders."

Duncan rushed off to do his bidding. Brock joined Joanna on his bed and carefully moved to lay her flat in his arms, making sure she was warm and comfortable. She murmured something before she curled into him, and he wrapped his arms around her.

My poor English flower. I will find out who did this, and they will pay dearly.

20

Brock spent three days feeding Joanna chicken broth and letting her drink water that had been boiled under Duncan's supervision. The cook was none too pleased, but she would adjust to his orders until he could figure out who was trying to harm his wife. There was a chance that Mrs. Tate was involved too, or the maid. What was her name? Maura? Yes, that was it. He'd rarely seen the girl; she was quiet and kept to herself. Once he discovered who was responsible, as the local magistrate, he would deal with the matter himself.

On the fourth day, he lay sleeping fitfully next to her and woke to the feel of her kissing his forehead. He blinked, wondering if he could believe what he was seeing. Joanna was sitting up, her face no longer deathly pale and her eyes neither cloudy nor overbright.

"Lass?" The word came out hoarse on his tongue since he'd barely spoken in days except for brief words with Duncan.

"I feel better, so much better." She brushed his hair back from his eyes, and his throat tightened painfully as he realized how easily he could have lost her, could have been digging a grave beside his mother's in the cemetery beyond the loch. The thought made his eyes burn, and a flood of dangerous emotions rose up and threatened to choke him.

"I'm relieved," he whispered. He sat up beside her, carefully pulling her into his arms. There were a thousand things he wanted to say. Instead he said, "More broth?"

"Please, no more," she begged. "I couldn't stand another bowl."

"The doctor said you should eat. It's important for your strength."

"Then bring me anything but broth." She ran her fingers up and down his chest, toying with the white shirt and the bottle-green waistcoat he presently wore.

"If you feel you can stomach it, I will bring you something heartier." He searched for any hint of uncertainty or signs that she was still ill. But he saw nothing except a bright smile and a rosy blush on her cheeks.

"Let me summon Duncan."

She moved away from him, climbing off the bed before he could stop her. She took her dressing gown off the nearest chair and shrugged it on. Her long blonde hair rippled down her back in a cascade. She looked at him over her shoulder.

"I can walk, husband. Now let's go. The walking will do me good."

He slid off his bed and joined her when she reached the door, ready to catch her if she were to suddenly faint.

"And after we eat, we could take the coach to the village."

"No, lass, not yet. I wish to have Dr. McKenzie return to check on you first."

"But"

"No arguing with me on this, lass. I will put my foot down, and I dinna want to be that sort of husband. I'm not above tying my pretty wife down to the bed if it means she will be safe."

Rather than be upset with him, she laughed. "Tie me down? Why do I think you would like to do that?"

He grinned. "I might indeed."

Raised voices greeted them as they reached the kitchen. Duncan and Mrs. Tate were squaring off with one of the wooden tables between them. The cook's face was red as she sputtered that the lad needed to mind his own business and keep to his own chores. Duncan held his ground, a blush staining his cheeks as he faced Mrs. Tate. The cook planted her hands on her hips and shouted at the lad to leave.

Joanna watched as Brock took charge of the situation. He towered over Mrs. Tate, not in an imposing way, but in a manner that distracted her away from Duncan.

"My lord, tell this boy to leave me be!"

"It's all right, Duncan. Go see to your duties. The lady is feeling better today, and we will handle the luncheon ourselves."

Brock took a wicker basket and began to fill it with roast beef, some apples, fresh strawberries, a few wedges of cheese, and a loaf of warm bread. Then he grabbed a bottle of wine and two glasses.

"Really, my lord, I should pack that for you. It is my job, after all."

"No, it's all right, Mrs. Tate." He curled an arm around Joanna's waist, and they went to the library, where they settled into two chairs by the fire. The afternoon sunlight poured through the windows, but he wasn't sure she would be warm enough.

"Shall I light a fire?"

"No, thank you. I feel fine." She had belted her dressing gown over her body, which he hoped provided enough warmth.

He prepared them each a plate, and after he finished eating, he chose a book from one of the few left in the library, a book of poetry, and read to Joanna.

Her face lit up as he read to her, and he vowed that they would do this often. Come to the library and read to each other. It made her happy, and that made him happy as well. It was especially a good thing to do to keep her resting for a time. She was still too pale for his liking.

"I should like to go to the village today and place some orders for more books. These empty shelves sadden me. Would that be all right with you?"

"Aye, it would be a fine thing to see the shelves brimming with books again."

"I'm surprised you had so many shelves, given how easily your father was willing to part with them. I would have assumed the castle wouldn't have had a large library."

"My father changed much after my mother died. Mr. Tate and his sister knew him a long time. They were still loyal to him, probably because he kept them around rather than let them go. It was a hard transition when I took over."

"Brock, that reminds me—I was trying to set the accounts straight, and..." She bit her bottom lip. "I believe Mr. Tate may be changing numbers. The expenses aren't as high as I think you've been told. Do you think he could be pocketing some of the money? I don't wish to accuse a man who has served your family for so many years, but perhaps we should consider talking to Mr. Tate about the accounts?"

He thought back to the arguments he had had with Tate, who'd insisted on handling the majority of the paperwork and the accounts, just as his father had.

Brock didn't want to admit that it was possible. Tate's behavior of late had been cold and secretive.

"I wonder..." He stroked his jaw thoughtfully.

"We need to find the books to be absolutely sure. They weren't in your study." Joanna started to stand, but Brock caught her wrist and pulled her back down.

"Eat first, lass. Then we can investigate."

She needed to regain her strength and wouldn't do so without eating. Only when Joanna cheekily flashed him her empty plate did he let her stand up.

"Can you dress yourself? Or do you need help?" He meant the question innocently, but when she fluttered her lashes at him, he suddenly had other thoughts.

"If you assist me, I rather think I'll end up with no clothes on at all." She laughed sweetly, and it made his chest tighten, and he found himself smiling for the first time in days.

"Why don't you go change? I want to have a word with Mr. Tate. Then I'll have the coach prepared."

The heat in her eyes dimmed a little, and she nodded in understanding. He headed to his study, not surprised to find Tate already there.

"My lord?" The older man rose to his feet and glanced over Brock's shoulder as though expecting someone. Joanna, perhaps? Brock kept firm control of his temper and his emotions. He had to let Tate keep thinking he wasn't suspected of anything. Not yet. There had been no more attempts on Joanna's life, but he needed Tate safely away so he could be sure while he investigated the estate account books.

"Tate, my wife has accounts with some Scottish banks. I would like you to go and make some withdrawals for me. I believe you'll need to take some signed letters to Edinburgh to begin the process. I'll have them ready this evening. Would that be all right?"

Tate swallowed audibly. "You wish for me to leave?"

"To retrieve some of my wife's money, yes. She has a trust, you see, and you need a letter from her asking for a withdrawal."

"But shouldn't I stay and help you here? What with Lady Kincade falling ill…" Tate's hesitancy only made his guilt seem more likely, but Brock kept calm.

"We will manage for a few days without you. You may hire a coach and stay at an inn along the way." Brock opened a drawer in his desk and retrieved a pack of banknotes he'd tucked away for emergencies and necessities. He thumbed several off the top, at least fifty pounds, far more than was needed, and gave the money to Tate. Tate's hands folded over the slim slips of currency.

"Very well, my lord. When should I leave?"

"This evening should do. When you return, we'll have much to do." Brock clapped him on the shoulder, perhaps a little too hard.

"Thank you," Tate said before Brock turned and left. He went to the stables and called for the groom to ready his coach. It required some service, but it would do. He was not going to let Joanna leave his side until he was positive that she was feeling like herself again.

And in the meantime, he would figure out what exactly Tate was up to and why.

21

Joanna climbed out of the coach and looked about the village. It was only three miles from Castle Kincade, and it was larger than she expected. There was a milliner's, a modiste, a blacksmith shop, a bookstore, and a market with quite a few inns. Boxes full of brightly colored flowers sat just beneath every window. Purple florets bloomed from Scottish thistles mixed with the red bog myrtles, Scottish bluebells, and the bright-yellow gorse blooms.

Brock noticed her studying the flower boxes as they passed by a window full of their fragrant scents.

"They keep the midges away." He chuckled and nodded to the bog myrtle.

"Midges?" Joanna hadn't heard the term before.

"Aye, you were lucky not to have seen a cloud of them yesterday while we rode. Wee biting beasties."

"They're insects?" She cringed, not liking the idea of a cloud of tiny insects swarming her at all.

"They aren't everywhere, mainly around the livestock and in the fields far from towns. The females are the ones that bite you. Bog myrtle has a honeyed scent, which confuses them. They canna smell a person whilst they're near this plant. The Kincade gardens are full of it, so you needna worry about feeding the midges, lass." He winked, and Joanna gently poked a finger in his ribs to tease him back.

"This is a lively town," she admitted, surprised to see the bustle of people and the relative quality of the buildings. She'd expected it to be more rustic, but it was far more like a small city than a village.

"Farmers come here to sell livestock, make breeding arrangements for their horses, or to buy whatever else they need. And since it's near a trade route, you have others stopping by on their way north or south." Brock offered her his arm as she gazed up at him. He was taller than most men and cut a striking figure among the men and women walking down the row of shops.

"It's a darling place." She smiled at a little girl who held her mother's hand as they passed Brock and Joanna. The little girl waved a chubby arm at her.

"I suppose it's small and rustic compared to what you're used to," he said with a hint of concern.

"I rather like it. To be honest, I never really was fond of the bustle of life in London or Bath," Joanna said softly. "I much preferred Hampshire but we rarely stayed in the countryside."

"Oh?" Brock paused in front of the milliner's shop, and she joined him at the window, gazing at the fancy hats resting on pedestals in the window. The poke bonnets with delicate lace, the shining satin ribbons, the intricate embroidery. They were just as well made as English ones.

"Well, I never really cared for all the balls and the dinners—or the gossip." They started walking again and paused only when they reached the bookshop. "I miss the dancing, I suppose. But being here... Things feel real." She laughed a little, knowing she sounded like a fool. "That doesn't make much sense, does it?"

Brock leaned against her from behind as she opened the bookshop door, and the press of his warm body made her burn with hunger. Yet she yearned for other, deeper things as well.

They entered the shop together, the musty smell of the books a comfort she had missed. The scent brought back memories of her curled up in bed, reading late into the night by candlelight, or the sunny afternoons in the gardens where she read until she drifted to sleep on a blanket beneath a tree, only to wake when she heard the steady hum of a fat bumblebee exploring a nearby flower. Reading had become a way for her to lose herself and forget the sorrows and the worries of her day. But now reading was a bridge between her and her husband. It was a way for them to find each other.

"I think it makes perfect sense," Brock said as they walked down an aisle. "But you don't have to give up dancing. I'm fond of it myself." He shot her a cocksure grin. "I'll even teach you cèilidh dancing."

She looked up at him, wanting to ask a question that had been on her mind since they had danced over a week ago. "How did you become such a good dancer?"

His lips twitched. "Shocked to find a barbarian Scot has more skill than those English popinjays?"

"Well, yes, exactly. Although I would never call you barbaric," she answered with a smile.

"Oh no? What would you call me, then?" He cornered her against the nearest bookshelf, and her body lit up with fresh desire. What was it about bookshelves that seemed to turn her and Brock into primitive creatures only focused on making love?

"Er..." She tapped her index finger on her chin, pretending to think. He curled one hand around her waist and leaned in, lowering his head, almost kissing her. "Exquisite, intense, brooding...sweet, protective, thoughtful." There were a dozen words she could put to him that would tell the story of what sort of man he was. But even those words were only the beginning.

"Is that all?"

"I've only started..."

He moved a hair's breadth closer, and she knew the

inevitable kiss would be worth the wait. The pull between them in that breathless instant before their mouths met was magnetic, an ancient force as old as the moon and tides. Her pulse skittered, and she closed her eyes. The heady sensation of his searching lips made her exhale in quiet joy. When he kissed her like this, it felt like the first caress of the morning sunlight when she pulled back the bed-curtains after a long, dark night in bed.

The kiss slowly burned her at the edges, making her feel alive. The warmth of his mouth welcomed her tongue as the kiss deepened. His hand on her waist tightened, yet he didn't do anything more than kiss her, albeit most sinfully. If she'd dared to do this in London or Bath, even with her husband, the scandal would have spread within hours, but here in this beautiful rustic village in a musty little bookshop, warm with summer sunlight...it seemed right.

It was perfect. *He* was perfect. And he was all hers. The swell of joy inside Joanna was unstoppable. She smiled against his lips, her lungs filling with laughter, and it made him smile as well when their lips broke apart.

"What is it?" he asked, still smiling as he pressed his forehead to hers.

"You...this... I'm so happy, Brock. I wish...I wish you could feel my joy." She meant that with every breath inside her. She would have given anything for him to feel what she was feeling.

He played with a loose strand of her hair around one of his fingers "I feel it too, lass. I was worried about bringing an English lady to my home. It isna like the life you're used to. I feared you would come to hate it—and me." He whispered his confession, and it fractured her heart with fine splintering cracks.

Hate this man? Her warrior? Her protector? Her Scottish lord? She saw so much of his people's past in him, the nobility of the soul that sometimes vanished from the men and women in English ballrooms. Here with him, she saw the people of Scotland and the ghosts of Culloden in his gaze. Yet he held no hatred toward her, no fury, only a plea for her to see. To understand. To love. To love the man he was and the place he called home.

I love him. I love him, and it cannot be undone. Come what may, he owns my heart, now and always.

"I love this place...and..." She held her breath before adding, "And I love you, Brock, my fierce badger."

His gaze softened in a way that made her melt into him. There were some smiles that existed in a secret place in one's heart, smiles that came to the surface only during moments of the purest joy. In that moment, she'd won such a smile from Brock, a smile that she wanted to burn forever into her memory.

"Oh, my sweet lass. I wish I could buy every book in the store for you."

He didn't say it, didn't tell her that he loved her, but

he hadn't shied away, hadn't denied her feelings. That at least was a start.

"Let me buy *you* books instead." She reached for the first title she could find behind him. When she lifted it up, the gilded letters on the spine flashed in the sunlight.

"*The Lady of the Lake* by Sir Walter Scott. He's one of us," Brock declared proudly.

"You know it?" she asked.

"I do." His gaze turned distant as he began to recite from memory.

Aloft, the ash and warrior oak,
Cast anchor in the rifted rock;
And, higher yet, the pine tree hung
His shattered trunk, and frequent flung,
Where seem'd the cliffs to meet on high,
His boughs athwart the narrowed sky.
Highest of all, where white peaks glanced,
Where glistening streamers waved and danced,
The wanderer's eye could barely view
The summer heaven's delicious blue,
So wondrous and wild, the whole might seem
The scenery of a fairy dream.

He finished his words by brushing the backs of his knuckles over her cheek, and she trembled with a force of affection for him that was so strong it made her knees buckle.

If she had not already been so in love with him, his recitation of poetry would have done it. She was hopelessly in love with her Scot. This man who only ever touched her with kindness and passion. His tenderness was infinite, and it filled her with endless wonder and fascination.

"We must take this one, then," she replied, blushing. He moved away a little and took the book, adoration in his eyes as he gazed at the spine.

"Any others?" Joanna asked him.

"Books? I've near read them all." He laughed, the sound washing over her like rich brandy.

"Your favorites, then? We must have those."

"Ach, but I want to know your favorites," he said earnestly. "You choose the next one. And then I will do the one after that. We shall have a library built upon our favorites."

For the next hour, she and Brock shared books and stories as they piled a massive stack on the counter for the owner to box up. The books would not all fit into the coach, so they would have to be delivered to the castle in a few days. Joanna snuck a few of their favorites into a small parcel and tucked it into the coach before they continued shopping.

After the bookshop, they bought some clothes at the modiste. Brock was insistent that she try on several dresses, and it took her an hour to realize he liked watching her face flush whenever she emerged from the curtain wearing something new. He insisted she buy a few of the ready-made gowns and order a few more to be made, particularly a riding habit. At one point, she saw him speak quietly with the modiste, a middle-aged Scottish woman named Agnes who blushed violently.

"What did you say to her?" Joanna asked as they arranged for the order to be placed on his account.

"That you needed a pair of breeches. 'Twill be much better for you to ride that way."

"Breeches?" Joanna laughed, remembering his earlier comment that he would love to see her in them.

"I canna have my wife showing her pretty bare legs to all the men as we ride about, and I willna let my wife ride on a bloody sidesaddle. You canna enjoy riding when your spine is all twisted and you can barely stay on."

She didn't argue with him on that. The last few days she'd gotten so much more comfortable riding, both because of him and riding astride, that she would have dreaded going back to riding sedately on a sidesaddle. She would never be able to gallop or jump or do anything fun.

"Where would you like to go now?"

She studied the shops around them and saw one that carried toys in the window.

"That one!"

Brock followed her into the shop, which sold a mix of toys, lovely woven tartan shawls, and jewelry. She studied the dolls carefully, trying to imagine little Elsbeth holding something new and beautiful rather than the rag she'd been carrying about. Then she found a set of toy soldiers for Camden and some for the other boys from the other tenant families.

"Do you think they'll like them?" She gestured to the large pile of dolls and other toys. She'd perhaps run a bit wild in the shop, but the thought of the children of the tenants having new toys to play with was incredibly important. It would give them some joy while they faced the hard times ahead until she and Brock could arrange for better housing and turn the crop yield higher.

"Aye, lass, you've too big a heart." His rough voice matched the sweet fire in his eyes as he pulled her to him in a kiss that made the shopkeeper grumble and look away.

It was nightfall when they finished their shopping and stopped by an inn for dinner. The inn's common room was full of men and a few ladies. A hush fell upon the crowd as Brock led her to one of the empty tables. Joanna felt a sudden tension thicken the air around them. Hard stares and dark-edged mutterings from some of the meaner-looking men made the hairs on the back of her neck rise.

"Pay them no mind, lass," Brock said as he shot a fierce glare back at the men.

She couldn't help but wonder what was happening. During their shopping, none of the people had seemed upset, yet here they were. Why?

A tavern maid brought them two glasses of wine and two plates of beef stew and bread. Joanna enjoyed the simple fare, despite her worries about the tension around them. Brock ate silently, his congenial mood gone, and that only worried her more. They paid for their meal and headed outside, where she waited for him to have their coach readied.

A tall man, a little leaner than Brock, came outside behind her and walked down the side of the inn. He glanced at her once before he vanished around the corner. A voice rose up inside her, whispering for her to take care. She had always listened to that instinct whenever it made itself known.

She kept a vigilant watch as a dozen other men exited the inn and followed the first man around the corner. All of them quite clearly looked at her—this was not some casual glance. Trouble was brewing. She just didn't know yet how it would manifest itself.

When Brock returned with the coach, she mentioned the men and her concerns. He pulled her onto his lap in the coach and kissed her.

"Dinna worry, lass. 'Tis nothing, I am sure." When he set her down on the seat beside him, she saw him touch his boot, and she remembered after so many days of traveling with him on the road that he kept a slim dagger there.

They were halfway home when Joanna heard rolling thunder. Only it wasn't truly thunder, but a herd of horses. Someone was following them.

Brock said with a growl, "Lass, I need you to remain calm and stay inside this coach. Do you understand?"

"Yes," she whispered, but her voice betrayed her, breaking on the single word.

Someone outside shouted in Gaelic, and the coach jerked to a sudden stop. If Joanna hadn't been prepared, she would've been thrown forward into the wall opposite her. Brock slipped the knife from his boot, the blade gleaming in the moonlight as he opened the coach door and leapt out, leaving her alone. She heard their coach driver shout, and the sound was muffled a second later. Fear shredded her nerves, and she bit her lip, listening in the darkness.

"Ewan, you bloody coward!" Brock's bellow ricocheted off the coach.

"*I* am the coward?" the man shouted back. "'Tis you and your family who are the cowards. Aye, we know the truth now. My father died fighting for a free Scotland, betrayed by *your* father." Shouting dissolved into the sounds of curses and scuffling.

Joanna pushed back the door's curtain and peered outside. She could see a dozen or so men struggling to catch hold of Brock in the fading light as the sun sank below the trees. He swung his blade with precision, cutting the arms of any who came too close. She had never seen violence before, not like this, but she had been right about Brock. He was indeed the warrior she believed him to be. None of the other men were a match for him, but he couldn't fight them all, not forever. He soon disappeared beneath a pile of bodies, and Joanna shoved a fist into her mouth to stifle a terrorized cry.

Stay in the coach, that's what he said. But she couldn't.

She opened the door farthest from the fighting and crept around the back of the coach. The men had dragged Brock to his feet, and one man, whom she recognized as the first man who'd left the inn, was punching Brock brutally in the face and stomach.

Brock spat out blood and laughed. "Ya hit like a wee bairn, Ewan!"

Stupid man! Joanna wanted to cry, but she had to think of a way to save him.

"Your father sold out my father and the others to an English spy. They were killed because of him, and you...*you* sit in that castle enjoying the lands and the money that were bought by the blood of good men."

The man, Ewan, retrieved Brock's blade from the ground, and the blade flashed again menacingly.

"My father was a monster," Brock said, and the grim humor vanished from his face. "I'll not argue with you on that. But I was a child then, as were you. I have no intention of carrying the sins of my father with me. I intend to wash the slate clean."

Joanna listened with bewilderment. Brock's father had betrayed men and sent them to their deaths? Why hadn't he told her?

"Some sins run too deep in the blood to ever be washed out," Ewan replied.

"So you'll slit my throat, is that it?" Brock challenged.

"You and that pretty *Sassenach* wife will meet with an unfortunate accident. The coach overturned in the dark of night, and no one heard you as you perished."

Brock's eyes widened. "Not my wife—she has no part in this."

"She's English. You married her, which as far as I'm concerned makes you as much a traitor as your father."

"Please, Ewan," Brock begged, and Joanna's heart tore. He had pleaded once before, when he'd thought her life was in danger from a highwayman. He put aside his pride for her life every time. Despite the icy fear twisting in her gut, she knew that meant something, that he cared enough to set aside his pride for her safety. A man only did that for someone he loved.

His pride... Suddenly an idea blossomed inside her, and she boldly stepped out from behind the coach.

22

"Stop this at once!" Joanna shouted with a deep, furious voice. Her mother would've been proud of the way the towering Scots all stopped and stared at her.

"Well now, there's the lassie! Saved me the trouble of going in there after you." Ewan laughed, the sound cold and cutting. A flicker of apprehension coursed through her as she stared him down. "Get her."

Two men took a step forward. Joanna had to work fast. "I have no intention of running, so you can stay right where you are."

The men stopped and looked at Ewan, uncertain. Ewan sized Joanna up and nodded for the men to step back. "You have courage, lass. I'll give you that."

"And you have a code of honor, do you not?"

Ewan glanced at his men before he met her gaze. "Aye. What of it?"

"I should like to challenge that honor."

Ewan threw his head back and laughed. "You?"

"Yes, me." Joanna had not been raised to be a cowering fool, no matter how much she quaked with fear on the inside.

"So what's it to be?" Ewan said with a sarcastic smirk. "Pistols at dawn?"

"I will fight you. If you fall to your knees even once, you lose. My husband and I will be set free, and the matter between you and him will be considered finished."

The Scots all started to laugh wildly.

"A wee lass like you will fight me? Oh, aye, that'd be something to see."

"I'm well aware you think I have no skills, but I might surprise you."

Ewan shrugged. "'Twill be a quick fight. One blow will knock you down. Then what? You agree to be dealt with by me and my men?"

Joanna tasted the bitterness of fear upon her tongue, and she tried not to think that losing meant her and Brock's deaths. But she felt no, she *knew*—she could do this. Ashton was an excellent boxer and fencer, but Rafe...the bounder turned highwayman had taught her far more valuable skills before her first season, such as how to stop a man from taking advantage of a lady.

"Joanna, no," Brock said. "I forbid it." One of the men nearest him punched him, and he grunted in pain.

"Gag him. I willna listen to him whine while I deal with her," Ewan snapped. Brock's mouth was forced open, and he was gagged with a cloth tied tight across his mouth. His hands were bound, and he was shoved hard to his knees.

"I should like to borrow the knife...if you please." Joanna held out her hand to Ewan.

He chuckled as he handed her the blade. "You mean to prick my fingers with it, *Sassenach?*"

She arched a brow at him, and his laughter died. Then she bent over and sliced her skirts and petticoats straight down the front and back, ignoring the whistles of the men. She needed freedom to move, and her skirts would only get in the way. Then she shoved the blade back into the ground and stepped away from it.

"Are you ready?" she asked Ewan. He stared at her.

"God's blood. You truly mean to fight me, *Sassenach?*"

She curled her lip in a challenge and replied in a mocking brogue, "Aye." Then she crouched, legs braced apart. The night wind billowed her split skirts around her ankles, but rather than slow her down it felt good. She was anticipating his actions now, just as Rafe had taught her. If she did this well, she could end the fight almost at once.

Ewan, smiling smugly, waved at her. "Come at me, English," he said with a sneer.

Joanna was grateful she had boots on rather than slippers as she approached him. When she was just out of reach, she waited. So did he. Then he swung a fist. Joanna ducked and came up fast, flattened her right palm and slammed that palm into the bridge of his nose. Blood exploded at the point of impact, and Ewan bellowed, clutching his face.

Joanna didn't stop. She jabbed a punch at one of his eyes, hitting the spot hard. He snarled and swung out, clipping her head, and she stumbled. Her ears rang, but she kept her balance and went back for another blow. She grabbed his shoulder to drag him down. The aggressive move caught him off guard, and he bent forward. She rammed her knee hard right into his groin.

A high-pitched keening escaped Ewan's lips. She ran around behind him and leapt on his back, getting a good suffocating hold around his neck. Between the pain in his groin, the bloody broken nose, suffocation, and her full weight on his back, he was having trouble focusing on how to defend himself. He clawed at her hands, but she ignored him and squeezed his neck with every ounce of strength she had. He stumbled, fell to his knees, and finally went down. She held on a moment longer and then let go. He collapsed facedown on the ground, gasping for breath.

The men around her stared at her, but not one of them moved on her.

She wiped at a bit of blood on her lips, panting hard.

She'd let her body get a bit too relaxed in the last year and wasn't as strong as she'd been when Rafe had first trained her. Her teeth had cut into the inside of her cheek when Ewan had hit her with that glancing blow. She looked at Brock, whose eyes were wide. He was just as motionless as the men who still held him.

"I won the challenge," she declared. "Your quarrel with my husband is over. Whatever sins his father committed are not Brock's. He is a good and loyal Scotsman, and you should be ashamed to treat him like a traitor. His father abused him. He had no love for that man, nor any control over what he did. In fact, he's more Scottish than any of you here. You are supposed to be honorable men and good warriors. Protectors. Not bullies, not men who murder in the night. That is cowardice."

She waited for Ewan to get to his feet and retrieved her husband's knife, tucking it into her own boot. In that moment she felt as wild as the wind upon the hills, as though she herself was a Scot. Which reminded her...

"And another thing. I am a Lennox. Scotland is in my blood. Think on that before you call me an outsider again."

She hadn't minded Brock calling her *Sassenach*, but she was not about to let these men turn it into an insult.

"Ewan?" one of the men whispered loudly.

Ewan smeared blood across his face as he dragged

the back of his hand under his nose. He winced, drawing in a deep breath.

"Let them go. 'Tis over, all of it. We will speak no more of the sins of Montgomery Kincade."

Brock was jerked to his feet and then released. Their coach driver was also released, and he joined them, his eyes still wide with fear. Ewan met Brock's gaze and nodded solemnly before he and his men mounted their horses and rode back in the direction of the village.

"I'm sorry, my lord," the coachman said as the others left. "I couldna stop them."

"It's all right, Hamish. Lucky for us we had a guardian angel riding with us." Brock turned to Joanna. "My God," he whispered, dragging her back into his arms, squeezing her hard enough that she struggled to breathe.

"I'm fine," she assured him.

"Fine? No, lass. You were brilliant, wonderful, fierce." He cupped her face in his hands, kissing her forehead. "Let's get you home. I need to make certain for myself that you are all right."

Joanna was more worried about him, because he was bleeding and bruised, but she didn't tell him that. She needed to ask him about what she'd heard Ewan say about his father. He owed her the truth.

The coachman climbed back up on his perch. She and Brock got back inside the coach.

"How did you learn to do that, lass? The fighting, I mean?"

"Rafe taught me."

"I see. I suppose if any of your family did, it would be him."

"He was worried I might be taken advantage of on some balcony or garden when I first came out. I haven't practiced the moves since I was seventeen. I was so afraid I might not do them correctly." It was only now sinking in that she could have gotten killed along with Brock if she had failed. She was just lucky Ewan had underestimated her, and she'd been able to strike before he'd had a chance to regain his footing.

"But you did, by God, you did. I married a warrior." He pulled her onto his lap again, burying his face in her hair.

"Why...why didn't you fight harder?" she asked. She was almost afraid to know the reason, but she had seen him hold back so many times before in a fight, even tonight. He defended only and had not pressed the attack when he could have. She knew he was not a coward, but his actions made little sense.

Brock's breath caught, and for a second she feared he would not answer her.

"My entire life, I lived in fear of my father's temper. The day my mother was laid to rest, I cast dirt on her coffin, and my father spoke cruelly of her weak nature for her to die of a broken heart." Her sweet, strong husband trembled as he spoke. "I couldna stop myself. It was as though a white haze, like early-morning fog rolling over the hills, filled my eyes. I struck out at my father, hit him so hard he fell and broke his nose. My brothers were barely able to hold me back. I was going to kill him. I wanted to feel the blood in his veins go cold on my hands." Brock's hands tightened slightly on her back as he held her closer to his chest.

"When I finally calmed," Brock said, drawing in a shuddering breath, "my father was laughing at me. *Laughing*. He said he finally had a son worthy of him, one with the same bloodlust as he. It made me sick to hear it. I made a vow upon my mother's grave never to harm anyone unless I had to. And tonight, when I needed to, the rage didna help. Ewan and his bloody fools were able to trap me all the same."

Suddenly so much about Brock began to make sense. He feared his temper, feared he would hurt people, especially those he cared about. Was that why he resisted her declarations? Was he afraid to love her in case he accidentally harmed her?

She met his gaze in the dim coach, peering into eyes that now seemed so dark and endless, like the sea lit by a sliver of moonlight.

"You are not your father, Brock. You mustn't worry about your temper. You have always done the right thing, even when it almost cost you your life. Promise me you will try to let go of your fear."

"I'm not afraid," he replied a little gruffly.

"Aren't you? Afraid of being like your father? You are not the first person to face that fear. Ashton was afraid for so long that he would become like our father, so much so that he became the opposite, which was little better. But meeting your sister, loving her, changed him. It made him into a better man."

Brock chuckled wryly. "A better man with a love for punching Scotsmen."

"Yes, well." She smiled. "You *did* carry me off into the night, marry me, and deflower me."

"All with your permission," he reminded her, grinning like a cheeky child.

"Aye," she teased him with a Scottish tone. "But really, Brock, you are not like your father. You are *everything* he is not."

"You never met him, lass. How can you say that?"

She traced his lips with a fingertip. "Because I know *you*, and you are *everything* to me." When she kissed him this time, she let him feel every bit of her love for him pouring out of her. She wanted to learn him by heart, to feel every bit of his body and have it etched into her mind.

"I can't believe you cut your skirts like that," he mused, lifting her shredded bits of gown as she straddled him on the coach seat.

"Stop talking and kiss me, husband," Joanna said, capturing his mouth with hers. He groaned as she rocked herself against him and deepened the kiss. There would be time enough for talk later. Right now she needed to show him how much he meant to her. And if she was being perfectly honest, having subdued Ewan and saved her husband had made her incredibly aroused. She didn't know if it was right or wrong to be so, but she was going to make the most of it. She arched against him and whispered in his ear, "Make love to me, *here*."

His soft answering growl vibrated through her as he lifted her hips and then reached for his trousers. She nibbled on his earlobe and neck, kissing him and teasing him. He cursed as he fumbled to free himself, and then he was pulling her down hard on his shaft. The unexpected sensation of being filled by him was glorious, if a tad uncomfortable in this position. She'd never been on top like this, but it was exciting.

"Ride me, lass. Like you were doing before." He lifted her hips, showing her how to rock against him.

"Like this?" She circled her hips as she moved up and down on him. He nodded, his eyes dark with hunger as he watched her. There was something utterly sinful about this, riding him like a prized stud horse, in a carriage of all places, while their gazes locked. It was simply savage and hard, and she had no illusion that she was the dominant one even though she felt empowered by her victory over Ewan. Brock was in control of her, like a magician who could lure a snake from a basket. She was under his spell.

Her heartbeat throbbed in her eardrums, and she reveled in the pure, sensual experience. She cried out as pleasure blackened her vision, and she fell limp against him. But Brock was far from finished. He thrust up into her over and over, using her now for his own pleasure, and it only heightened the rippling aftereffects of her own release. He panted hard as he came and held her tightly to him. She laid her head on his chest, feeling the rapid beat of his heart as he came down from the sweet high of their lovemaking.

Joanna felt her blood surge from her fingertips down to her toes. He brushed a thumb over her lips, sighing in contentment.

"Lassie, you will be the death of me, and what a sweet death it will be."

She chuckled, letting go of the last bit of tension inside her. She would ask him about his father's betrayal soon enough. But right now, she was going to fall asleep in her husband's arms and not worry about anything else.

✣ 23 ✣

Brock smiled as he felt Joanna fall asleep in his embrace. He moved her only once to fix his trousers and her dress before he pulled her back into the cradle of his arms. He had bruised ribs and an aching jaw, but it had all been worth it. His English lass had saved him, and while he did not like to think that he had been unable to protect her, he was glad he had married a woman with a warrior's heart. He would never forget the sight of Ewan Campbell on the ground, clutching his bollocks.

My sweet Joanna, you are indeed sent from the heavens.

He held her tightly until the coach stopped at the castle entrance. He carried her out, whispering thanks to the driver before he took the coach and horses around to the stables. Brock carried his sleeping wife inside. Duncan held the door for them, and the lad's eyebrows rose as he saw Joanna's torn skirts and Brock's bruised face, but he didn't ask any questions.

"Get some rest, Duncan. We will see you in the morning."

"Aye, my lord." The young man left for the servants' wing.

The cook, Mrs. Tate, was in the great hall by the stairs. When she saw them, she frowned.

"Has your brother left for Edinburgh?" Brock asked.

"Aye." Her brows knit in concern at both him and Joanna before looking up at him. "Are ye both all right? Should I send for the doctor?"

"No, no, we're quite fine, Mrs. Tate. We just ran into a wee bit of trouble on the road. But we're none the worse for wear. You may retire to bed." He left her at the bottom of the stairs as he carried his wife up to his chambers.

He laid Joanna on the bed and took care of her clothes, removing the ruined gown. She stirred as he unfastened her stays and mumbled something adorably grumpy about not being able to breathe. Then he slipped off her stays, stockings, and boots, and he removed the pins from her hair without waking her.

Poor lass, she was exhausted. She'd been deathly ill from the wolfsbane, then she'd spent much of the day on her feet in the village, then she had battled Ewan, and, well, there had been their time together in the coach...

Lord, she had ridden him with wild abandon, the way

he imagined a Scottish lass would her husband. There was no timid, blushing English bride here, and for that he was grateful. He wanted Joanna to feel free to demand his body when she desired it. He was more than happy to comply with any request where he ended up inside her.

When he was with her, it felt like the clouds had parted and carried him straight to every sweet, beautiful dream he had ever had. When she kissed him, it made him dizzy with want, yet there was a softer urge buried inside that, the need to whisper her name as a fervent prayer. What would it be like years from now, when they both knew each other and their deepest desires perfectly?

He looked forward to finding out everything about her. His wife. His partner. For the first time he was no longer lonely. As the oldest child, he had carried so many burdens alone on his shoulders. Brodie, Aiden, and Rosalind never truly knew how hard it had been for him to be the next Earl of Kincade, to know that their father had run their lands on spilt Scottish blood, and to feel the weight of judgment from men like Ewan.

Brock lit a candle by his bed and stripped out of his clothes. Now that he was home, he would wear the Kincade kilt again. He had never dared wear it in England. The Dress Act of 1746, which had outlawed kilts, had been repealed in 1782, and far too many Englishmen still felt it should be law. He'd had no wish to cause trouble for Rosalind, so he'd worn trousers. But that would change now that he was home.

He couldn't stop grinning as he tried to predict her reaction to the change. Shocked, scandalized perhaps, then intrigued. What would she think when he showed her how much easier it would be to claim her when he didn't have to mess with cumbersome things like trousers?

When he climbed into bed beside her, he pulled his wife into his arms.

He chuckled and kissed the shell of her ear. "My Scottish lass."

She sighed dreamily, and the sound was so sweet it made his body hard with hunger, but they were both exhausted and she was already asleep. There would be plenty of time tomorrow for more of *everything* with her.

He rolled over and blew out the candle, then pulled Joanna tight against him, so that they nestled like spoons in a silver drawer.

"Good night, wife," he breathed, feeling a peace so profound that it would have stunned him if he hadn't been so exhausted.

Minutes or maybe hours later, he woke with a start, his heart racing and his head tight with a headache. He was feeling hot...too hot. He wiped a layer of sweat from his brow. *What the devil?* He leaned over, checking on Joanna, and she was covered in sweat as well. Perhaps if he threw open a window he could let in a breeze.

Brock slipped out of his bed and was halfway across the room when he saw a glow beneath the edge of his bedchamber door. Had someone relit the wall sconces in the corridor outside? He changed direction and started toward the door. When he touched the handle, it was surprisingly warm.

He opened the door and gasped. Smoke, thick and dark, poured into the room. Through the haze he saw flames at the far end of the corridor where his father's bedchamber had been. The castle was on *fire*.

He rushed back to the bed, hastily gathering her dressing gown and boots, and shook her awake. "Joanna!"

"What's the matter?" she asked drowsily.

"There's a fire. You must go now. Put these on—don't bother to tie the laces. You need only to protect your feet from the burning embers." He pointed at the boots.

"Fire?" She understood right away the seriousness of the situation. If they didn't move fast, they could die. Joanna slipped on her boots, and Brock quickly pulled on his kilt and boots and then a shirt.

"Follow me," he commanded as they stepped into the corridor. The flames were moving quickly, devouring the old carpets lining the floor. Through the blaze he thought for a moment that he saw his father's face. But that was impossible. The man was dead and cold in the ground.

"Brock!" Joanna pointed to the roof above them. Fire

was snaking its way along the beams. Thankfully, that high ceiling also meant the smoke wasn't smothering them.

"Run!" He shoved Joanna in the opposite direction of the fire. When he turned to follow, he stumbled into her back and steadied himself.

"What the—?" The words died on his lips as he saw what had stopped his wife in her tracks. Mrs. Tate was there, wide-eyed, her hair loose from its tiny bun, and she held a long knife in her hand.

"What are you doing? Can't you see—?"

Her harsh laugh cut him off. "The castle is on fire, my lord," she sneered. "But ye aren't *my* lord, and ye never were." The sly, wide-eyed look transformed to one of madness.

"Mrs. Tate!" he snapped, and stepped in front of Joanna, putting himself between her and the cook.

"I've had to listen to ye give me orders, tried to see ye in his place. But ye aren't him—ye could never be *half* the man he was."

Brock's gaze darted above them as sparking embers began to flutter down like black moths with their wings on fire.

"Ye are but a pathetic fool to think ye could ever be like yer father," Mrs. Tate screeched. "Ye are your mother's brat, you and the others." The cook's eyes were near black, and she began to laugh wildly.

"You were the one who poisoned Joanna."

She snarled. "Bit of monkshood to start—wanted to take my time with it. But ye brought Dr. McKenzie, and he knew..." She curled her lip in a sneer. "Not that it matters now." She laughed again. "Ye sent my brother away. He couldn't stop me, not tonight."

Brock grasped Joanna's hand, keeping her behind him. They tried to slide past Mrs. Tate. She lunged, slashing out with the knife. Brock pushed Joanna, and she stumbled out of the way behind him toward the open corridor. Then a sudden crash sounded, and he spun around. Part of the ceiling had collapsed, just half a dozen feet beyond his wife. Joanna looked between him and the flames. They were trapped.

"Jo—" Pain tore across his back, and he crashed against the wall. He grasped the edges of his mother's beloved unicorn tapestry, the silver and white threads glimmering in the raging fire. Everything seemed to slow down, unfolding like a terrible dream. Mrs. Tate stepped in front of him, the now bloody knife clutched in her hand. She must have cut him deep if his sudden dizziness was any indication.

The crazed cook spat at him. "*Filth!* Weak-hearted brat! Ye are na worthy of yer father's blood!"

Brock stared at her, still stunned. He had always known Mrs. Tate had liked his father, but this woman's obsession with the brutal man made little sense.

"Brock!" Joanna cried out. "There's no way out. We can't go this way."

Mrs. Tate turned toward Joanna's voice, and Brock knew he had to distract her away from his wife.

"I do not *want* my father's blood. He was a rotten bastard, a cruel monster. A betrayer of his people!" His shouts drew the cook's focus again.

"He was a prince among ungrateful swine!" Mrs. Tate lunged for him. Brock readied himself for the blow, but Mrs. Tate screamed and vanished from view as she flew past him and stumbled into the fire beyond. Brock blinked. Joanna stood there, panting. She had shoved Mrs. Tate into the flames at the other end of the hall. Her body writhed on top of the fallen wooden beams, her clothes catching on fire. She staggered out, fully ablaze, and fell over the banister to the ground far below. Joanna turned away, covering her mouth.

"Come, lass." Brock grasped her hand as they rushed back to his chambers. They closed the door to keep the flames and smoke out for as long as possible.

"I have an idea." Joanna pulled the sheet from the bed, dousing it with water from the basin on the nightstand, and then she rolled it lengthwise and pushed it under the door where smoke had started to curl its way in.

"Good thinking, lass," he said. "That will buy us a little time." He winced as he felt his back split in two with pain.

Joanna looked around, trying to think of a means of escape, but she was unable to find one. They were too high up to jump from the window. "Brock. We can't go anywhere. We...." She came over to him, shaking violently as she embraced him. He swallowed the cry of pain, and she buried her face in his neck.

"I'm sorry." He had let her down. He had made a vow to protect her, to give her a life of happiness here in the Highlands. But all he had done was bring her to an early end. Tears blurred his eyes, and he blinked rapidly, uncaring as they fell to his cheeks. The moonlight cut through the open window, catching his attention.

"Wait, I have an idea." He pushed her away as he tore the bed hangings from the bed and began to string them together into a loose rope. If he could lower her down, at least she could climb to safety. And perhaps he could find a way to fasten it somewhere so he could follow.

When she realized what he meant to do, they worked together. Distant crashes outside the chamber made them both jump. His hands shook as he carried the makeshift rope to the window and opened it. The drop was a good twenty feet, but if he could get her most of the way down, she would be all right. He tossed the rope out and held on to one end.

"Start climbing," he ordered. Joanna stared at him.

"You must tie the other end to the bed."

"No, we need as much rope as possible. Now climb." He couldn't meet her gaze. If he did, it would crush his resolve forever.

"Brock, you're coming with me, aren't you?" Her words trembled in the air between them.

"I will, lass, but only after you're safe." It was all he could say before he feared his voice would break, just like his heart. She was his beautiful dream, the gift he had never deserved, and now he was losing her forever. But at least he would save her.

"Then I'm not going. We'll find a way out together. We—"

He dragged her to him for one brief, hard kiss before he pushed her back and thrust the rope into her hands.

"You'll go because you might very well be carrying our child. Do you hear me? The life we might have created between us. I'll not have you destroying that because you want to die with me."

Her lips quivered, and her eyes filled with tears. "But I love you, Brock." She almost whispered the words.

"And it is on that love you must obey me now. You ken?" He dragged her to the window's edge, wound the rope around his arms, and braced himself.

"Climb. *Now*."

Her gaze met his as she climbed over the edge of the window. "Find a way out. Do you hear me? I will not bury you," she shouted at him as she climbed down the rope. Pain tore through his back as he held the rope in place while she climbed down. When the pressure finally eased, he moved to the edge of the window and peered down. She was on the ground, looking up at him, her face lit with the glow of the fire coming from behind him and the castle roof far above.

"Brock!" she screamed. He left the window, carrying the rope to the bed, and he tried to tie it around a bedpost. The knot held, but he couldn't drag the heavy four-poster bed closer to the window with his injured back. He couldn't even climb part of the way and jump, because the distance was too high. Defeat smothered him like smoke, choking him as he slumped down by the window ledge.

Smoke now started to fill the room, slowly choking him. His only comfort was knowing he would be dead before the fire ever reached him. He closed his eyes, picturing only Joanna's face. Then something nudged his leg, and his eyes jerked open. Freya was by his ankle, the badger whining softly and nudging him with her striped snout.

"Ach, I'm sorry, wee one." He chanced being bitten by her and lifted the badger up into his arms. The door to his chamber cracked and groaned as flames exploded into the room. He buried his face in the badger's fur, holding on as he closed his eyes again. The smoke thickened, and his head grew cloudy. His thoughts scattered as the heat climbed around him. A soft humming began to grow in his head, like music, the notes of a long-forgotten melody, one his mother used to sing to him.

Do you trust me?

Her voice, that question, one she'd asked so often

when he'd been a wee lad and she tended to a skinned knee or a splinter in his finger.

"Aye, Mother." Even now, facing death, he trusted the phantom memory of her in his head.

Then jump.

"Jump?"

Go... Now!

He opened his eyes, seeing only fire, not the ghost he longed to see. Death was coming, and he could not stay to burn. He faced the window, clutching the badger. He could see nothing below him, only smoke and flames. If he jumped, perhaps death would be swift. Freya shifted in his arms, and he knew that if he landed on his back, he might at least save her life.

"Hold on, my sweet." He took a few steps and leapt through the open window. The smoke swallowed him up as he fell into darkness.

The moment Joanna realized Brock would not be able to get out, she screamed his name. Duncan found her trying to claw her way back up the stone walls. The heat of the blaze was fierce, and the castle seemed to swell with the heat beneath her hands, but it didn't stop her. Her husband was going to die if she couldn't find a way to save him.

"My lady! Be careful!" Duncan shouted. Pieces of wood and stone fell from the battlements, landing with heavy thuds on the grass around her.

"Duncan! Thank God! Brock is trapped up there. We must find a way to save him!"

"How? We canna get back inside." Duncan stared up at the cloud of smoke billowing out from the window above them, his face ashen. Joanna watched the flames lick along the stones in terror. She'd never thought stones could burn, but the amount of timber inside the castle was feeding the fire.

If only they hadn't run out of rope. If only he'd been able to get out the window and jump. But it was too high. If only... A sudden burst of inspiration hit, and she grabbed Duncan's arm, pulling his focus back to her.

"The wagon! Get the hay wagon from the stables! He might be able to jump into it."

"Aye. I'll be back." The lad sprinted into the darkness.

Joanna searched the smoky haze for the window to Brock's chambers. Smoke billowed out so thick now, and it mixed with the building storm clouds that were swallowing up the moon and stars overhead.

"Brock! Hold on!" she called out, hoping he could hear her. Duncan came barreling around the edge of the farthest tower of the castle, driving a pair of horses and pulling a wagon brimming with hay.

"Beneath the window!" She pointed to where she wanted it, and he halted the wagon just below.

"What now, my lady?" Duncan asked.

"I don't know." She looked up. "Brock! If you can hear me, jump. It's your only chance!"

A shape flew through the pouring smoke and came crashing down into the hay. Joanna and Duncan rushed to the edge of the wagon and peered down at the hay. Brock lay on his back, eyes closed, a stunned badger curled up in his arms. For a second Joanna couldn't speak, couldn't even think. Shock electrified every cell in her body as pure joy collided with pure terror. Were her eyes betraying her? Did she actually see her husband alive and well, or was she dreaming?

"Brock?" The name had barely passed her lips when the skies opened up and a torrential rain began to fall.

Brock jolted up in the wagon and cursed. The badger scrambled free, burrowing deep into the hay.

Duncan climbed up on the wagon and grabbed the reins of the horses. "We should get to the stables."

Joanna leapt onto the open end of the wagon and held on as Duncan drove them to safety, staring at her husband, speechless. He stared back at her, just as wordless. Unable to wait any longer, she crawled toward him across the hay, and with a shaking hand she touched his ash-covered cheek, making sure he was real. The moment her fingertips touched his skin, he opened his arms she threw herself against him. He caught her as they fell back into the hay.

"Ah!" He winced. "Don't forget my back, woman."

"I'm sorry," she said, unable to let go of him. She ignored the prick and crinkle of the hay against her skin as it poked her through her thin chemise. Nothing in the world mattered except her husband lying beside her, safe. *Alive.*

"Never apologize for that. I would take every pain in the world to hold you in my arms." His voice was low and raspy. His gray-blue eyes seemed all the more intense now that they were red-rimmed from the heat and smoke. He coughed violently. Ashes feathered the top of his head, and a layer of soot coated his skin. And yet he looked like the most handsome man in the entire world.

Joanna thought of all the things she had never said before she climbed out the window. But she had told him the one thing that mattered.

"I love you," she said again, holding her breath, hoping she'd finally hear him say it in return.

He held her gaze as the wagon entered the barn, but just as he opened his mouth to speak, Mr. Tate, the groom, the driver, and the maid were all gathered around them. Brock's servants were safe.

"My lord!" Mr. Tate climbed onto the back of the wagon. "I turned back from Edinburgh. I had an awful feeling—"

"I'm sorry, Tate," Brock said on a sigh, the sound so very world-weary. "Your sister is gone."

Mr. Tate's face fell, and he looked to the burning castle. "In there?"

Brock nodded. "She... She went mad. Tried to kill us all."

Mr. Tate looked to the ground. "Then it was even worse than I feared."

"You knew?"

"I had my suspicions. She never got over Lord Kincade's death, ya see. She was always quite taken with him, and well..." Tate sighed. "He *used* her, played upon those affections. Tossing her aside and then wooing her back on a whim. I didna know she was still so focused on him that she would try to kill you and my lady. I discovered she was stealing from the estate, changing the account books when I was in the village."

"Why?" Brock asked.

"I think she felt it was owed her. She hated him as much as she loved him. I learned it was best not to talk about the man when she was around. I feared someone would discover the theft, an' I was trying to find a way to make things right. Then you sent me to Edinburgh before I could explain." Tate shot them both an apologetic glance. "I feared for you, my lady. I thought she might have tried to hurt you. I visited your chambers, looking for her, fearing what she might do if she were ever alone with you. I didna think about the tea she prepared. It is my fault you were sick...and now my fault the castle is burning."

Brock placed a gentle hand on his shoulder. "It is my father's fault, not yours."

"The rain is quenching the fire!" Duncan called.

They all stood at the edge of the barn door, watching the castle for a time. There was little to be done right now. They didn't have the numbers to fight the fire themselves. Nature would decide the building's fate.

Brock slowly lay back down into the hay, pulling Joanna with him so she lay against his side. Neither of them had enough energy to move for the moment, and if the castle continued to burn, that was something they could not stop.

"I'm sorry about your home," she said. The rain rattled against the wood roof of the stables above them. The sound was soothing, and she was so very tired. If she dared to close her eyes she might slip into sleep, and she didn't want to, not when she wanted to watch over Brock and make sure he was all right.

"I'm not," he said after a while. "It was filled with so many bad memories. Now I have a chance to build something new."

"*We* do," she corrected gently.

"Aye. We do," he agreed, and they listened to the rain and waited for dawn.

۞

THE NEXT MORNING, BROCK AWOKE TO THE SOUNDS of men shouting. He sat up in the hay, aching all over. His back was wrapped with clean cloth where he'd been cut, which meant Joanna must have tried to tend to him. He was alone. There was no sign of his wife or his few servants. He stumbled out of the wagon to push the barn doors open.

His mouth fell open at the sight before him. Men and women were everywhere, removing rubble from the castle. Most of the stone structure was still standing, but anything that had been built of wood had vanished into ash. Joanna was calling out instructions, which Mr. Tate then repeated to the men in the midst of the stones of the castle, and Duncan passed along instructions to the women who were in charge of removing furniture. Brock recognized their faces. People from the village, his tenants, and even the children were there. Joanna noticed him and smiled. She gave a few more instructions before walking over.

"Dr. McKenzie has just arrived. I didn't want to wake you until he was here. You looked so tired, husband."

He tried to ignore the sting of shame he felt that he had slept through all of this. He had been unable to protect his wife last night, and now he was late to helping this morning.

"Tell Dr. McKenzie I'll see him later. I should help move the stones."

"You'll do no such thing," Joanna growled at him, her face suddenly fierce as a Highland wolf. "Any heavy lifting could damage your back, and I will not allow it until the doctor has had a look at you." She crossed her arms over her chest, giving him a heavy scowl. He wasn't sure whether he wanted to laugh or growl back at her.

"Ach, fine, woman. Bring me to the doctor," he grumbled. But secretly he rather liked that she was bossing him about and caring for him. It was new, this feeling of being looked after, and while he didn't like to feel weak, he definitely liked feeling *loved*.

Joanna grinned at his acquiescence and escorted him
to Dr. McKenzie.

Half an hour later, he stood, stitched and bandaged,
one arm in a sling to prevent the shoulder from moving
while the cuts on his back healed. He wasn't allowed to
help at all. Which meant he was left to watch the
others clear out the rubble from his home. But at least
he was able to see Joanna take charge. She was as fierce
as any Kincade chief to ever protect his clan in the
long history of his family. His mother would have
loved her.

He stilled as a flash of memory came back from the
night before. He had heard his mother's voice, telling
him to jump. And Joanna had been waiting below with
the wagon. He'd thought he'd been going mad, but
perhaps he had just heard her calling to him from the
window to jump?

Or perhaps...

Perhaps he had been so close to death, he had
somehow stroked the invisible curtain that lay between
the living and the dead, and his mother had come to his
aid. She had saved him from beyond the grave, just as
Joanna had saved him from certain death.

A faint prickling of the hairs on the back of his neck
made him shudder. Perhaps the ghosts of his parents had
finally been freed from this place. He wanted to think
so. The ruins of his home felt different already. There
wasn't a darkness that seemed to edge out of the

shadows any longer. Everything now was exposed to the sunlight, and that darkness was gone.

We can start over. All of us.

"Brock! Come look!" Joanna was standing with a group of women. They were all looking at several portraits that had been retrieved from the castle.

"These were stowed in a heavy oak cabinet that was drenched with rain. The wood didn't catch fire, but it also didn't let any water inside." Joanna gestured for him to come closer. There were three portraits. His mother's and two others. One he hadn't seen in many years. His ancestors on his mother's side, Ramsey and Torin, twin brothers who'd fought at Culloden; they were both posing beside their wives. The elder, Ramsey, had been Lord Kincade. Then when his family believed him killed in Culloden, the younger brother, Torin, took over as Lord Kincade.

"Who are they?" Joanna asked. "The paintings are very old."

"Aye, nearly ninety years old. They were my mother's family, the last true Kincades to rule over these lands. My mother was the last of her blood. Because she wasn't born a son, they sought a husband for her, someone with some Kincade blood, however faint. It was how she met my father. He was a distant cousin."

Brock stared at the two men and their wives. Proud, noble, pure of heart. They had both been captured after Culloden and sentenced to death. But a kind English

soldier had spared one brother's life, allowing him to
work as a servant on his estate until it was safe to return
to the Highlands. It was a story that someday he would
tell Joanna, while they sat by the fire. It was a romantic
tale, after all, one she would enjoy hearing. He turned his
focus back to his wife, and she was watching him, a
worried look in his eyes.

"Brock, we never had a chance last night to speak
about your father and Ewan. I want to know the truth.
What happened?"

He motioned for her to walk a little way away from
his people so they could speak privately. She tucked her
arm in his, and they moved fifty yards apart from the
workers so that they might be alone. Only then did he
speak.

"My father was always motivated by greed. When I
was younger, I learned that he'd sold out his friends
who were forming a rebellion against the Crown. He
worked with an English spy and betrayed them to that
man. They were all killed. Great men, the leaders of
their clans—what remains of us, anyway, after
Culloden."

"And Ewan's father was one of those men killed?"

Brock nodded, a bitter taste in his mouth as he
thought of how Ewan must feel, knowing the Kincades
had betrayed his family.

"When we came to rescue Rosalind from your
brother, that same English spy who'd worked with my

father convinced me that Lennox was harming my sister. He played me for a fool."

"Who is he? This English spy?"

"A man named Hugo Waverly. I wanted to kill him, but your brother assured me that he would take care of him. I trust him. Your brother and his friends have a deeper reason for needing to handle that man, and I am glad to give them that responsibility. I want no more blood on my hands."

He looked down at Joanna, his brows drawing together as he gazed at her. How could he tell her that all he wanted now was a life of love and joy with her? The last of the darkness that had followed him had burned up in the castle, and a new Kincade family was rising from the ashes. He and Joanna would be the start of it all.

"Are you well?" she asked, not wishing to embarrass him in front of his people.

"Aye. Very well indeed." He crooked his finger, indicating that she should lean in. When she did, he cupped her face with one hand and kissed her. It was a kiss he would never forget, because it was a kiss that wasn't just about physical passion. There was far more to it than that.

"I love you, lass," he said, and he was rewarded with her bright-blue eyes widening.

"Truly?" she asked, the word quivering with hope.

"Aye. I suppose I loved you the first moment I kissed

you. But I was too afraid to say it until now." He knew now that he was not his father, that he had no monster within him. He was like his mother after all, but unlike her, he was not going to die from a broken heart. He trusted Joanna to love him as fiercely as he loved her. There was no room for any more doubt. There was only endless love, just as his mother had said.

When you loved someone, truly loved them, there was no room for anything else in your heart, even for your enemies. And Joanna's smile was like a burning flame in the darkness, calling him, guiding him home.

EPILOGUE

Two months later

"They're here!" Brock bellowed from upstairs.

The castle rebuilding was almost finished. It was no longer a crumbling ruin, even the way it had been before the fire. His tenants had worked hard, and Joanna had hired many more local men to help. The promise of decent wages along with noon and evening meals had drawn men from miles.

Now the castle was a source of pride, not something which drowned him in guilt and shame. Each night he and Joanna had stayed up late in the new library, which was quickly filling with books, reading to each other, sharing food and smiles before they retired to his...*their* bedchamber to make love.

Joanna rushed downstairs, wearing a dark-blue gown

accented with a tartan sash bearing his family's pattern of red and green. "They're here already?" She had taken to wearing his family's colors whenever she had the chance. He smiled as she flew into his arms. He caught her, and she kissed him hard, laughing as he swung her around.

"I admit, seeing you in Kincade colors..." He smiled and stole a kiss. "Did I ever tell you the central seat to the Kincade lands is connected to the Scottish Lennox clan?"

"My family, you mean?"

"Aye. For many centuries, our families have come together. Kincade and Lennox. I guess we are continuing a grand tradition." He lowered his head to hers, claiming her lips in a way that left him forgetful of what they were supposed to be preparing for.

"Ahem." The sound of someone clearing his throat broke them apart. He found Ashton and Rosalind standing in the entryway, watching them.

"Sister!" Brock waved Rosalind to him, and she ran to embrace him and Joanna.

"Did you travel well?" Joanna asked.

"We did," said Rosalind. "Your mother and Rafe should be in shortly. Aiden returned with us as well. Brodie has decided to stay in England a few more weeks."

Ashton nodded to the large family traveling coach

outside. Rafe and Aiden were talking quietly, and Rafe said something that made Aiden laugh.

Brock clapped Ashton on the shoulder. "Brodie stayed behind, you say?" Brock asked, a little concerned. Brodie had a habit of attracting trouble when left to himself, particularly the feminine kind. "Did he happen to say why?"

Ashton shook his head. "Only that he wished to see what England had to offer."

Brock groaned. Things never ended well when he said that. "He isn't seeing anyone in Bath by chance, is he? Or is anyone showing interest in him?"

Ashton shrugged. "Well, there was talk of a young lady who'd set her cap for him, Miss Portia Hunt..."

"Portia?" Joanna nearly shrieked. "Oh no, Brock, you must send for him at once. Portia is the most dreadful, insipid, and cruel little creature I've ever met. I do not want her to be a part of this family. Her sister Lydia is quite wonderful, but ever so shy, but Portia..." Joanna groaned. "Lord save us if he becomes entangled with her. If we could perhaps allow him to meet Lydia though..."

Ashton and Brock stared at her, and then Ashton burst out laughing. "You've been married only two months, and you're already matchmaking your brother-in-law? God help the man." He and Brock shared a grin before Brock reassured his wife.

"Dinna worry, lass. I'll see that Brodie comes home...*without* a wife unless its one you approve of."

Joanna breathed a sigh of relief, and Brock fought off a smile. He turned back to Ashton. "We're glad you came, brother."

Ashton's pale blond brows rose. "Brother?"

"Aye, you're family now, whether you wanted it or not."

With a chuckle, Ashton studied the castle. "Well, we do have a bit of Scot in us, so I'll accept it. You've done well repairing the castle. It's not..."

"A crumbling ruin, unfit for Joanna?"

Ashton's face reddened. "Er...yes. It's quite suitable now."

"Well, the lass is the one who did it all. She's quite talented at many things."

Joanna's mother bustled inside with a hint of impatience. "Where's my child?" When she caught sight of her daughter, she held out her arms. Joanna approached her mother demurely, the way a fine lady of any house would.

"Joanna," Regina said uncertainly. "I hope you've forgiven me for not listening to you, my dear. I had no idea how unhappy you were at home. I'm so sorry."

Joanna embraced her in a tight hug. "It's all right, Mama. I'm ever so happy now. *Deliriously* happy." She shot Brock a smile, and he returned it.

"So things are going well?" Ashton asked Brock.

"Very well. She is the best part of my life. I hope you will see how happy she is while you're here."

"I already see that," Ashton said. "The way she looked at you just now...it's how I feel when I see Rosalind." He looked toward Brock's sister, who was praising Joanna on the improvements to the castle.

"When you love someone, they become everything to you," Brock said.

Ashton nodded. "On this we can agree. *Everything* and more."

Brock stood proudly in the entryway of his home, the sun beaming in through their new high windows. Joanna had redesigned the old medieval structure and had given it a more modern look. The effect was incredible—more light, more space, more *everything*.

But the truth was, none of that mattered to him. He would've given it all up and more, just to have one more moment to know and love her.

His mother was right. Love left no room for hate. And Joanna filled him with love unending.

THANK YOU SO MUCH FOR READING *NEVER KISS A Scot*! Don't worry, Brodie and Aiden will soon have their stories! The next book however will be about *The Earl of Kent* as part of the Wicked Earls' Club series and the League of Rogues which will be about Phillip and Ella (Charles's little sister)! It comes out October 2019.

If you love this story and want to read more

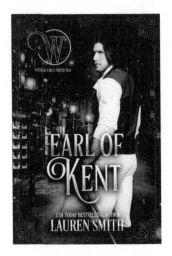

about passionate historical romances, please leave a review for it and tell your friends! Showing a book love by reviews and telling friends, helps me write the next book in the series!

The best way to know when a new book is released in this series is to do one or all of the following:

Join my Newsletter: http://laurensmithbooks.com/free-books-and-newsletter/

Follow me on BookBub: https://www.bookbub.com/authors/lauren-smith

Join my Facebook VIP Reader Group called Lauren Smith's League: https://www.facebook.com/groups/400377546765661/

If you like what you've read, feel free to explore another delicious and romantic series: Sins and Scandals!

Feel free to fall in love with Leo, the british

Earl and the half gypsy woman from his childhood, Ivy as they rekindle their romance! Turn the page to read the first 3 chapters of *An Earl By Any Other Name*! Come on, you know you want to turn that page...

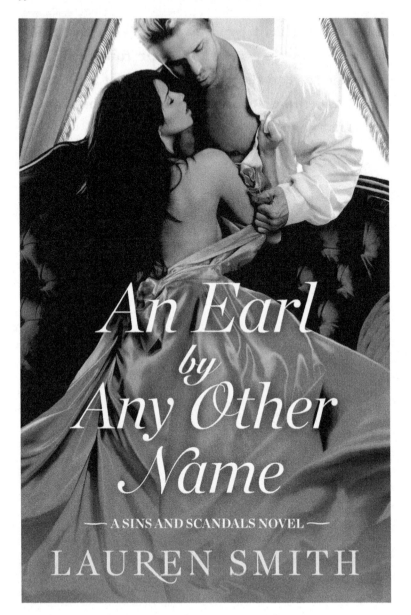

An Earl
by
Any Other
Name

— A SINS AND SCANDALS NOVEL —

LAUREN SMITH

AN EARL BY ANY OTHER NAME

CHAPTER 1

England, October 1911

"You know what they say about the old boy..." Lord Caruthers murmured as Leopold Graham stepped into the main reading room of Brooks's Club on St. James's Street. The words stopped Leo cold.

"No...what do they say?" another man whispered, his face half hidden behind a newspaper. The two men were sitting close to a fireplace beside the door. They were both older, with graying hair and extended waistlines that showed their well-off lifestyles. Leo scowled at them, but deep inside he was afraid of their whispers.

"Kept an Italian opera singer in a cozy little love nest in Mayfair. Can you believe it?" Caruthers chuckled. "Damned if I'm not jealous of old Hampton for carrying on like that with a wife and son at home. Quite a bold move to bring down scandal like that so publically."

"Wait..." The other man gasped, his paper rattling in his hands with excitement as he leaned closer to Caruthers. "The old fellow who died in his mistress's bed? I heard about that!" The older gentlemen were leaning close to each other, gossiping like a pair of old ladies, using their newspapers much the way women would use fans.

"Yes! The late Lord Hampton...Had to carry him out of that woman's house. She didn't even care about him. I heard she was determined to keep the home. Messy business leaving that to the son to deal with. Even now that the family is out of their year of mourning, everyone hasn't forgotten old Hampton's sins." Caruthers sniffed pompously. "I wouldn't let my son be seen at dinner with that family, not with that sort of talk still hanging about."

"Indeed," the other man agreed. "Quite so—"

"Ahem," Leo growled softly as he stalked past the two men, his fists clenched in rage. Both of them jumped; apparently they'd deceived themselves into thinking he couldn't hear them. *Deaf old fools*. Even at his own bloody club, he couldn't escape the rumors, the whispering, the damned utter black scandal that his late father had brought down on his head. He didn't want to remember having to deal with his father's mistress or paying her off by letting her keep the house his father had purchased. The need to silence her and quiet the scandal as quickly as he could hadn't been as successful as he'd hoped. London ballrooms and dinners caught rumors and scandals, spreading them like wildfire.

Caruthers and his companion, now silent, watched him with keen interest as he settled in the only empty seat, one by the window facing St. James Street. On the street there was a mixture of motorcars and carriages. London was always busy in the fall with the season in full swing. For a brief moment, he let his thoughts wander away from the pain of listening to his family's private business be fodder for entertainment. If only he could get in his car and drive away from it all...

Despite the silence in the room, Leo knew that every man was focused on him.

He raked a hand through his blond hair and stifled a groan. He'd been in London for all of three days, feverishly trying to secure investment opportunities and join in speculation schemes but it was no use. No one would work with him.

Father has damned me and Mother for his selfishness!

The spike of rage inside Leo was startling and so unlike him, but after having more than one door closed in his face today, he was exhausted. Even though it had been a year since his father had died, the scandal and the fervor behind it had yet to fade. His poor mother, Mina, refused to leave the countryside, knowing she'd have no real friends left in London who would allow her entrance to their homes. All because his father hadn't been faithful. It was an accepted albeit awful practice for a man to carry on an affair, but a man didn't die in his mistress's bed after a night of bed play, and he certainly didn't wrack up debts to pay for the care and keeping of that mistress. Yet that was exactly what his father had done.

Leo reached into his pocket and removed a letter that his footman had delivered to him before he'd left for the club. He opened it, smoothing out the paper and reading the hastily written lines from his banker, praying for much needed good news.

Lord Hampton,

It is with my deepest regret that we cannot extend any of your family's lines of credit at this time. We will be happy to discuss more credit if you can bring us new collateral but until then, the estate and all of your tenant farms connected thereto are fully mortgaged and cannot be further used to obtain additional credit.

Sincerely,

THOMAS ATKINSON

The words filled Leo's stomach with an empty ache. He had to find a way to stabilize his family's estate or he would risk losing his mansion in the country. Hampton House was his home, more so than London ever would be, and to think of creditors pawing at his family's furniture and running amok through the rooms of his childhood...

I won't let it happen. He would find someone to invest

with, and he would bury his father's scandal in whatever way he could by living a life above society's reproach. He was going to marry a good English rose and not make the same mistakes his father did by allowing himself to become obsessed with some exotic beauty. Those sort of women were *always* trouble.

He had always believed he might marry someday for love and have a wife who was as passionate as he was, but those dreams were dashed now. He had chosen a neighboring viscount's daughter as his future bride for financial reasons. It was a chilling thought that he would soon tie his future to a woman without love, but it must be done.

"Hampton?" A familiar voice shook him from his dark thoughts. Striding toward him was a man he recognized.

"Hadley!" He grinned as relief at his friend's appearance swept through him. He got to his feet and shook Owen Hadley's hand. His dark-haired friend was smiling widely. Once, as boys at Eton, they had been inseparable, but then Owen and their friend Jack had gone off to fight in South Africa in the Second Boer War. When they returned, Jack and Owen had...changed. Leo hadn't been able to leave to go fight; his father hadn't allowed it. The estate was entailed to a male heir and as the only son, if Leo had perished beneath an African sun, some distant cousin would have taken over Hampton.

"Haven't seen you at the club in ages." Hadley sat

across from him at the small table beside the window. It didn't escape Leo's notice that Hadley's clothes, while finely tailored, were a season out of fashion. Money troubles were apparently all the rage this season for young bachelors. Leo had enough money to pay his creditors now, but if he didn't find a way to produce new income soon, he would be in trouble.

"I've been in the country." Leo hastily tucked the banker's letter back into his coat pocket.

Owen's keen eyes missed little but he didn't ask what the letter was about. "You look tired, old friend."

"Do I?" Leo mused glumly. "Since my father died, it has been a trial to set the estate to rights."

"Are you afraid you'll lose it?" Owen asked quietly.

"No...at least not yet." Leo sighed. "But I cannot get a single man in London to let me partake in investments or speculation. The economy of the tenant farms simply isn't what it used to be and we need more stability." He leaned back in the leather armchair, wishing he could stay here in the club and not have to face the world outside.

"Cheer up!" Owen grinned. "Why don't we go find something to entertain us? It's been months and you could use some fun."

Leo shook his head. As much as he wished to throw his cares to the wind, he couldn't. His father's scandal had forced him to live a life of boredom. It was the only way he might find favor with society again, and that was crucial if he was to preserve Hampton House and everyone who depended on him.

"Perhaps another time. I suppose I ought to get back to Hampton at any rate. Lord knows what Mother will have gotten up to while I was away."

His friend laughed heartily. "Your mother is a dear. Any trouble she causes is a delight."

Leo brushed his hair back from his eyes. "You don't have to live with her."

"Touché." Owen shrugged. "At least she's not involved with those suffragettes. You know they're having meetings all over the country right now?"

"Lord, don't even breathe a word of women's rights around my mother." Leo and Owen both glanced around the club to make sure no one was listening. Talking of suffragettes had a way of rousing trouble in a gentleman's club, one of the few places that completely barred women.

"Well, I won't keep you, Hampton, but write to me the next time you're in town. We should have a drink."

"Agreed." Leo shook Owen's hand and they both rose from their chairs. It would have been a fine thing to sit and talk with his old friend. They'd survived much together, but after today with his failures and knowing the talk of scandal was still clinging to his family even after a year, he was ready to run home with his tail tucked firmly between his legs. Tomorrow he would find another way to protect his home...tomorrow.

CHAPTER 2

"Now that your father is dead, I intend to indulge in scandalous behavior."

Leo choked on the sandwich he'd just bitten into. He'd been back from London for only one day, and his mother was already trying to kill him. His gaze shot to her face. The Dowager Countess of Hampton slid into a chair opposite him at the large oak dining room table where he was currently eating luncheon. She smoothed her lace tea gown over her lap and fixed him with a steady gaze.

Blood roared through his ears as he struggled to dislodge the bit of sandwich from his throat. *Damn cucumber...can't get it out...*He coughed violently and was finally able to get a bit of breath back in his lungs.

"Breathe, my dear, breathe," she intoned gently as though instructing a child of four, not her grown son of thirty-two. He adored his mother, but she had the uncanny ability of rankling him when he least needed to be rankled.

He reached forward and snatched his water goblet, hastily gulping the liquid. A cold nose nudged his other hand and he glanced down, seeing Ladybird, his chocolate-colored English cocker spaniel, lean against his knee. She whined softly when their eyes met. At least there was one sympathetic female in this house that wasn't determined to do him in.

"Mother," Leo finally got out. "What on earth are you talking about?" Could a man not enjoy a simple meal in peace? His eyes flicked heavenward as he prayed for patience. He supposed he should count himself lucky.

Before his father had died, he, Owen, and Jack had been constantly treading the line between propriety and scandal. He had caused more than one lady's father to eye him askance during a house party or a ball. Leo openly admitted he loved pleasure and the challenge of wooing a woman into his bed. But those days were gone. He was supposed to be keeping out of trouble to restore the family name. The last thing he needed was his mother getting into more trouble than usual.

The dowager countess perched regally, and one hand brushed a few loose hairs back into her elaborate coiffure. The light threading of silver amidst the gold was the only hint of her middling years having just passed. Considering how unhappy her marriage had been to his father, it was impressive that she still looked so well. It never ceased to upset him to think his father had spent nights in the arms of another when he had a beautiful wife at home. But then again, his father had been quite a fool.

"We are finally out of our year of mourning, and I wish to *enjoy* life." Her words were wistful in a way that made his chest tight. Her eyes narrowed as she continued. "I wasn't allowed to do so while the old tyrant still lived." The biting edge to her tone made him wince.

He had known his parents suffered through a loveless marriage, but her frankness about it was a little unsettling. One was not supposed to talk of such things so openly, but his mother had always been open. She was wild where his father had been cold and calm. He'd taken after her in that regard, and she'd never once challenged him on his rakish ways or his tendency to break the hearts of young ladies. But that was because he was a man; a lady had a higher duty to herself and to society to avoid scandal. If his mother was talking of living recklessly, he did not want to know the details. Leo dreaded whatever scheme she was planning now that she could enter society again without violating the strict dictates of her mourning period.

"Well?" She lifted a teacup to her lips, sipping it patiently.

"Well what?" He drank his water and studied her over the rim of the crystal glass. Since his father had died, he'd grown closer to his mother and he'd learned to read her. Right now, she was waiting for him to make the first move in this game she was playing.

For the last few months she'd been working tirelessly to get him away from Hampton House and to return to London. He knew he should be suspicious of her schemes but he wasn't going to fall back into old habits, no matter how tempting it would be to call upon his friends, spend nights at his club, live the life of a wild bachelor as he'd done well enough before his father died. Things were different now.

I cannot be that man anymore, the carefree fool who didn't know his life was on the brink of collapse.

His father's passing had left a hefty amount of death taxes that could bankrupt Hampton, and it was Leo's duty to find a way out from under that crushing weight. After the last three days in London and his continued failures to find a source of additional income, he was afraid for the future of his family. His estate wasn't the only one in danger of being broken by debts.

Only last week he'd visited the neighboring property to the west and learned that the Ashfords were selling their house because Lord Ashford's death had left them deeply in debt. An auctioneer had been examining family portraits and the collection of china and silver while Lady Ashford wept quietly in the corner of the drawing room, her two children sitting beside her, faces drawn tight with grief. It was a bloody bleak affair and

Leo would not let that happen to Hampton. Even if it meant sacrificing his own happiness, he would see the estate remain intact.

His mother cleared her throat when he failed to respond. "Let's hear your objections. I know you wish to stop me and will insist we both live frugally and quietly."

Those very words had been on the tip of his tongue. He was a man of business and was keeping the Hampton estate alive based on such notions. Still...he preferred not to face his mother's obvious scorn over the valuable life lesson his father's passing had taught him. To care for a vast estate, a man could not simply gallivant about and live like a veritable rogue as he had when he'd been younger. It was even more important that he work to clear the Hampton name in society or they would be in dire straits before long. His father's mistress and the unsavory way he'd passed in her bed had set tongues wagging and doors slamming in his face so hard that Leo was afraid he might never be viewed reputably.

His days of wildness were behind him. He had his duty to his lands and to his family. They could not let this house be sold or their lives destroyed by losing a home that had been his family's for three hundred years.

"What"—he paused, hoping his concern didn't show —"exactly do you intend to do by indulging in scandalous behavior?" It was entirely possible that his mother's idea of scandal was far tamer than his. They were called the gentler sex for a reason.

"I am going into the village to attend a little political meeting. I've arranged to meet some ladies who share my views and—"

"Good God! You aren't talking about that women's suffrage nonsense, are you?" Leo set his napkin on the table and scowled imperiously at his mother.

Mina's brows arched and her spine stiffened. "I most certainly am. I am quite moved by their cause. Did you know we once had the right to vote? Back in the days of feudal society?"

Leo groaned and nearly smacked his palm into his forehead in frustration. God's teeth, this was not a matter he wished to be dealing with.

"Mother, you cannot go to any such meeting, and I don't give a bloody damn if women were voting back in the days of mud and squalor. That was the damned middle ages for Christ's sake. People were dropping dead of plague and nothing in life was certain. Now things are safe; there's no need for women to have a vote. The men of this country are quite capable of deciding matters of state for you."

The stark look of pain and rage in his mother's eyes was startling. He hadn't expected to see her react so... openly to his words.

"How can you say that...to *me*? After the way your father made us live, you would continue to deprive me of a voice?"

Leo rubbed his temples. "*No*, that's not what I

meant, Mother. Please, try to understand. I have much to do and I cannot be worrying about you. People in London are talking..." He didn't want to continue but he had to make her understand that her actions could make matters worse.

"Talking? About what?" she asked quietly. Her blue eyes were dark and shadowed now.

"Father, about him and that woman. I couldn't get in to see half the gentlemen I used to before."

His mother seemed to understand now, her blue eyes wide with worry. "It's the money, isn't it? You're worried and we've lost so much face because of...*him*."

His throat tightened painfully and he nodded. He had let her down, had failed to do what he needed to in London, and it was destroying him to see her realize that.

She leaned over and placed one hand on top of his on the table, squeezing it. "Then I shan't go to the meeting. I would like a house party instead. Surely we can afford that?" she asked, hope brimming in her tone.

He smiled a little. "Yes, we can certainly afford a house party, Mother."

She brightened again, the worries chased quickly away. "Excellent! I wish to have it next weekend. Guests will arrive here on Friday and stay through Monday. I'm planning to invite all sorts of people, including Mr. Leighton. He owns the *London News Weekly*, which has all of those sensational articles regarding social and political intrigue. He has a lovely daughter—"

Ahh, therein lies her true goal. Not scandal, but marriage. He almost wondered if her plans to join the ranks of the suffragettes was merely to rile him up. No doubt she assumed he would agree to a house party instead because it was much less scandalous...and it would give her a chance to throw eligible ladies at his feet.

Leo's lips twitched. She was clever, his mother, but not clever enough to fool him into putting himself up for sale on the marriage mart. He waved a hand in the air.

"No. No matchmaking. You know full well that I intend to propose to Mildred Pepperwirth." He had been planning this for the last two months. He'd been to see their neighbors in Pepperwirth Vale and had made his intentions to Viscount Pepperwirth quite clear. Mildred was a good, solid choice for a wife. Beautiful, intelligent, and with a clean established English pedigree that would raise the Hampton title back up in the eyes of society.

An extremely unladylike snort escaped his mother's lips. "Bah! Mildred Pepperwirth. Leo, dear, are you determined to give me dull, witless grandchildren? Don't repeat my mistakes." Her eyes darkened and the lines around her eyes and mouth seemed more pronounced as she frowned. "Marry for love. Marry a woman who makes you furious, who drives you mad, a woman who makes your heart bleed if you even think of living one day without her. Don't marry some simpering fool with a hefty dowry simply because you feel compelled to do your duty to your father and this house. She isn't the woman for you. You need someone forward thinking, dear, and Mildred...well...She is far too traditional."

"Traditional is exactly what I need, Mother. You'd have me marry some suffragette who'd tear down the laws and rules that keep our society intact? It would destroy my estate." How the devil had his mother circled back to the topic he wished for her to forget?

"I think those women who fight for the vote are wonderful!" His mother's voice rose a little and color deepened her cheeks. If he wasn't careful, he'd upset her again and he didn't want to do that. *Best to concede some battles in order to win the war, as Owen Hadley would say.* Owen would know, of course, seeing as how he'd fought in the war where battles had been all too real.

"They are indeed brave ladies, Mother. I wouldn't disagree on that. I simply think they would not make the most respectable of wives. I need someone I can depend upon to support my decisions for the estate, not undermine them." A woman with her head in the clouds, dreaming of voting and equal rights was...trouble. He could admire a woman for fighting for something she believed in, but he certainly didn't want to marry a woman like that.

"You'd doom yourself to a life without love?" Her

voice trembled slightly as though she were deeply wounded by his reaction. She made as if to stand, but he reached out, caught her hand, and held it.

"Mother, sit. *Please*." Her words stirred something in him, and he wasn't sure if he liked the idea...to get so lost in another person that you could not live without them. His father had done that with his mistress, a woman who hadn't cared for him the moment she knew her furnished lifestyle was at an end. Leo wanted to avoid such a fate with every fiber of his being.

Living a reckless bachelor life was one thing, but he'd never been foolish enough to allow himself to fall in love. It would be far too dangerous to open one's self up to such a weakness. He didn't want anyone to have power over his heart. His mother had loved his father, and she'd ended up perfectly unhappy when he'd abandoned her for a mistress. Love was a risk he would not take. He shoved the idea out of his mind, focusing on things he knew he could control.

"I think a house party is a wonderful idea, Mother. But do invite some people *I* know. I saw Hadley at the club yesterday. Drop him an invitation for me. In fact, invite the Pepperwirths as well." He winked at her. She rolled her eyes and sighed dramatically. He swore she muttered something about Mildred under her breath. Leo stifled a laugh. As long as his mother was in a mood to fence with him verbally, that meant she was all right and he hadn't upset her too terribly by refusing to let her attend the suffragette meeting.

He wasn't thrilled about the social obligations that houseguests would create, but he couldn't deny he had been burdened lately with far too much work. A party might improve his mood if only for the distraction it would provide. It was a pity he was no longer able to indulge in old habits. The Leo Graham he'd once been would have made it his mission to bed every willing and lovely lady under his roof.

Damn being respectable. It was going to kill him.

I'll have to find some other means of entertainment.

Keeping his mother from marrying him off to someone during the party would be his chief objective, and it would be amusing to see what schemes she came up with.

"You really insist I invite the Pepperwirths?"

He nodded, biting his lip to hide a smile as he enjoyed her squirming. He knew she liked Lord and Lady Pepperwirth, but she balked at his idea of marrying Mildred, simply because she found Mildred boring.

His mother threw up her hands and huffed. "Leo, shame on you. I expected more of a reaction than that. How is it you're a child of *my* blood?"

She stood to leave, and he could only sit back in his chair and glance down at Ladybird. Her canine brown eyes met his, and she seemed just as perplexed as he was by the entire situation. Her tail thumped the ground rhythmically and she nudged his hand until he stroked her head.

His mother wanted him to run off with a woman who made his blood burn. He couldn't afford to. Hampton needed its earl to be calm and in control. Many of his peers were not adjusting to the new age and thus were losing everything their families had built over centuries. His mother was too old-fashioned to see the changes sweeping England. Farmland was less valuable, and the tenancies on the estate weren't prospering as they had in the past.

Leo couldn't even begin to count the hours he'd spent working until the last candle burned out in his study. Or the endless meetings he'd arranged with his steward, Mr. Holmesbury, as they tried to salvage what they could of a crumbling way of life. *Their way of life.* Everything that mattered to him. They could lose it all if he didn't succeed. Grand houses cost far too much, as did the servants they employed.

Running the tip of his finger over the white china plates fringed with a blue flower pattern, he drew in a deep breath. A heavy weight settled over his chest and shoulders, an invisible burden he could not remove, not so long as he continued to love Hampton House and the people who lived within it. They were a part of this place, a part of its history, just as he was.

If any sacrifices could be made, he would fight to keep Hampton just as it was for as long as possible. He had made his plans. He would marry Mildred, use her fortune to sustain Hampton during the transitions taking place in England, and that would be the end of it. Nothing would change his mind. *Nothing.*

WILHELMINA, DOWAGER COUNTESS OF HAMPTON, peered around the door to the dining room, watching her son finish his luncheon in silence. Ever since he'd returned from London a week ago, he'd been glum and predictable in his daily routine. Working from morning till midnight.

Leo took another bite of his lunch before he reached for the stack of letters on the silver tray to his left, a soft sigh escaping as his shoulders drooped. Ladybird sat at his side, tail swiping across the floor in gentle swishes as she waited for crumbs. The dog whined softly and he petted her absently.

He painted a perfectly boring picture of country life, and it deepened the ache in her heart for him. Leo had been a wonderful child, always exploring, always questing for adventures and causing trouble, the way any good lad should. Mina hadn't been deaf to the rumors of his many paramours or the broken hearts he'd left behind him. At least he'd been a man of passion and action.

Now he was...not. This new Leo was not a son she

wished to call her own. He was world-weary, his eyes dark with sorrow and his lips perpetually pursed as he let worries and anxieties drown him. How could he not see that only the bold and courageous men would continue on in this new world, where the ancient houses were crumbling and being broken apart?

She shuddered. The Ashfords had heard their home would be gutted and the grand staircases, the tapestries, even the marble tiles would be sold off to different bidders. Nothing would be left of the grand house or the family who had lived there nearly as long as the Grahams had lived at Hampton House.

We are soon to be ghosts of a forgotten era. We must change; we must adapt. It was one of the reasons she was so determined to attend the suffragette meeting in the small village close to Hampton House. A good number of ladies were coming down from London to attend in order to escape the harsh reactions their gathering would draw in London. Things had to change; *people* had to change. Men needed to recognize that women were just as smart and as valuable in society.

Leo could not marry a traditional woman. He needed someone who would stand at his side and face the future without fear. Mina would do just about anything to see him married to a fierce Amazon who would battle at his side.

"My lady?" Mr. Gordon, the butler, whispered as he joined his mistress by the door.

She turned and placed a finger to her lips and pointed to Leo.

"Have all the preparations been made for our guests?"

Gordon's face, usually a study of seriousness, softened with pride, and he puffed his chest a bit. "Of course, my lady. I received a telegram from Mr. Leighton. Miss Ivy is coming down early in her father's motorcar."

Mina moved back a few steps from the door as she clapped her hands together in silent glee. Her plan was coming together perfectly. She'd invited Ivy down to Hampton on the pretext of attending the suffragette meeting together, and she'd convinced the young lady that visiting for the house party would be fun.

"Did Mr. Leighton say if he was able to tamper with the motorcar?"

Gordon frowned a little, concern darkening his expression as he handed her the folded telegram. He had known Miss Ivy as long as Mina had and the idea of putting her at risk seemed to upset him.

"Mr. Leighton assured me her motorcar would be close enough to the house but that she'd be stranded. We should make sure to suggest his lordship take a drive around half-past two on Friday. He'll be sure to come across her on the main road."

She hastily read the note herself, grinning a little before slipping it into her dress pocket.

Poor Leo. He was most determined to marry that awful Pepperwirth girl. If all went according to Mina's plans, his intended betrothal would soon be at an end, and her son would fall in love with a woman far more worthy of him. A girl he'd known many years ago, one who'd loved him with all her heart before tragedy had forced their destinies apart.

Ivy Leighton was a modern woman who shared Mina's views on women's rights and would be the best match for her son. Assuming he could see past the fact that she was a suffragette. Mina's lips twitched. No doubt when he met Ivy again, he would find her very grown up and very much changed from the little girl who used to stare at him with stars in her eyes and her heart on her sleeve. She only hoped he would see Ivy as Mina did, as the woman who could save his soul and save Hampton House.

Perhaps I am a meddlesome mama, but Leo should know that I won't leave his choice of wife up to fate.

CHAPTER 3

Ivy Leighton swiped at the billowing black clouds smothering her. Coughing, she removed her driving goggles and tossed them onto the seat of her new Hudson Speedabout. The *broken* speedabout. Her father was going to be furious. She'd asked to drive it, and only a few miles from her destination, the engine had made a ghastly screeching sound like a dying falcon. Dark smoke plumed out from beneath the yellow hood, painting a dark picture against the deep blue sky.

"Oh dear," she groaned.

She wiped her brow with the back of a gloved hand and it came away dirty. A cool September breeze teased at a loose tendril of her hair from beneath her flat hat. She tried to brush it away, but the thick veil tied around her hat made it more than a little complicated. She unbuttoned her tan linen duster, feeling a little flustered by the Hudson's sudden failure.

What on earth was she going to do? Walk to Hampton House? Why had she thought coming early by herself was a good idea? Because she was plagued by curiosity. Sixteen years ago she had left Hampton, her mother's body barely cold in the ground. How much had the place changed? How much had *he* changed?

Leo...his name still made her shiver.

Handsome, charming Leo. When she'd been eight, he'd been sixteen, and a lifetime seemed to have separated them. Now she was twenty-four and he had to be... she did the math. Thirty-two? Would he still have the ability to consume her soul with those fathomless blue eyes? A part of her was afraid to see him again after all these years. Had her girlhood memories been the stuff of fantasies or was he still the man she'd always loved?

After six Seasons in London, she hadn't found anyone who measured up to Leo Graham, the Earl of Hampton, and she feared she never would. But...what if she arrived at Hampton House and found that he wasn't the man she believed him to be?

With a little shake of her head, Ivy recalled the way he used to tease her, tap the tip of her nose with a finger and call her Button.

"Button indeed," she muttered.

Her nose was no longer buttonlike, at least not completely. Leo hadn't seen her since she'd outgrown her oversized eyes, knobby knees, and pert nose. Ivy tried to quell the fleet of butterflies that stormed against the battlements of her stomach.

She was nothing like the English beauties who were so favored by the gentlemen at the balls during the Season. That was the problem with being half Gypsy rather than a full-blooded English rose. Still, she knew she was pretty, in an exotic sort of way, but would Leo think her desirable? Ivy had been a favorite of many men. Her father's position, as well as her own heritage, made them believe she had no morals.

A non-Romani or *gadjo's* sense of Gypsies was always wrong. Women of the Romani culture were anything but loose. Still, that awful cultural misunderstanding led to more than one man to offer her a position as his mistress. An offer that she had to politely refuse without making a scene, even though such a request deserved a slap.

Hopefully Leo would be different.

Not that I should truly care, she reminded herself. She was only coming to Hampton House to see the dowager countess and to attend a suffragette meeting with her. Lady Hampton had insisted that Ivy stay for the house party. She'd reminded Leo's mother that she wasn't coming to husband hunt but to see old friends. Ivy firmly believed a modern woman couldn't have a husband, at least not a man born into the British peerage. They stood against women's rights and that was something that she could never reconcile.

She'd watched her mother work tirelessly as a servant for years in a world where her voice hadn't mattered. Witnessing her mother's inability to live the life she truly wanted before she'd died had changed Ivy. Without the right and the power to speak, a person ceased to exist.

After her mother died, she'd been reunited with her father and it had become clear just how powerless she was as a woman. Although he loved and adored her, even he could not give her power over her own life in the way men had. She could not even control her own inheritance; it had to be held in trust by a man. It seemed like everywhere she turned was a dead end. No way out. To be ensnared in a gilded cage meant she was still trapped. The thought made her recoil. Marry a man who would trap her and destroy her independence? No, she would never agree to that. But still...seeing Leo again after all this time would be nice.

Turning her attention back to the Hudson, she knew she'd have to leave it on the shoulder of the road for now. As she reached for her valise, the gravel on the road slipped beneath her boots. A panicked cry escaped her lips as she fell headfirst into the space behind the driver's seat. Her legs wiggled in the air as she struggled in vain to propel herself back upright.

"Blast and hell!" she cursed, fighting wildly to get her

body into a position that could leverage her back down. Her dress and coat tangled around her knees.

The purr of another motorcar's engine made her freeze. A cool breeze caressed her where her travel dress bunched around her thighs. Whoever had just stopped on the road had a prime view of her legs.

The motor died. Footsteps crunching on gravel warned her of someone's approach, and her body went rigid in apprehension. Fear ratcheted up inside her until she was gasping for breath and thrashing to get back on her feet.

"Er...excuse me, miss. May I help?" a rich, smooth voice asked.

"Oh, yes, please. I'm in a spot of bother it seems."

"I'm going to touch you, miss. Please do not panic." The man's gloved hands settled on her ankles, then slid to her calves as he pulled her down. Tingles of awareness shot through her body, making her twitch in the oddest places.

Ivy tried not to let it ruffle her that some strange man's hands were on her legs. She'd never liked feeling vulnerable, and this was perhaps the most exposed she'd ever been in her life. It was unsettling to say the least. She slid down the side of the Hudson, her face heating and the blood pounding in her ears. When she turned to her rescuer, her heart skittered to a stop, and she sucked in a breath.

Leo.

For a long moment she couldn't think, couldn't breathe. She was a girl again, crying as her mother lay dying. Leo's long, muscular body had been solid and warm behind her as he held her while she wept. He'd been comfort and heat and light where she'd only endured darkness in her mother's last hours.

Of course it would be *him*. He'd be the one to find her covered in road dust, legs flailing in the air, and stuck with a broken down motorcar. She was always at her worst when he was around. Lady Fate evidently didn't like her.

Is there no end to my bad luck?

"Thank you," she said, uncertain if she should say her name. Would he even remember her? Surely not...

With an unexpected deftness, he adjusted her hat, which had been knocked slightly askew during her tumble into the motorcar, and pushed the sides of the veil back as though to get a better look at her face. His lips kicked into a grin, and her heart fluttered back to life. Lord, the man was handsome. His aquiline nose and strong jaw, lips a little thin, but no less appealing, and a halo of golden hair blowing in the breeze. And those eyes, eyes she'd dreamt about for years. More beautiful than she'd remembered.

"You're welcome, Miss..." He waited for her to introduce herself.

So he didn't remember her, then? It stung, yet perhaps that was for the best, given the secret mission

Leo's mother had entrusted her with. It was best he did not recognize her and she did not wish to be remembered as "Button."

"My name is Ivy Leighton."

Her name had no effect on him, not that it should have. She'd taken her father's surname after she'd left Hampton and she couldn't remember a time when Leo had called her Ivy. Perhaps he didn't even know it was her name. She hadn't mentioned her mother's maiden name, Jameson, so there was the real possibility he wouldn't recognize her at all. Ivy wasn't a unique name, not really.

Leo captured one of her gloved hands and pressed a kiss to her knuckles. "It's a pleasure to meet you, Miss Leighton, even under such trying circumstances." His lips twitched at the last few words as though he was doing his best not to tease her. "I see you are having some difficulties with your automobile." His eyes roved over the state of the smoking motorcar behind her, assessing the situation.

She tilted her head to the side. Something was different about him, and it wasn't simply that he'd grown into a man and left the last traces of his boyhood behind. No...he had changed, and she couldn't put her finger on how. There was a seriousness to him, a grave solemnity of a man who'd suffered tragedy and loss and now bore a heavy burden. It gave her a bittersweet longing for the young man he'd once been and a respect for the man he'd become now. One thing that had not changed was the effect of his devastating smile. He could have made a fortune bottling it and selling it to lonely hearts throughout England.

In his unbuttoned Burberry motoring coat, trousers, and cap, Leo looked every inch a man of leisure. Yet a silver pocket watch chain glinting in the sunlight lent him an air of authority and precision. An altogether different impression from the boy he'd once been who'd spent an evening capturing glow worms with her in the garden or comforting her after she'd had a rough day and scraped her knee while running about.

She remembered grinning at him so broadly her cheeks hurt as he bent down to show her a captured insect between his palms. The green light had illuminated his face as he studied the black insect. In that moment, they'd been bound together by a spell of twilight and an effervescent glow. Having to stay still, breaths held, so as not to frighten the shy glowworm into darkening her shine. Her heart clenched in longing for warm summer nights like those again. She swallowed the sudden sense of homesickness for a place she'd forced herself to try and forget.

"It was very kind of you to stop and help a lady in distress." She offered a smile, hoping the action would lift her spirits. She had to put memories of that sixteen-year-old boy with merry, twinkling eyes and a tempting smile behind her or she'd be lost. *He's not for you; you cannot fall in love with him, not again.* The Leo she faced now was businesslike and polite, with only a hint of that charming, troublemaking boy she remembered so well.

What had changed him? Had his mother been right that his father's death and the pressures of running the estate had turned him cool and passionless? She'd heard some of the rumors about his father but wasn't sure if they were true. Given how the whispers of his father's mistress had persisted, it had likely affected his reception with most of the respectable families in the city. Even now she could see a hint of that resigned expression in his beautiful eyes. Where was the fiery young man who'd stolen her heart? *No wonder Lady Hampton begged me to come visit him.*

"I'm sorry, I haven't introduced myself. I am the Earl of Hampton. I would be delighted to help, though I confess to knowing nothing of motorcar engines. If you permit, I shall escort you to your destination and send my mechanic to repair your automobile and return it to you." As Leo spoke, he leaned in, placing one hand against the car beside her hip, and she shivered at the scent of him and his warmth. She had always been aware of him; like a planet hugging a distant star, she was connected to him in ways she'd never been with any other man. And that was what made him so dangerous to her. He was perhaps the one man in all of England who could tempt her into falling in love. And love would ruin all of her dreams for a brighter future as a woman with rights. Still, she had promised Lady Hampton she would visit the house and see Leo; she simply needed to guard her heart while she was here.

"My lord, it seems we are both fortunate. My destination is in fact Hampton House. I was invited by the countess for her house party."

This caught him by surprise. His eyes narrowed slightly as his gaze swept her body. Within her tan duster covered in dirt, Ivy must have looked a fright. Not that she could have helped her appearance, but she would have loved to have met him again under better circumstances.

Comprehension showed in the widening of his eyes as he made some mental connection. "My mother invited you? You aren't the newspaper fellow's daughter, are you?"

The newspaper fellow? So Lady Hampton had mentioned her coming, then. Over tea, Lady Hampton had outlined a scheme to play a game upon Leo that required some level of discretion as to Ivy's identity. Leo's mother was convinced he would be too well behaved if he realized Ivy had once been the child he'd looked after. It would be better to hide her identity for a time so she could be treated like any other lady he might meet. The idea of deception hadn't set well with Ivy, but she had to admit she did not want him thinking of Button during the house party.

I'll tell him who I really am, after he has a chance to know me as a woman.

"My father is indeed the newspaperman." She chuckled. He wasn't the first to react that way to her father's background. Leo's eyes were still fixed upon her face and she tried not to wriggle under the intense scrutiny of his gaze. It made her feel warm in the oddest places, and it was much more like the Leo she'd known as a girl.

"Fortunate indeed that I found you, then." He looked over her shoulder into the motorcar. "Your luggage?"

Before she could step out of the way, he moved, accidentally pressing her against the door. A flush of heat coursed through her in a sudden rush when he didn't immediately step back. His eyes blazed with an unexpected interest that made her feel small and vulnerable. As though he could see through her, pick apart her soul, and study the pieces and understand her. What a terrifying thought...Never had she wanted a man to evoke such a feeling, but with him, it was exciting, rather than frightening. Ivy licked her lips and his eyes tracked the movements the way a lion would a mouse.

"Your"—he breathed deeply—"bag," he murmured, sliding past her to reach into the Hudson. He retrieved it without any of the trouble she'd had. "This way."

He gestured toward his auto, which was parked next to hers.

It was a lovely black Stanley Touring motorcar. Her

father had almost bought the same model instead of the Hudson, but in the end he'd opted for the striking yellow auto, valuing the flash more than the extra seats.

Leo walked ahead of her, placing her luggage behind the front passenger seat.

Ivy retrieved her eye goggles and hastily got into her side of the Stanley, which earned her a raised brow by Leo, who had only just turned to try and open the door for her. For some reason, she needed a moment of space between them, at least long enough to get her breath and her good sense back. How was a woman supposed to concentrate around such an irresistible man? When he was too close, she seemed to think only of him and wonder if his lips were as soft as they looked.

Once they were driving back down the road, he turned to look at her.

"Are you traveling alone? Mother mentioned your father was coming. I'm sure she would have insisted you be escorted." There was a note of disapproval to his voice that she didn't like.

She hesitated before replying. "My father is coming tomorrow afternoon on the train, and he's bringing my lady's maid and his valet. Your mother said one of her upstairs maids could wait upon me until they arrived."

"So was that your father's Hudson?"

The question prickled her because his tone seemed to imply a woman could not own a motorcar. It was her father's but only because she insisted they share a vehicle, when he offered to buy her one of her own. They didn't need two; that would have been silly.

"It is," she replied a tad stiffly. "But I have plenty of experience driving it."

Let him think what he will about that.

Leo was silent for a moment. "So...you are...friends with my mother?"

Ivy nibbled her bottom lip, considering how best to answer that. Lady Hampton had always looked out for her as a child, especially when her mother fell ill. The countess was the one who had located Ivy's father and informed him that he had a daughter. For such a service, the word *friend* hardly seemed adequate. Leo's mother was a veritable godsend. But she was supposed to remember the little prank they were to play upon Leo by keeping her real name a secret for a time.

"We met in London three months ago at a charity function held by Lady Buxton." A lie. The countess had crafted a story to explain how they met to keep Leo from discovering Ivy's true identity. She also didn't want Leo knowing that she and Ivy were involved in the Women's Social and Political Union together. When Ivy had questioned the deceptive plan, Lady Hampton had explained her predicament vaguely, saying Leo had become too rigid, too driven, and wasn't open in his thinking, especially toward the suffragette movement.

"He needs adventure and mystery, my dear, and you can

provide both. It shall be a fun game. He needs to be shocked for
his own good."

But Ivy had grown up at Hampton House and
worried the servants would recognize her. The countess
had insisted that the servants who'd known her as a child
had been instructed to treat her as they would any guest,
not as the child they had helped raise.

Ivy had no desire for "Button" to be resurrected in
Leo's mind, and a few days of simply being herself would
be fun. She would not play the deceiver long, though.
She would tell Leo who she was soon; she would simply
leave out his mother's involvement in the local
suffragette gathering.

Lost in thought, she didn't immediately realize she
was being a poor companion to him. A lady of good
breeding would never let herself get lost in thought in
the presence of her future host. She glanced at Leo and
discovered he was watching her when not checking the
road ahead.

"And your father? How did he meet my mother?"

"At the same event. She seemed to enjoy discussing
his paper."

Leo's bark of laughter made her frown. "The newspaperman. Mother mentioned he was coming and is quite
looking forward to it."

She hoped her father had the good sense to follow
the instructions Lady Hampton gave him and not betray

Ivy's true identity by mentioning her mother and Ivy's past at Hampton.

Ivy shivered, now feeling the chill in the air, and rubbed her arms.

"There's a lap rug beneath the seat." His hand bumped into hers as they both reached for it.

"My apologies," he murmured, and withdrew his hand. Ivy's gloved fingers brushed over the blanket. She hastily arranged it over her lap and legs, feeling instantly warmer.

"Thank you, my lord."

He merely nodded. The Stanley rattled and bounced worse than a coach on the road. After a few minutes, Leo spun the wheel and turned onto a gravel drive that stretched toward a massive manor house in the distance.

Hampton.

The vision of it always stole her breath. The tan stones were warm in the September sun and afternoon light glinted off the windowpanes. Fir trees dotted the open grounds in patches like spikes of deep green paint across a lighter emerald canvas. She had forgotten how vast the house was and how beautiful.

Nature blended with the house and the gardens, making it a private world where anything seemed possible. Memories of early morning mists curling around the grounds like milky tendrils stirred within her. She used to chase the peacocks across the lawn with Old John, Leo's old butterscotch-colored cocker spaniel, the dog nipping at the thousand-eyed plumed tail feathers of the ill-tempered birds. Old John had always been called that for as long as she could remember. Had he ever been Young John? She hadn't thought to ask. The silliness of her thoughts made her smile. Hampton had a way of reminding her of being a child again, in small ways that made her heart tighten in her chest. Like dancing rainbows in the library caught from a spinning diamond chandelier, or digging in the cool soil to plant seeds with the ancient gardener, Mr. Matthews.

A little sigh escaped Ivy as she thought of all the hours she'd spent there, the minutes ticking away, never knowing her mother would soon die and she'd lose part of herself forever. Or that she'd lose Hampton forever. Yet here she was, sitting in an automobile with Leo, *coming home*.

Want to know how it ends? Get the book HERE!

ABOUT THE AUTHOR

USA TODAY Bestselling Author Lauren Smith is an Oklahoma attorney by day, who pens adventurous and edgy romance stories by the light of her smart phone flashlight app. She knew she was destined to be a romance writer when she attempted to re-write the entire _Titanic_ movie just to save Jack from drowning. Connecting with readers by writing emotionally moving, realistic and sexy romances no matter what time period is her passion. She's won multiple awards in several romance subgenres including: New England Reader's Choice Awards, Greater Detroit Book-Seller's Best Awards, and a Semi-Finalist award for the Mary Wollstonecraft Shelley Award.

To connect with Lauren, visit her at:
www.laurensmithbooks.com
lauren@Laurensmithbooks.com

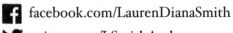 facebook.com/LaurenDianaSmith
twitter.com/LSmithAuthor
instagram.com/LaurenSmithbooks
bookbub.com/authors/lauren-smith

OTHER TITLES BY LAUREN
SMITH

Historical

The League of Rogues Series

Wicked Designs

His Wicked Seduction

Her Wicked Proposal

Wicked Rivals

Her Wicked Longing

His Wicked Embrace

The Earl of Pembroke

His Wicked Secret

The Last Wicked Rogue

Never Kiss a Scot

The Seduction Series

The Duelist's Seduction

The Rakehell's Seduction

The Rogue's Seduction

The Gentleman's Seduction
Standalone Stories
Tempted by A Rogue
Sins and Scandals
An Earl By Any Other Name
A Gentleman Never Surrenders
A Scottish Lord for Christmas

Contemporary
The Surrender Series
The Gilded Cuff
The Gilded Cage
The Gilded Chain
The Darkest Hour
Love in London
Forbidden
Seduction
Climax
Forever Be Mine

Paranormal
Dark Seductions Series
The Shadows of Stormclyffe Hall
The Love Bites Series
The Bite of Winter
Brotherhood of the Blood Moon Series
Blood Moon on the Rise (coming soon)
Brothers of Ash and Fire

Grigori: A Royal Dragon Romance
Mikhail: A Royal Dragon Romance
Rurik: A Royal Dragon Romance

Sci-Fi Romance

Cyborg Genesis Series

Across the Stars

Krinar World

The Krinar Eclipse (coming Fall 2019)

Lauren
SMITH
TIMELESS ROMANCE

Made in the USA
Monee, IL
17 September 2021